She closed her e  and waited for the impact. It was not what she expected! She hit against a warm solid something that knocked the breath out of her. Two bands of steel clamped around her and held her still. She opened her eyes cautiously and found herself nose to nose with a very handsome man. Two dark blue eyes gazed intently into hers. Laughter crinkled the corners of his eyes. Locks of black hair fell across his broad forehead.

"What did you catch, Val?" an amused male voice behind them asked the question.

Val was taking a heated inventory of the woman he held in his arms. He focused on the disarray of her hair, the fullness of her breasts, the narrowness of her waist, and then the soft pink lips so close to his own. He pulled her close against him, amused and intrigued.

"I merely asked the gods for their favor on our hunt, and they dropped a goddess right into my arms." He tightened his hold about her waist and leaned in for a closer look.

Desire slammed into him like a battle-ax. He liked what he saw. This angel that dropped from the sky was beautiful with her long ebony hair, green eyes, and pert little nose.

Bewitching. He stared at her mouth so close to his and wondered if she tasted as good as she looked. He wanted this enchanting girl.

The Wicked Sister

by

Virginia Barlow

This is a work of fiction. Names, characters, places, and incidents are either the product of the author's imagination or are used fictitiously, and any resemblance to actual persons living or dead, business establishments, events, or locales, is entirely coincidental.

The Wicked Sister

Cover Art by *Kristian Norris*

The Wild Rose Press, Inc.
PO Box 708
Adams Basin, NY 14410-0708
Visit us at www.thewildrosepress.com

Publishing History
First Tea Rose Edition, 2019
Print ISBN 978-1-5092-2821-8
Digital ISBN 978-1-5092-2822-5

Published in the United States of America

Dedication

To my daughters, for believing in me.

Chapter 1

Covington Estate, Oldenburg
A long time ago

Lady Anastasia stopped on her way past the entry hall. The loud pounding started again. *Why is someone pounding on the door? And where is Henry, the butler?* Her curiosity piqued; Lady Anastasia decided to answer the door herself. She quickly crossed the ornate entrance hall with its gleaming Italian marble and golden mirrors. She swung the heavy oak door open and spent the rest of her life wishing she had gone in search of Henry instead.

Several soldiers stood outside the door, covered in mud. They carried a man on a wooden slab. Blood was everywhere. Major Mikeal Kavendish, commander of His Majesty's army, stood at attention; his fist poised to pound once more.

Anastasia stepped back in alarm, gripping the door hard with both hands. Major Kavendish followed her inside, ushering the soldiers past him. He tried unsuccessfully to block her view of the wounded man with his tall lanky body.

"Where's Lady Evelyn, lass?" The major's frantic blue gaze darted here and there searching for the lady in question. He swiped a hand at his silver tipped hair, removing his hat.

"She is…." As the soldiers rushed past, Anastasia got a look at the man's face, stopping the words in her mouth.

"Papa!" Both hands came up to cover her mouth as she tried, unsuccessfully, to swallow the scream that rose in her throat. She stared, her mind refusing to understand what her eyes were telling her.

Major Kavendish watched the girl warily, hoping to God she did not swoon.

"Can I help you, sir?" Dimly Anastasia was aware of Henry entering the hall.

Major Kavendish turned with relief toward the butler. "Lord Covington has been gravely wounded. I am looking for Lady Evelyn to tend to the wounded man until the king's physician arrives."

Anastasia eyes were riveted. Papa's usually jovial face was ashen gray. He lay as still as death.

"This way, sir." Henry led the way out of the entry hall and toward the stairs.

Major Kavendish wanted to avoid parading Lord Covington in front of his family, but that could not be avoided and dammit, time was running out. He had to get Lord Covington some help before he bled to death from his wound. The soldiers followed Major Kavendish with their burden.

Anastasia was awash with a sense of unreality. This could not be happening. *Why did I not tell Papa I was sorry? Why did I not tell him I loved him or explained what happened?* Anastasia stared at a drop of blood on the tile. She was numb, and her heart beat loudly in her head. In the background, she heard Beatrice with her singing lessons and the pianoforte music as Rella practiced. They did not know of the terrible thing that was happening.

"Miss Anastasia." Henry was at her elbow, a frown of concern on his face.

She was in shock. The last time she saw that much blood, she lost everything. She trembled violently, and her stomach threatened to upend its contents all over the entry hall.

Henry tried again.

"Miss Anastasia!" He placed a hand on her shoulder and shook her gently.

She jumped. Her gaze slowly turned toward him.

"Your mother asks for her herbs and her medicine bag. She wants you to fetch them for her," Henry said.

Anastasia stared at him. She heard sound but could not make any sense of what he said. Another knock sounded at the door. Anastasia jumped again. She was still in the entry hall, and Henry was speaking to her.

"Your mother needs her herbs and medicines, Miss Anastasia. Could you fetch them for her?"

Henry opened the door for the king's physician and glanced back at Anastasia as he took the man's coat and hat.

Anastasia nodded, suddenly coming to the present. Papa needed the medicine. She hurried from the room to fetch the herbs. Guilt ate at her while she searched for her mother's bag of medicine. What if she was too late? What if she never got a chance to talk to Papa, to explain? Anastasia found the bag of medicine and hurried to her mother.

****

What seemed like a long time later, the door to the master chamber opened and Henry stepped out into the corridor, a bundle of bloody linen in his arms.

Anastasia jumped to her feet when she saw him. His weathered face was drawn with grief and his gray eyes bright with emotion. She stifled the sob that rose in her throat. The distress in his expression confirmed what she already knew to be true. *Papa is dead.* This was the worst possible sort of nightmare, the worst, because it was real.

Anastasia had waited outside the chamber door for hours listening to Papa moan and cry out. She paced and wrung her hands in agitation as she listened, her mind going over a thousand scenarios with each moan. Guilt ate at her with each imagined scenario. She should have gone to the library the last time Papa was home and begged his forgiveness for being a disappointment to him. She should have tried harder to please him. She should have listened to him, and she never should have run away after he scolded her. Anastasia absently rubbed the hideous scar on her forearm through her sleeve and silently wept. Her arm had finally healed; but the scar on her heart and in her mind was still raw and aching. The cuts there were much too deep. For most of the night, she sat lost in her own painful thoughts.

Then, after all the long hours, there was nothing, only silence. Anastasia had crept closer to the door, her heart beating loudly in her ears with the hope that somehow Papa was going to live, that the king's physician managed to put Papa back together. Anastasia would remember the sound she heard next for the rest of her life. Her mother was weeping. It was not the weeping itself that was so hard to bear, but the agony in the cry that tore at Anastasia's heart. She had never felt so helpless, so vulnerable, so alone, or so afraid in her

4

life. *Papa is dead.* She knew it, and her whole world turned upside down and inside out. Anastasia sank into the nearby chair and tried to breathe. She was limp with the onslaught of emotion that crashed over her.

"I thought you went to bed hours ago, Miss Anastasia," Henry scolded.

Anastasia lifted her head slowly; soul shattering sadness filled her. "I would not be able to rest with Papa in so much pain," she said softly.

Henry handed the bundle of linen to a nearby footman, and knelt in front of Anastasia, his work worn hands reaching for hers. "I have something I need to tell you, Miss Anastasia," Henry began.

"I understand, Henry. Please do not say the words. I do not think I can bear to listen to them. I am aware that Papa is…"

Anastasia could not finish. She was not able to say the words either. She glanced down at their hands, where his much larger ones covered hers, and began to cry. Papa had been her comfort before all this. Sobs shook her thin shoulders, and soon her whole body trembled violently. Anastasia put her hands over her eyes and wept as if it were the end of the world. For to Anastasia, it was.

****

Henry patted her hands awkwardly and let her weep.

He had been with the family since before Lord Covington married his first wife Agnes and had Lady Rella. He had been the one to cater to Lady Agnes after Lady Rella's birth as she struggled to hold on to life. For eight long years, he fetched and carried for the sickly woman until her health finally failed her. Henry had been the one to tell Lady Rella of her mother's death and then stood in awkward surprise when the girl showed no emotion at all to the news. Lady Rella simply shrugged and continued to play with her cat as if they were discussing which type of cake she would like to have with her tea.

Henry then looked after young Rella in her papa's frequent absence, smoothing over the upsets the girl delighted in causing among the servants and townspeople. He thought life was finally smiling upon his good master when Lord Covington married the lovely widow, Lady Evelyn Dunbar, and brought her home with her two gentle daughters. The days became brighter, happier, and Henry had been most pleased with the love that grew between the widow and his lord. The daughters proved to be as sweet and gentle as their mother, and Anastasia quickly carved a niche for herself in his heart.

Henry sighed wearily; this was a devastating blow. Dark days were once more settling in on Covington Estate. It was his duty now, to tell the family of the lord's death. It was a very dark day indeed.

Henry let Lady Anastasia cry for several more minutes before he gently squeezed her hand and said, "You must go to your mother, miss. She will need you now, and I must tell your sisters that your papa is gone."

Anastasia briskly rubbed the tears from her cheeks. "Did Papa hurt much…at the end?" she whispered.

"No, Lady Evelyn gave him a draught and it took his pain away. He passed, Miss Anastasia, in your mother's arms. His Lordship had a smile on his face. His last words were about his precious girls and his love for you all." Henry patted her hand once more and got to his feet.

Anastasia closed her eyes, drawing in a shaky breath. "Thank you, Henry. I shall go to my mother."

Henry nodded his head and started off down the corridor. *Miss Anastasia always was a strong little thing; bless her heart.*

****

Major Kavendish stood right inside the chamber door shaking his head over the tragedy and loss of Lord Covington. "What a bloody shame," he repeated for the hundredth time.

He opened the door for Lady Anastasia with a bow and a fatherly pat on her shoulder.

Lady Evelyn sat on the bed silently weeping. Papa lay deathly still beside her. The king's physician was gathering up the last of his tools and medicines.

Anastasia hurried to her mother's side and wrapped her arms around Lady Evelyn's shoulders.

"I am sorry, Lady Covington," the physician began. "The wound proved to be too deep. The musket ball was lodged too close to his heart, and I was not able to reach it where it lay. There was nothing I could do. Please accept my deepest regrets." The man snapped his bag shut and sighed a long weary sigh. "He was a good man and he shall be greatly missed."

Lady Evelyn looked up at the physician and nodded her head graciously. "Thank you, sir, for all you have done."

Major Kavendish also bowed to Lady Evelyn. "It is with great regret, my lady, that I beg your leave. I must relay the sad tidings to His Majesty. The king is anxious to hear of the welfare of Lord Covington and will be most upset by the terrible news I bring. Please accept my deepest sympathy for your untimely loss."

Lady Evelyn nodded. "Thank you, Major."

"I am sure you can expect His Majesty in the next couple of days. His Majesty will want to convey his sympathy in person. Lord Covington was one of his most trusted diplomats and a dear friend. Only Lord Covington could have prevented war with Lichtenburg and negotiated for a peace treaty the way he did. With Lichtenburg's anger over the new tariffs, war was imminent. The entire realm owes a debt of gratitude to your husband. We have all suffered a great loss with his death."

The two men bowed again and left the room.

"How can this happen, Mama? How can Papa be dead?" Anastasia whispered in bewilderment.

"Lord Kavendish tells me Papa and his guards were attacked in the mountains going through the pass. Snow was piled so high through that area that they were trapped and at the killer's mercy."

"Does the major think it was Lichtenburg that attacked?"

Lady Evelyn shook her head. "The major does not think so. They do not know who the men were, and the king has sent soldiers to the area to scout for clues."

"But Papa is always so careful. I do not understand how this happened! Papa is an excellent swordsman and he has never lost a battle yet. How did he lose this one?"

"The men had muskets, darling, and your papa was shot. The king's physician did everything he could, but the ball was too close to his heart." Tears ran down Lady Evelyn's face as she said the terrible words.

"I shall miss him dreadfully," Anastasia said.

"As will I, my darling. Papa has been so good to us, has he not?"

Anastasia nodded her head. Papa certainly had. She couldn't even remember a time when Lord Edward Dunbar, her real father, had made time for her like Papa had. Lord Edward had been gone so much of the time, and when he had been home, he had been so busy with the estate business and social events, that she hardly even saw him except for family gatherings, and formal occasion. She and her older sister Beatrice always had their meals in the nursery. They had tutors and nannies to see to their needs. Lord Edward died when she was eight years old. Anastasia only had a handful of memories of him, most of them fuzzy. Anastasia stared into the fire as memories of shared laughter with Papa filled her thoughts.

Lady Beatrice walked into the room then. Her hair, black and glossy like their mother's, was unbound and hanging down her back. Her brown eyes were full of tears, her face red and swollen from crying. She, too, hurried across the room to hug Lady Evelyn.

Lady Rella was right behind her. Her golden hair plaited down her back; her blue eyes filled with hate as she crossed the room slowly. Rella's hands were fisted at her side as she surveyed the scene before her. Lady Evelyn was still holding Papa's hand. Beatrice and Anastasia were on either side of her, their arms about her.

****

Rella remembered the first time she saw Lady Evelyn. It was the day her papa brought home her "new mama" and her "new sisters." Rella stood at the

9

window in her papa's upstairs room watching, as he laughingly helped the three demons from his new carriage. Rella hugged her cat Satan and stroked his soft fur as she watched. She thought Lady Evelyn resembled a witch with her long dark hair and green eyes. Her daughters looked exactly like her, dark and thin, with long fingers, and long dark hair. Rella hated them then for taking her papa away from her, and she hated them even more, now.

Through tight lips, Rella said, "How...lucky my papa was to have you, Lady Evelyn." She paused and stared hard at the scene before her. That should be her next to her papa, not this witch and her two evil daughters. The way the witch touched her papa made Rella furious. They did not need to pretend that they cared anymore; Papa was no longer here to be tricked by it.

"I heard it was a draught you gave him that...eased his pain." *It was probably some witches' brew Lady Evelyn concocted to kill my papa*, she thought.

"Yes, darling, I gave Robert a draught for his pain." Lady Evelyn rose from the bed and stepped back making room for Rella.

Bitterness, and five long years of jealousy and hatred loosened Rella's tongue. "Did you poison my papa with your hateful herbs and draughts? Did you do it on purpose? Did you kill my papa? Were you hoping to take all my papa's money? To take all his jewels and paintings? I know that is why you tricked him into marrying you. You only pretended to love my papa and now that he is dead you think to take everything away from me! Well, I won't have it! I can tell you right now everything in this house is mine. I will never let you have my papa's money, the jewels, or anything else. They are mine! If you try to take so much as a candlestick from me, you will be sorry you ever stepped foot in my house."

Rella's voice had gone shrill as she yelled her accusations.

Lady Evelyn was speechless.

"You killed him. I know you did," Rella said.

"Darling," Lady Evelyn stepped toward the angry girl, disbelief and pain etched on her face. "How can you ask such a thing? How can you think such a thing?" Lady Evelyn choked on a sob. "'Twas not the herbs that killed your papa, but the wound in his chest. A bullet the king's physician could not remove. I would never do anything to hurt Robert. I loved him more than life itself! You know that. Why would you think...? How can you ask?" She broke off; her face went a ghostly white. Taking a shuddering breath, Lady Evelyn hurriedly sat on the edge of the bed as if she didn't have the strength to continue standing.

"Either way, it doesn't matter does it?" Rella asked angrily. "My papa is dead, and I believe you killed him."

Lady Evelyn went paler still and Anastasia quickly stepped to Lady Evelyn's side and put an arm around her mother's shoulders, letting the older woman lean on her. Tears ran down Lady Evelyn's face.

Rella stared hard at Lady Evelyn, turned on her heel, and stalked from the room.

****

Lady Evelyn gazed after Rella, confused and shocked. Her whole body shuddered with sobs. Beatrice came over to her other side. Both the girls held her while she wept.

After a while, Lady Evelyn stopped crying and took a long calming breath. She sat motionless for a minute or two. Then a profound sadness settled upon her, and her shoulders dropped as if the weight of the world suddenly descended upon them. Beatrice was the first one to break the silence.

"I am sure that Rella did not mean all those hateful things she said. I think she…hurts inside, and it makes her angry, and so she says hateful things. Maybe she is frightened and feels all alone," Beatrice whispered.

Beatrice would of course see only the good. She was very like their mother.

"I know, darling," Lady Evelyn answered. "The poor dear is out of her mind with grief and doesn't know what she's saying. We must be especially kind to her my darlings, and make sure she knows that she has us and that she is very loved and needed."

"She shouldn't have said those things to you, Mama," Anastasia began. "It was not your fault! You did everything—"

"Shshsh," Lady Evelyn interrupted. "I won't hear another word about it. We are going to pretend it never happened." Lady Evelyn was once again in control of her emotions. "Poor darling, I am sure she only needs time and rest. She will need to grieve for her dear papa. She will be fine after a bit, I'm sure."

****

Anastasia wasn't so sure. Rella had been very careful in the last five years since they had come to live at Covington House to never let either parent see her cruelty. Rella often said and did cruel things to Beatrice and herself and then lied about it. It was surprising that she showed Lady Evelyn she was not the sweet girl her stepmother believed her to be.

Chapter 2

"Miss Anastasia, Lady Evelyn is asking for you in the red salon." The footman spoke from the kitchen door.

"Tell her I am coming," Anastasia said.

Holding the silver tray with both hands, Anastasia concentrated on walking from the kitchen and down the corridor to the salon. The two days since Lord Covington's death were both long and empty. Anastasia was numb all over. She needed to pay extra attention to her surroundings, for she tripped over everything lately. She wanted this once to be helping, not making it worse.

The blue salon stood in the front of the huge stone house facing the driveway. The guests sitting inside had an excellent view of the cobblestone drive and the beautiful flower gardens that bordered it.

The heavy tray had another tea arranged upon it. Cook had nearly been run off her feet preparing refreshments for the guests who now filled the salons at Covington House.

The footman opened the door for her as she approached the blue salon. Anastasia walked over to the settees arranged around the tea table and set the heavy silver tray down. She shook her head at Beatrice, who motioned for her to sit and help pour tea.

"Mama wants me in the red salon," she explained,

nodding at the guests. She turned to leave, but Lady Darling stopped her.

The old woman held onto her arms. "There you are, dear; I've been searching all over for you."

"Lady Darling."

"How are you holding up, my dear?" she asked and peered at the girl over the rims of her gold spectacles.

"I am coping," Anastasia lied.

"Nonsense, you are as pale as the snow in January."

She pulled Anastasia into her grandmotherly arms for a quick hug. Her silver head bending close to the young girl as she held her. Then Lady Darling pulled back, her silver eyes shining with unshed tears.

"Your mother is a strong woman," she stated, "and you inherited her strength. I think you shall be fine, after a time. We thought we lost you several times last winter, but here you are, as sound as before. You have only to keep yourself busy and before long, your heart will be all right and will not hurt as bad as it hurts at the present. Only time can heal the pain and the sadness. I have extensive experience in situations such as this." Lady Darling paused.

Anastasia doubted Lady Darling had experience with this kind of guilt and disappointment.

"Come and visit me anytime, there are very few people I invite to disturb my peace, but you are one of them," Lady Darling added with a nod.

Having delivered her words of wisdom, Lady Darling patted Anastasia on the shoulder and turned away to talk to Lady Dravenski.

It took Anastasia several minutes to escape the crush of guests gathered in the salon. Each one with a story or an anecdote they wanted to share about Lord Covington. Though she loved stories about Papa, she wanted to be alone for a few minutes to regain her composure. A lump had been forming in her throat all day, and with each shared recollection, it became a little harder to push the feeling back down. Finally, she reached the door and hurried into the red salon.

Lady Evelyn looked up at her entrance and smiled, extending her hand to Anastasia. "Come, darling, I want you to sit beside me for a few minutes." Anastasia nodded at the guests that sat about the salon and settled herself on the cream satin settee next to Lady Evelyn.

"Are you well, my darling?" her mother inquired. "You are quite pale."

"I am fine, Mama; I thought to go sit in my window seat in the library and catch my breath when you called me." *It is the only place I can be alone and feel close to Papa.*

"Then go, darling. We will manage without you for a bit."

Anastasia squeezed Lady Evelyn's hand and hurried out of the room. She walked back down the corridor, across the entry hall, and down the next corridor until she came to the library. She was exhausted, physically, mentally, and emotionally. Anastasia had no idea so many people knew Papa. He had many close friends and acquaintances, of course, but seeing them parade through the house over the last two days had been quite trying. Even considering his relation to the king, she was simply astounded at the onslaught of mourners that came to pay their last respects.

Now, all she wanted was a few minutes alone. Her

window seat in the library was the one place that offered her the comfort and quiet her emotional state needed. Anastasia had loved Papa with all her young heart, and he loved her back. She knew he did. It was that knowledge that helped Anastasia deal with the other things in her life. She closed the library door quietly behind her. Walking past the tall oak shelves filled with expensive leather-bound volumes, she skirted past the satin settees and leather armchairs and hurried to her favorite spot.

Papa caught her hiding one day behind the heavy brocade draperies not long after they came to Covington House to live. She had a book in her lap, and Papa chuckled to himself when she told him she intended to read every single book in the massive library. Lord Covington commissioned his workmen to build a window seat into the corner of one of the long paned windows. The seat had been built so light from outside would fall softly through the window, onto the seat. The seat was completely hidden behind the ornate woodwork and draperies that covered the window. No one could see it and its occupant unless standing directly in front of the window. Anastasia hid there often as a girl. It was a safe place to hide from Rella, especially when Papa was sitting at his huge desk going over estate business. No one dared to bother him by walking further into the room and checking the window seat, and if he knew she hid there, he never let on.

She hid there now, clutching a velvet pillow to her chest and crying as the ache of her loss ate at her heart. Everything she cared about was gone. Anastasia sobbed as she thought about the words she wished she could say to him. *Oh God, how I miss him!* The loneliness overwhelmed her and sitting here seemed to bring his presence close, offering her the love and comfort she needed.

The door to the library suddenly swung open and a high-pitched woman's voice said, "Where is my niece?"

Anastasia jumped at the sudden intrusion.

"If you will wait in here, my lady, I shall find Miss Rella," Henry's deep voice answered the woman.

Anastasia sat up and tried to decide what to do. She wiped her wet cheeks with the back of her hand. Henry must have decided to put Rella's visitor in here since both salons were already full of guests. Anastasia did not want to be caught in here with Rella and one of her visitors. There were things Rella did and said that it was better not to see or hear. Most of the visitors that came to see Rella were mean nasty people anyway. Anastasia was about to emerge from behind the draperies, when she heard the door open again and then the loud click as it was shut firmly behind whoever had entered.

"What are you doing here, Aunt Connie?" The sound of Rella's voice made it clear she was not happy in the least with her aunt's presence.

Anastasia slid back against the seat, trying to make herself as small as possible. It would not go well if Rella found her here. There was silence for a minute or two. Anastasia tried not to breathe.

"I have come to visit my only niece, and to offer condolences to her on the death of her dear papa," the lady drawled, "and to offer my shoulder for you to cry on."

"Since when do you care whether my papa is alive or not?" Rella's shrill voice carried across the room.

There was a moment's pause. "What are you really doing here?" Suspicion laced Rella's words.

There was the sound of footsteps and then the rustling of skirts. The aunt's voice now came from the direction of the settees.

"I told you, I am offering my services," the lady said. "With your papa dead and no male heir available to inherit the title, I thought perhaps we could come to some sort of arrangement."

Anastasia leaned forward a bit to catch more of the conversation. *What is this aunt up to?*

"Why would I need you or any arrangement?" Rella asked.

"Do sit down, my dear, my neck is beginning to ache looking up at you."

Anastasia heard Rella move toward the settees and the rustling of her skirts.

"Well, Aunt Connie?" Rella asked again.

"Traditionally, titles are only passed from male to male. Since you are the last of the Covingtons, the title reverts to the crown until you marry. Then the king will most likely give your husband the title, and all that goes with it. However, since your papa remarried, Lady Evelyn is considered your guardian and therefore the keeper of the estate until you either marry, or the king grants the title to someone else. Your uncle and I are offering our services to you...for a fee of course."

There was a long awkward silence. Anastasia held her breath as she waited for Rella to answer. "Why? Once the courts are satisfied there is no male heir, the title and the wealth shall all be mine. It is only a matter of time. I do not need you."

"Perhaps," Lady Constance paused, "but then how

do you know they will rule in your favor? A young unmarried woman with no family is hardly able to find favor with the courts. Besides, what if your dear papa left everything to that harlot he married and her two simpering idiots? Without any male relative, the courts would respect his wishes in the matter."

Anastasia swallowed her gasp of surprise at the aunt's comment. *Would Papa do that?* It was an interesting idea to consider. They would find out soon enough one way or the other. The solicitors were due to arrive following the funeral. A fly landed on Anastasia's nose and she tried to flick it away before it made her sneeze.

"Papa would not dare! No other person alive has Covington blood flowing through their veins, only me! Covington House and Estate shall belong to no other. It cannot! It is mine!"

Anastasia heard the fury in Rella's voice and shrank against the cushions.

There was silence following Rella's outburst, then the aunt asked, "Do you?"

"Do I what?" Rella asked.

"Have his blood in your veins?"

The silence was so loud it deafened Anastasia. She was confused by the aunt's question. *Why would she ask? Rella is Papa's daughter.*

"Of course, I do! Why would you ask such a silly question?" Rella answered vehemently.

Anastasia leaned forward once more, straining to hear. There was more silence, then the rustling of papers.

"I was looking through my letters from your mama the other day, and I came upon this one." Lady

Constance stopped, pausing for dramatic effect.

The fly flew off right then, and Anastasia breathed a tiny sigh of relief. The last thing she needed was to sneeze and give her presence away. She should not be listening, but she could not escape either. She desperately wanted to leave and yet, at the same time, wanted to see how the conversation ended. What if everything the aunt said was true? Anastasia held herself still. Regardless of the outcome, Rella must never know Anastasia heard.

"And?" Rella asked impatiently.

"It seems that there was an event some seventeen years and three months ago, give or take," Lady Constance said.

"Apparently, a particular gentleman caught your mama's eye. The gentleman's wife criticized your mama publicly at an important social event. Your mama decided to take her revenge by sleeping with the woman's husband, right in their own bed. Your mama never expected anything to come of the encounter except to teach the man's wife a lesson."

The aunt's voice paused again, letting her words sink in. "But here you are, a result of that incident."

Anastasia put her hand over her mouth to keep silent her squeak of surprise.

"Exactly what are you implying, Aunt Connie?" Rella asked angrily.

"Oh, I am not implying anything, dear. It is all in here. The party, the gentleman, the mating, the pregnancy, even the birth. It is the truth, and it is *all* in this letter. So, you see, my dear little niece, you do not have Covington blood in your veins, and should the truth of your lineage be revealed, the courts will more than likely grant Lord Covington's wishes in his choice of successor. You will *never* inherit Covington lands and estate. If he did leave his title to his wife, the courts will honor that decision. On the other hand, if you were to go to the courts and request your uncle and me as your new guardians, this letter shall disappear. I believe the courts will be swayed in accepting your uncle's petition for the title. Titles are passed from man to man, after all." The aunt sounded quite happy as she delivered the news.

Anastasia's eyes widened. She had both hands over her mouth now. This was worse than she thought. She really needed to escape before either lady realized the conversation had been overheard.

"And if I do not request a change of guardian?" Rella asked thinly.

A tinkling laugh came from the direction of the settees.

"Well, my dear, unless you plan to wed tonight and hand over your claim to the Covington wealth to your husband, the courts will grant your stepmother guardianship. You shall never receive your inheritance. That greedy woman and her loathsome daughters will run the estate into the ground."

Anastasia leaned back, shocked at the venom in the aunt's voice. They did not even know the woman and she spoke of them in such a horrid, critical way.

"How much is your help going to cost me?" Rella asked at last.

"Half of everything!" the lady responded.

"Half!" Rella's scream of indignation echoed loudly. Anastasia covered her ears. "You greedy, wicked woman! How dare you come in here and threaten me!" Rella roared. Anastasia made herself as little as possible.

"Careful, my little niece, you do not want to anger me. Not while I hold such valuable information about you here in in my hand. Think, my dear, your whole world will disappear with one little reading of this letter."

There was the sound of scuffling followed by a yelp of surprise.

"You have a gun?" Rella's voice rose in fear.

"Yes. I do and I am not afraid to use it if I must. You cannot have this letter; it is mine, and I intend to keep it very safe." Anastasia tried not to breathe. Rella must have tried to get the letter causing the aunt to pull out a gun!

"What is it you intend, Aunt Connie?" Rella's voice dropped to a whisper. It barely reached Anastasia's terrified ears.

"Only this, either your uncle and I become your new guardians and you agree to give us half of Covington and all the wealth, or the contents of this letter shall become public knowledge within the next day or two. Is that what you want? You shall be branded as a bastard, you know."

There was a long silence following Lady Constance's announcement.

Anastasia shrunk on the seat. Perspiration broke out on her brow. She had to escape. Rella would make her life a living hell if she ever found out Anastasia knew all that happened here.

"We both know how that will end for you. Can you do without your fancy dresses? Your fancy house? Your fancy name and rank? The honor Lord

Covington's name gives you?" Lady Remington laughed. "I think not, my dear little niece. You would live in the streets. No one would help you. No one would want you. No one would marry you or treat you honorably. The only thing you could do to earn the bread you eat and a roof over your head, would be to lift you skirts for every man that has the coin to pay to get between your legs. I would think carefully about your decision, if I were you."

"How do I know that letter is real? How do I know you did not make all this up to get your hands on what is rightfully mine?" Rella spoke bitterly from her position on the settees.

"Oh, it is real enough. No court in the land will deny what is written right here in your mother's own hand! What do you call this sort of thing?" A long pregnant pause followed. "Oh yes, a confession. That is what it is, a confession."

Anastasia heard the malice in Lady Constance's voice and shivered. This woman was Rella's relative. She shared the same dark frame of mind. Rella must not find her here or know Anastasia had been here, ever.

"What do you want me to do?" Rella's voice was clipped now. Anastasia recognized the tone. Rella was making plans.

"I want you to name me as your guardian, your only blood relative. Your uncle and I shall petition the courts for your inheritance, and you shall give us half of everything."

"And if Papa left everything to Lady Evelyn?"

Anastasia's ears pricked. Surely this was not happening! What if Papa *had* left Mama everything?

"It will not matter. We will claim your inheritance

on blood rights. Besides, the courts are far more likely to grant our petition and bestow the title on your uncle. It will work out splendidly! Your uncle and I shall move in here. We will, of course, require the master's suite. You shall have your pick of the other chambers. Oh, I simply cannot wait to feel the Covington jewels about my neck!" The aunt's voice rose as she spoke.

Anastasia sat perfectly still. Such a thing was not possible was it? They had nowhere to go and Papa had only been dead for two whole days.

Rella screamed with fury. "You cannot have them! I will not let you touch them! They are mine!"

There was more scuffling. Someone hit the floor.

Anastasia heard a click, as the hammer of the gun was pulled back and she sank even farther into the window seat. *Dear God, the aunt is going to shoot Rella*!

"Need I remind you what will happen if the contents of this letter are revealed? You will have nothing, absolutely nothing! Do you understand what I am saying? Not even your name. Think carefully before you answer. Do we have a deal or not?" The woman spoke firmly. She meant business.

There was a longer pause. Anastasia looked at the latch on the window. Locked! If only the door were not so far away. She felt faint with terror. She wished she had gone somewhere else to be alone. Listening to Rella's aunt threaten her with a gun made Anastasia nauseous. *What if she shoots Rella?*

"Yes." Rella's whisper floated toward Anastasia.

Anastasia held her breath, waiting for the response.

"Meet me in town at the inn tomorrow evening after the will has been read, and we shall discuss this further." Lady Constance was all business now. Footsteps moved away toward the library door.

Rella must have nodded for Lady Remington spoke again.

"Good. I shall see myself out."

The library door closed with a thud. Anastasia shakily let out the breath she had been holding. Had they both gone or was Rella still in the library? Anastasia waited for another couple of minutes, listening intently for any sound indicating Rella was still there. She heard nothing. Cautiously, Anastasia peeked around the drapery. The room was empty. She drew in a shaky breath and stepped from her hiding spot. Her legs shook as she began to walk toward the door.

Thank God Rella had not thought to check the window seat!

Anastasia was aghast at what she had heard! What if it was true and Rella was *not* Lord Covington's daughter? She stopped for a few moments and thought. Was it true? How could Rella be anyone other than Papa's daughter? He certainly loved Rella the same as if she were. It was a puzzle to be sure, but not one to be solved in the library. Anastasia shook her head. It would be best to leave before anyone found her here. She reached for the handle on the door as it opened and Rella walked back inside!

Her eyes narrowed at the sight of Anastasia. Rella looked behind Anastasia at the large windows and understanding dawned. A cruel smile twisted her mouth. Rella shut the library door with a dull thud and stood in front of it, blocking Anastasia's only escape.

Chapter 3

"What are you doing in here?" Rella's eyes narrowed as she took in Anastasia's expression.

Anastasia shivered even though the room was very warm. The magnificent marble fireplace gave off inordinate amounts of heat.

A small smile curved Rella's mouth, realization dawning in her eyes "You have been here the whole time, have you not?"

Rella must never know I overheard the whole conversation. Anastasia did not answer. She stood there looking back at Rella. In truth, she did not know what to say, and if she said the wrong thing, Rella would pounce on it like the hens with their morning feed. She learned a long time ago during her first few situations with Rella to be still. Whatever Rella did or said, it only became worse, much, much worse if she said a word.

"Answer me." Rella took a menacing step toward Anastasia, but Anastasia held her ground.

When Anastasia refused to answer, Rella changed tactics and stepped back against the door, effectively blocking Anastasia in again. "I can see that you overheard my conversation," Rella said.

Anastasia did not move. She really should have stayed in the window seat for another few minutes.

"I suppose you think you are a very smart girl, hiding in the window the whole time Aunt Connie and I talked," Rella continued, her eyes narrowing.

Anastasia did not move. She knew Rella hated her with all her heart and the last thing she wanted to do was make Rella angry.

"Where were you going in such a hurry?" Rella taunted. "Were you going to run to your mama and tell her about the letter?"

Anastasia still did not answer. Rella eyes glowed with anger.

"Let me save you the trouble." Rella tossed her head as if the whole thing was a mere annoyance. "The letter is a complete fake. Aunt Connie is trying to take my papa's money. She always was jealous of Mama and her money. Aunt Connie has tried to take the money before and this is another scheme she came up with to steal my inheritance," she said.

"Now that Papa is dead. Aunt Connie thought she could come here and blackmail me while I suffer over his death. Well, it won't work. I am stronger than Aunt Connie thinks, and I will not be used."

Silence. Anastasia refused to let Rella see the horror she felt at what she overheard.

A crafty smile curved Rella's mouth. "You are too late, again."

Anastasia felt the blood drain from her face.

"I already solved the problem, and if you tell Lady Evelyn what you heard, you will only be a disappointment to her again. No one will believe you. I will deny it all, and they will believe what I tell them." Rella sneered.

It was true. Whenever Anastasia went to Lady Evelyn over the years, to tell her about the things Rella did, Rella always twisted the truth and told the story with so many little lies, that Lady Evelyn believed Rella, and told Anastasia how disappointing she was. Nothing Anastasia said would convince her otherwise. It did not help that Rella pointed it out to her now.

"So, I would not bother if I were you. Besides, it is all a lie." Rella laughed a cruel little laugh, her eyes sparkling with malice. Then she turned deadly serious; her gaze pinned Anastasia to the floor.

"This is what will *not* happen." Rella stared into Anastasia's eyes. "You will *not* talk about today, about what you heard, or about Aunt Connie, *ever*. Do you understand me? You will *not* breathe a word of this to anybody."

Rella held the stare intently for several seconds. "If you say a word, I will tell Lady Evelyn that you hid your stitching square so Papa would not find it."

Anastasia flinched at Rella's reference to the sampler and that horrible day, but she did not answer her. She stared straight back at Rella, exchanging stare for stare. She showed no emotion, nothing. She had been threatened many times by Rella, and she knew the fastest way to deal with her, was to show no feeling, until Rella got tired of taunting her.

"My aunt is going to pay dearly for trying to blackmail me," Rella promised darkly, "and you will too if you say a word."

"I am not scared of you." Anastasia swallowed.

"Aren't you?" Rella laughed, her gaze on Anastasia's throat.

"No. I am not."

Rella dropped her smile. "You should be. You have no idea how sorry I can make you. You will regret ever knowing anything about me or my private affairs."

Anastasia did not answer.

Rella glared at Anastasia. She moved away from the door and walked to the blazing fire. Rella held her hands out to warm them. Then, she turned back toward Anastasia.

"I shall have my inheritance. It will all be mine and there is not anything Aunt Connie, you, Beatrice or your mother can do about it. I shall stop anybody that gets in my way," she promised. Her blue eyes sliced a glacial look at Anastasia. Rella was as aloof and cold as the ice that now covered the pond outside.

Anastasia made for the door. With Rella across the room, she could make her escape. The library door closed behind Anastasia with a thud. Only then did she notice how her hands shook.

****

The funeral for Lord Robert Covington was an elegant affair. Flowers appeared out of nowhere and covered every inch of the little village church. His Royal Highness, King Alexander Kazimir Augustine, was in attendance with a whole squadron of soldiers in freshly pressed red and black uniforms to honor the king's fallen diplomat. The entire village was aflutter with excitement and awe at the presence of their royal visitor. Residents for miles around made it to the church in their Sunday best clothing, with their hair slicked back. Some of them even wore shoes. Most of them came to mourn their lord. Some of them came merely to say they sat in the same church as His Royal Highness. All of them came to pay their respects.

Seating had to be set up outside to accommodate the crush of mourners and although most of them could not hear the service, they were glad to be in attendance.

Even the vicar outdid himself, giving the finest eulogy anyone ever heard.

After the service concluded, the guests pressed toward the king, and the king's soldiers formed a defensive barrier between King Alexander and his loyal subjects. Many of the villagers got to kiss the royal hand and considered it an unspeakable honor to pay their respects to Lord Covington alongside His Majesty.

Soon after, the king held his arms up, indicating he had something to say, and everyone fell silent. The king presented Lady Evelyn with a unique round gold medallion. The royal seal was affixed to one side of the medallion; Lord Covington's seal was affixed to the other. The king held the medallion up for all to see and then he turned to Lady Evelyn.

"We gift this medallion to you, Lady Evelyn and to the family of Lord Covington, as a small token of our royal love and devotion for Lord Covington. Lord Robert Covington was a good and honorable man. He was a dear friend and a loyal subject. He gave his life for his king and his country. Lord Covington possessed diplomatic skills without compare. We narrowly avoided war on many occasions, thanks to this man. The entire kingdom owes him a great debt of gratitude. And so, to show our royal appreciation for all Lord Covington has done, we present this medallion with the promise of our royal favor. If you are ever in need or in trouble, present this medallion, and you have our royal word that whatever favor you seek, it shall be granted as long as it is within our power to grant it." King Alexander extended the medallion toward Lady Evelyn and bowed to show his love and respect.

Lady Evelyn accepted the medallion with a low

curtsy.

"We shall all miss him," the king said.

King Alexander kissed Lady Evelyn's gloved hand, and with a wave to his many loyal subjects, he climbed into his royal carriage and settled back against the red velvet cushions for the return journey to Larenia. The royal guard in their red and black uniforms, gold braids gleaming in the sunlight, mounted their large white stallions and formed a protective line about the royal carriage. The squadron of soldiers brought up the rear. On Colonel Stolinski's command, they set forth.

The mourners all returned to Covington House for refreshments and conversation. They also came for the reading of the will. Everyone was curious about who the courts would award the title and lands to, with no living male heir to inherit.

The solicitors arrived at the house later that evening, in their black shiny coach. Four black horses pulled to a stop in front of the massive oak door of the two-story stone structure of Covington House. The elder solicitor entered first; a long parchment held reverently in one gloved hand. His three partners, all attired in black coats, black breeches, black boots, and black hats followed him. Identical black gloves upon their hands, identical frowns upon their faces. They stoically took their seats on the four cushioned chairs Lady Evelyn had placed in the red salon.

The will was written on parchment, rolled up, and sealed with two wax seals. One bearing the Covington seal and one bearing the solicitors seal, ensuring the will remained legitimate and had not been opened or altered.

Lady Evelyn and the three girls sat on chairs in the

front row, facing the solicitors. After the two seals were examined to verify their authenticity, the family and the solicitors signed legal papers as witness to the fact.

Mr. Primm, the oldest member of the distinguished firm of Primm, Knight, Langley, and Kelch, did the honors of the reading.

His voice droned on and on as he went over all the preliminary sections, then on to the responsibilities of the House of Covington, and finally, to the immediate family.

****

Rella dozed off in her chair; she was so bored. She wasn't entirely sure why she needed to be here at all. Everybody knew the whole of Covington Estate belonged to her now, or would as soon as the courts made up their mind,

"...do leave Covington Estate and all that is entailed to said estate, having no other blood relative to take possession of the Covington title, house and Estate, as well as all of my worldly goods and possessions to my loving wife, Lady Evelyn Covington. She shall care and watch over our three girls. She is the most loving and honorable of companions and so I leave the welfare of my only descendants Lady Beatrice Covington, Lady Anastasia Covington, and Lady Rella Covington in her capable hands."

Rella sat straight up. "What did you say?" she shrieked.

Mr. Primm stopped reading and glanced over the silver rim of his glasses at the young blonde girl seated in the first row. Then he looked at Lady Evelyn. "My Lady, would you be so kind as to control the young miss so I might continue?"

"Of course," Lady Evelyn replied. "Rella, dear, perhaps this is a little much for you. The recent affairs have been a strain on us all. Perhaps you should go lie down for a bit. Would you like to be excused, darling?"

"I would not!" Anger made Rella's face hot and her hands fisted tightly in her lap.

Lady Evelyn studied Rella for a minute then said, "Please forgive the interruption, sir. Pray continue."

The solicitor resumed reading after a long solemn stare at Rella.

Rella fumed. *How dare they take Covington Estate! The House! The Covington Lands! The Covington jewels! The paintings! The furniture! It belongs to me! It is my inheritance! My right! What does it matter that most of the wealth is tied to the Covington title? It still belongs to me! Look at them. I shared everything with them! My house! My papa! And my money!* She glared at the trio of demons who ruined her life. She needed to pretend not to care for Papa's sake. How had Lady Evelyn convinced Papa to leave her as guardian and in control anyway? Lady Evelyn was a witch. Rella gave Lady Evelyn a long considering look. She was more devious than Rella gave her credit for. Rella stamped her foot. Clever or not, if Lady Evelyn thought Rella was going to sit meekly by and let her take Rella's inheritance, she was sadly mistaken. *I will make them all pay for this!*

****

Anastasia watched Rella's face. She saw the emotions chasing themselves around and around. She never saw Rella lose control before. Usually Rella only showed the emotion she wanted others to see. Anastasia watched with dread. She saw surprise, anger, hatred, anger again, and then steely determination. A knot formed in Anastasia's stomach. She needed to be especially careful from now on. Anastasia knew Rella blamed them for the change in Papa's will. She could see it on Rella's face. Rella intended to make them pay for whatever it was she decided they had done. Rella excused herself, claiming a headache and went off to her chambers after the reading concluded. Anastasia watched her go with trepidation.

Lady Evelyn glanced after Rella with concern etched on her face, but agreed with a soft, "of course, darling."

There were papers to sign and witness.

The solicitors shook Lady Evelyn's hand and left soon after, entreating her to call if she needed anything.

****

Later that evening, after all the guests and visitors left, Lady Evelyn, Beatrice and Anastasia retired to the red salon. Lady Evelyn sat upon a settee, her hands clasped in her lap. She quietly stared into the merry fire blazing on the hearth. Beatrice was beside her, reading quietly.

Cook set a tray of sandwiches on the gleaming table at their knees.

"You must eat something, m'lady. You will become weak and sickly if you do not." Cook placed a dainty sandwich and a slice of lemon cake on a small plate and held it toward Lady Evelyn.

"Come, m'lady, try some tea and cake; it will help you get your strength back."

Lady Evelyn took the plate and smiled. "Thank you, Diedre." She took the cup of tea Cook held out for her and sipped it slowly.

"What is wrong, Mama?" Beatrice looked in concern at Lady Evelyn's face.

"Mr. Primm had a private word with me before his departure. It seems that we are not as well off as I thought. According to Mr. Primm, Robert spent so much time away from his fields and from the distillery following the death of Lady Agnes, his first wife and Rella's mother, that the production of the Covington Brandy is not what it has been. Because it takes a minimum of five years to age the brandy, we have very little to sell. It shall get better, of course, as the brandy we made since then comes of age. But for now, there is not much. Up until now, we have been living off the money the king paid Robert for his service as diplomat. Now, without that money from Robert's service, we have almost nothing to live on." Lady Evelyn's face was pale, the worry evident around her eyes.

"What are you saying, Mama?" Beatrice asked.

"I am saying that without your papa we do not have much money."

Beatrice was bewildered, "But we do have brandy we could sell."

"I sold what we had on hand to pay the outstanding household bills. I also paid for another load of coal."

"Do we have any left?" Anastasia inquired.

"A little," Lady Evelyn answered.

"How can we be poor when we have so much around us?"

"Could we not sell some jewelry or something?" Beatrice inquired.

"It is all entailed to the Covington Title," Lady Evelyn explained. "Since your papa left all of Covington Estate to me, perhaps I could sell something that is not entailed. But, oh my darlings, I would rather not. It hurts me to think of selling something so important to your papa. I would much rather try to make do without selling any of the wonderful things that belonged to him."

Lady Evelyn sighed. "I had a meeting with the staff, after dinner, I explained that we do not have the coins to pay them their wages, and most of them agreed to find other positions. Henry and Cook shall stay, of course, and the gardener, but I had to let everyone else go." Lady Evelyn studied the girls. They were both lost in thought, their faces very sober. So much had changed in the last few days.

"We shall be fine, my darlings. It is not as bad as all that. We have food in the larder, coal to keep us warm, and I believe if we practice a little economy, we will get along splendidly."

Anastasia looked up as the door swung open and Rella stepped inside the room.

"I shall sleep downstairs in the kitchens," Rella said, "I believe it will help conserve fuel if you have one less room to keep warm."

Anastasia stared. *Is Rella suggesting she sleep downstairs with Cook?*

Rella was taking this surprisingly well. Never in the five years since they lived together had Rella done anything to jeopardize her own personal comfort.

"Oh, my beautiful darling," Lady Evelyn got up and hugged the girl to her heart, "what a sweet loving girl you are. To think you would make such a sacrifice! You truly are an angel! But really, darling, while I appreciate your sacrifice with all my heart, things are not as bad as all that. We can afford to heat your room.

You need not sleep downstairs."

"But I want to, and so I shall." With that Rella turned and began to walk out at the same moment Henry walked in.

"Forgive me, my lady, there is a message here for Miss Rella." Henry handed Lady Evelyn the missive he held in his gloved hand.

"It seems that Lady Constance Remington has been found dead in the alley behind the inn in town," Henry informed them.

"Lady Constance Remington? I have not heard that name for quite some time, and you say she was here? at the inn in town?" Lady Evelyn's brow wrinkled with perplexity. "and she is dead? How can that be?"

"Aunt Connie? Are they sure it was her?" Rella seemed to be surprised.

"Who is she, Mama?" Anastasia could not resist asking.

"She is the sister of Lady Agnes, Lady Rella's mother, dear," Lady Evelyn answered.

"She was stabbed, my lady," the butler announced. "The constable was just here. They are doing all they can to find the killer."

Lady Evelyn put a delicate hand over her heart. "Oh my," Lady Evelyn turned in concern to Rella.

Anastasia glanced at her, too. *Does Rella know something about Lady Remington's death?* Suspicion flowered as the threats Rella hurled at Lady Remington went around and around in Anastasia's mind.

A sudden scream echoed around the room, causing the other occupants to jump at the sound.

"She cannot be dead! She cannot! I cannot lose Aunt Constance too! Not so soon after losing Papa! It is too much! I cannot do it!" Rella threw herself onto the settee facing Lady Evelyn and began to scream even louder.

Lady Evelyn jumped to her feet and hurried to the screaming girl. "Run quickly, Anastasia, and fetch my herbs. I shall need something for the poor darling to calm her nerves. I am afraid she has suffered too many upsets in these last few days. This last one may send her over the edge."

Anastasia ran from the room to do her mother's bidding. Anything to get away from Rella's screaming was welcomed.

When Anastasia returned with the herbs, Rella was seated next to Lady Evelyn, sobbing uncontrollably against the older lady's shoulder while Lady Evelyn smoothed Rella's hair back from her forehead. Big tears streamed down Rella's cheeks. Beatrice stood over them wringing her hands looking unsure of how to help.

"There, there, my darling. It shall be all right," Lady Evelyn murmured into Rella's blonde hair. "Now help me, girls, get Rella up the stairs to her bed."

Beatrice went to one side of Rella, Anastasia the other, and with their arms about her waist, they got her up the stairs, down the long hall, and into bed.

"Hand me the poppy, dearest." Lady Evelyn took the bottle from Anastasia and deftly prepared a draught for the still sobbing girl.

After Rella drank the draught, Lady Evelyn laid her gently back against the mountain of soft pillows. "There, my darling, that should help," she murmured. Then she turned to Anastasia, "Stay with your sister, dearest, until she is asleep. I must put my medicines away."

Beatrice followed Lady Evelyn out the door, while Anastasia blew out the candles burning by the bed. The only light came from the fire that burned in the hearth. The door closed behind them, and Anastasia was alone with Rella.

A high-pitched laugh came from the bed. It rose and mingled with the shadows causing an eerie darkness to settle on Anastasia. Rella sat up, a sinister smile splitting her face.

"Poor Aunt Connie is dead," Rella softly sang. "Who would have supposed she would die so suddenly?" Rella sang out.

Anastasia shivered; a cold feeling settled in her chest.

Rella laughed again and jumped from the bed. She began twirling around and around the floor, laughing as if possessed.

Anastasia stood still beside the chest where she had blown out the last candle. Her eyes widened with astonishment as she watched Rella twirl about the room in her night rail. The darkness around her was heavy, forbidding. Anastasia moved a little closer to the hearth as she watched. Rella had changed dramatically once Lady Evelyn and Beatrice left the room; her shadow made frightening images on the chamber wall. *Has she gone mad?*

"I do not see what is funny about Lady Remington's death," Anastasia said.

Rella stopped twirling and stared at Anastasia. "Don't you?"

"No, death is not something to laugh about and how Lady Remington died is terrifying. She should not have died all alone in an alley." Anastasia shivered at the thought. She faced death by herself once, and it was the most frightening thing she'd ever experienced.

Rella laughed cruelly and started to twirl once more. The shadows lengthened and grew more grotesque.

"She did not deserve to die in such a brutal manner," Anastasia insisted.

"Yes, she did. She tried to blackmail me. It is exactly what she deserved," Rella said.

"How can you say such a thing? She was your aunt!" Another shiver went down Anastasia's spine.

"And she wanted to use me to take my inheritance." Rella smiled in satisfaction. Rella stopped dancing about and walked to her bed. She reached under her mattress and brought out a folded letter. "Look what I have." Rella waved the letter slowly in Anastasia's pale face.

"What is it?" Anastasia asked.

"What do you think? Aunt Connie should have known better than to try to match wits with me."

Anastasia felt the darkness of the room press down on her, making it hard to breathe. She wanted to leave but Mama asked her to stay until Rella was asleep.

"This is the very letter Aunt Connie wanted to blackmail me with." Rella flapped the letter in Anastasia's face one more time. "The one with all the proof." An evil smile twisted her lips.

Anastasia looked at her. In truth, she was horrified and more than a little bit afraid.

Rella bent down and threw the letter into the flames, watching as the letter burned. "There," she said, "that takes care of that." Rella smiled in smug satisfaction at the ashes the letter left.

Rella must be mad. Anastasia continued to stare at her. Rella was laughing like a lunatic. Her blue eyes shining with malice.

"Where...how did you get the letter from your aunt?" Anastasia asked.

Rella turned toward Anastasia, the darkness casting eerie shadows across her face. A slow smile spread across her face. "I found it on my pillow," Rella lied.

Anastasia shivered.

Rella climbed back into bed and pulled the bedclothes over herself.

"Do you know who killed her?" Anastasia whispered; her mouth suddenly dry.

"Do you?" Rella returned. Her eyes were narrow slits, and Anastasia took a hasty step back.

"No, how would I?" Anastasia asked.

"I could ask you the same question. How would I know?"

"You had the letter, so you must know something," Anastasia reasoned.

"Must I?" Rella fired back.

"You do not appear to be that upset about your aunt's death." Anastasia was surrounded by the darkness and she felt the evil closing in on her.

"On the contrary, Lady Evelyn, Beatrice, and the whole household believe I am extremely disconsolate over her death. In fact, Lady Evelyn is wondering if my aunt's sudden death disturbed my mind," Rella said. "I fear she may be right," Rella added. Then Rella yawned. The poppy was starting to take effect. She fluffed her pillows and lay back down.

"I do not feel sorry for Aunt Connie at all. She deserved to die. She threatened me." The sinister whisper floated in the darkness toward Anastasia.

Anastasia looked at Rella as terror squeezed her chest. "Are you not sad in the least bit that your aunt is dead?"

"Why should I be? She knew too much. You heard her," Rella said with irritation "This is what happens when someone knows too much." She stared eerily at Anastasia.

Anastasia swallowed her fear. "Are you saying I will die too, if I tell someone what I heard?" Anastasia asked quietly.

"I did not say that. I am saying you better keep your mouth shut. We do not know who killed Aunt Connie, but with her dead, that only leaves you and I that know what was in that letter!"

Is Rella threatening me?

Rella settled herself back against her pillows, an evil satisfied smile on her face.

Anastasia was frozen with horror at the turn in the conversation. She knew Rella did not like her. When they were alone, Rella made no secret of her dislike, and she got such enjoyment out of orchestrating scenarios that got Anastasia into trouble with Papa and Mama. But did she dislike her enough to threaten her life? Surely not. Rella liked to be difficult and to cause scenes, but she was not an evil person, was she? Anastasia looked over at Rella. Her eyes were closed now and her breathing even. Rella was finally asleep, thank God. Anastasia slipped from the room, her mind racing. Did Rella know something about Lady Remington's death? She did not seem the least upset with the news. Nor was she surprised. In truth, she almost seemed pleased her aunt was dead. And where did Rella get the letter from? Rella's tears had been for Mama's benefit, Anastasia knew. She witnessed many scenes like this over the years. But what about the gleam in Rella's eye when she spoke of her aunt's death? Was it satisfaction, perhaps? Anastasia quickened her pace. She felt something evil in Rella's room she could not explain. She hoped it was only her imagination at work again.

Chapter 4

It was finally spring. After a long cold winter, the sun came out from behind the clouds, and the birds started to sing. Flowers sprang from the ground with wild abandon. Green appeared in the trees and in the fields.

Anastasia leaned on the makeshift counter. She pulled her tight sleeve further down her arm and rubbed at the scar to ease the ache. The stall they rented at the local market was not much, but it served as a place to sell the fruit and vegetables they grew. She sighed as she thought about the last few months. A lot of things changed in her world since Papa died. It was difficult, at first, to learn to do some of the things they always had servants do for them, such as washing and ironing, for instance. Those tasks were not easy ones. Who knew too much lye in the water with the clothing caused holes? Or that a hot iron burned through cloth in a few seconds? Well, Anastasia did, now. She grimaced at her calloused hands and chipped nails. She learned to sweep, to mop, to dust carpets, to clean wood paneling, and to clean the drapery. She even knew how to polish the silver. It had been a long winter.

Anastasia lifted her face toward the warmth of the sun and wanted to sing with the birds. It was wonderful to be outside and feel the gentle breeze across her face.

"'Ello dear. What yer sellin' today, aye?"

Anastasia turned. Mrs. Wilton, the butcher's mother, stood before her counter. She was bent with age and blind in one eye, but she got around.

"Cherries, tomatoes, and fresh eggs," Anastasia answered with a smile.

"Ow do ye have tomatoes, aye? It ain't been warm long." Mrs. Wilton tapped the counter with her wooden cane.

"I planted them early and kept the plants in little pots in the kitchen where it is warm," Anastasia said.

"Yer a smart one," the old woman cackled, "wouldn't a thought o' that meself."

Anastasia smiled again. "How is your leg?"

Mrs. Wilton took a tumble two days before when some unruly village boys accidentally ran into her as they raced through the street. "'Ers doin' fine now. Thanks to yer ma fer the liniment." The old lady tapped her leg with her cane. "Nary a pain."

"That is wonderful, Mrs. Wilton. I shall tell Mama the news."

"Yer ma is a good woman. Ye tell 'er 'ello, aye." With that Mrs. Wilton left, toddling along with her cane.

"This is a complete waste of time," Rella announced as she came walking toward their stall from the dressmaker's shop. "I do not understand why you insist on standing out here like a commoner. I will not. The sun is ruining my complexion and I want to go home."

Anastasia sighed. With Rella, it was always the same thing. "It is not a waste of time. It is how we eat and keep a roof over our heads."

"Well, I for one am not standing out here and

subjecting myself to the commoners, or the smell. I am going for a walk." Rella turned and walked up the street to the shoemaker's shop.

Anastasia sighed again.

Beatrice finished helping her customer and put the coins in her pocket. "All the eggs are sold and almost all the tomatoes. Mama will be pleased."

Anastasia nodded and moved the basket of cherries to the front of the counter.

Two village boys ran by, grabbing the basket of cherries as they ran past.

"Hey! Put that down!" Anastasia called as she hurried around the edge of the stall. They lost all their cherries last week too, and to the same two boys she suspected. They certainly seemed familiar enough.

"Do not chase them, Anastasia, what will everyone think?" Beatrice wrung her hands and called after her, but Anastasia was already running down the street after the two boys. She chased them through the alley and over a couple of fences. She cleared the fence quicker than the straggler and nearly caught him by his shirt, but the little devil caught the edge of a porch and pulled himself onto a low roof. *He must do this a lot.* Anastasia thought to herself as she pulled herself onto the same roof and began climbing. It felt wonderful to use her arm again. She spied the boy balancing along the peak of the roof as he hurried to the other side. *Little rascal.* She would have given the boys some of the cherries if they but asked. She made it to the top of the roof and began to walk along the edge. She was half-way across when her foot slipped, and she went tumbling head over heels down the steep slope of the roof.

Drat!

She closed her eyes when she went over the edge and waited for the impact. It was not what she expected! She hit against a warm solid something that knocked the breath out of her. Two bands of steel clamped around her and held her still. She opened her eyes cautiously and found herself nose to nose with a very handsome man. Two dark blue eyes gazed intently into hers. Laughter crinkled the corners of his eyes. Locks of black hair fell across his broad forehead.

"What did you catch, Val?" an amused male voice behind them asked the question.

Val was taking a heated inventory of the woman he held in his arms. He focused on the disarray of her hair, the fullness of her breasts, the narrowness of her waist, and then the soft pink lips so close to his own. He pulled her close against him, amused and intrigued.

"I merely asked the gods for their favor on our hunt, and they dropped a goddess right into my arms." He tightened his hold about her waist and leaned in for a closer look.

Desire slammed into him like a battle-ax. He liked what he saw. This angel that dropped from the sky was beautiful with her long ebony hair, green eyes, and pert little nose.

Bewitching. He stared at her mouth so close to his and wondered if she tasted as good as she looked. He wanted this enchanting girl.

****

Anastasia could not move. He studied her through half-closed eyes, like a predator studies its prey. She drowned in the heat of his eyes and all around her was his scent. He smelled of the woods, sunshine, and danger. Her lips parted and her breathing quickened. A tingling sensation began somewhere in the region of her stomach and spread through her whole body. White-hot heat pumped through her veins. Her body hummed with excitement and danger. His gaze moved from her lips, to her heaving chest, and then back to her mouth. He leaned closer still. Every nerve she had screamed with sensory overload. She felt as though she were a tender piece of meat being offered to a hungry wolf. She waited for his touch, her breath coming quickly. His full mouth hovered above her own. If either of them moved the smallest bit...

"Will you put my sister down?"

Anastasia jumped at the sound.

Beatrice stood right behind her now, her voice indignant.

The man lifted his head slowly and turned to face Beatrice. "I caught her; now she is mine to keep," he teased.

Beatrice did not look amused at the situation. "Put her down at once," she commanded. "You cannot hold my sister like that, sir, it is not proper. People are beginning to stare."

"The lady is right, Val. We are about to be the talk of the village," the other voice said.

Val glanced around with a frown of annoyance and set Anastasia on her feet.

Anastasia dragged in a hard breath. She was dizzy. When her feet touched the ground, her legs wobbled like a young colt.

He stared down into her eyes again, hypnotizing her with his heat. Anastasia blinked up at him, trying to reason beyond the spell he wove around her. She grabbed hold of him to keep her knees from buckling. His arms were thick with muscle, and the fire he radiated almost burned her fingers. He was so tall that his shoulders blocked out the sun. The top of her head did not reach his chin. Anastasia boldly let her eyes wander over his massive chest and the bulge of muscle visible beneath the coarse tunic he wore. Lord, this man was fit and large. She shivered. Heat pooled into her stomach, as she stood on liquid legs. Was he a soldier of some kind? Surely, nobody could be this well-defined unless he trained regularly. Anastasia tried to speak but her mouth was dry, and her tongue way too big. She licked her lips. Val's gaze flickered to her mouth. Val leaned toward her. Anastasia began to quiver against him with some nameless desire.

"Anastasia, will you let go of that man and come with me? Have you taken leave of your senses? What will Mama say when I tell her of your lack of decorum today?'

Anastasia jumped again at the sound of Beatrice's voice. She looked down in bemusement. Lord, she had hold of his tunic with both hands. She blushed and made her hands let go of him.

"What is your name?" Val asked.

"My name is Anastasia," she answered. She felt the heat in her cheeks. "Thank you for catching me," she managed to whisper.

"My pleasure," he drawled. "Anytime you need catching, I will be there, Anastasia."

His voice held a velvet promise, and Anastasia felt her stomach clench. She did not know what to say. In truth, her mind seemed to have deserted her altogether.

Val winked at her, a slow provocative gesture, then

turned to his companion. "Come, Vroknar, there is other game to be caught."

Only as the beautiful man walked away did Anastasia's breathing return to normal. Then she became aware that he had not one companion but several.

"What is wrong with you today?" Beatrice chided. "Have you taken complete leave of your senses?" she asked for the second time.

Confused, Anastasia looked at her. "What senses?"

"I am beginning to wonder the same myself," Beatrice muttered as she grabbed Anastasia's arm and dragged her back to their stall.

"How could you let a stranger hold you like that? It is not proper for him to be so forward with you. And he is so big. What if he had evil intentions toward you?"

Anastasia had no idea what an intention was, so she asked.

Beatrice rolled her eyes.

"Did he try to kiss you?" Beatrice sounded more interested now than outraged. But then she bounced back to the outrage. "Why were you not trying to get away? Mama is going to be disappointed in you."

It was worth it. Anastasia closed her eyes and thought of the strong warm arms that held her, and the beautiful eyes that sucked her soul right out of her body. The heat and the danger made her breathing erratic. Besides, she was getting used to disappointing her mother.

Beatrice shoved her shoulder. "Here comes a customer. Pay attention, Anastasia. We have almost sold everything. In a little while we can go home."

It was Mrs. Griffin the dressmaker. She walked

right up to the booth and put a finger in Anastasia's face. "You should be ashamed of yourself," the thin little lady said without preamble. Mrs. Griffin looked down her thin nose at Anastasia and adjusted her glasses. "How could you treat such a gentle, sweet girl so poorly? She is such an angel and she deserves better." Mrs. Griffin sniffed.

Anastasia was confused. "What gentle sweet girl, Mrs. Griffin?"

"She loves you so much. It shows on her face when she talks about you, and it breaks my heart to see her suffering. Her losing her mama at such a young age and now losing her papa, too!" Mrs. Griffin brought out a handkerchief and dabbed at her eyes. "After all her suffering, and all the sacrifices she made for you and your sister, for your family, how could you make her sleep in the kitchen with the staff? How could you make her wait on you and treat her like a servant?" Mrs. Griffin wailed.

Understanding inserted itself into Anastasia's muddled mind. *Rella.*

"Oh yes, I know all about it, and you do not fool me one little bit with your innocent act." Mrs. Griffin tapped Anastasia on the chest, punctuating her words with her finger. "I can see right through you."

"You have got it all wrong, Mrs. Griffin. Rella does not work—"

Mrs. Griffin cut her off. "I do not want to hear your lies Anastasia Covington." Mrs. Griffin adjusted her glasses once more. "That girl is truly an angel and you should be ashamed, deeply ashamed of yourself." She wagged her finger in Anastasia's face once more "The poor dear came to my shop to get a drink of water.

Your mother must not be thinking clearly to send poor Rella out with the likes of you. She says you will not even give her a drink of your water to wet her parched throat. I have to say I am extremely disappointed in you, Anastasia. Your poor papa would be too. Thank the good Lord he is not alive today." With that she walked away.

Beatrice was astounded, "Why would she think we would do such a thing? Rella does not do one thing to help…"

"I know."

"And what about the water? She has not been here all day to even acquire a parched throat!"

"We can talk later. Look at how the villagers are watching us." It was true. The villagers were in huddles whispering, and all gazes were upon them.

They sold the rest of their goods soon after and hurried home. Rella met up with them once they were outside the village. She followed idly along behind.

"I see you have been busy while we were in town," Anastasia remarked.

Rella swung her hat by its strings and hummed to herself. "Of course, I was busy; we all have to pitch in now that Papa is gone."

Anastasia rolled her eyes. Rella knew what she meant.

"Why did you tell Mrs. Griffin we force you to live downstairs and that we treat you like a servant?" Beatrice wanted to know.

"I do live downstairs."

"She said you had to get water from her because we would not give you any!"

"I was thirsty."

Beatrice appeared annoyed. "You do less work than anybody else."

"Says who?" Rella demanded. "I help all the time. In fact, all I do is help!"

They turned the corner and started up the long driveway to their home.

"Mama is going to be very upset when she hears all this talk. You know she loves you and she has not asked you to do one thing since Papa died."

"So?"

"So how can you say such ugly things?"

"Well, let me see." Rella stopped and put a finger against her chin pretending to think. "You took my papa away, you took my house away, you took my inheritance away; you took everything away. Your mama even sold some of the paintings right off the wall. My papa's paintings! My paintings! So why should I say nice things?"

Both the girls were surprised by the venom in Rella's voice. "Mama only sold those two paintings so we could have coal during the winter."

"And food," Beatrice added. "You saw how she cried when she took them off the wall. It broke her heart."

"So you say," Rella said. "I shall never forgive her for selling them."

"You ate the food they bought, too," Beatrice said.

"The coal kept you warm as well," Anastasia added.

"Whatever! They were my paintings and she had no right to sell them. She only did it to hurt me!"

"That is not true..." Beatrice began but Rella hurried away. She circled the lake and disappeared behind the trees.

"What will Mama say?" Beatrice whispered.

Anastasia was worried. Lady Evelyn was not sleeping. She was hardly eating, and she worked harder than anyone attending to the needs of the estate and the household.

"We will not tell her," Anastasia said. "She will not believe us anyway. Trust me; I have tried. Rella has done this many times over the years and Mama always believes her. Papa believed her, too." Anastasia was silent for a minute then asked, "Did you know Rella can cry at a moment's notice? Tears running down her face and everything."

"Oh, nonsense." Beatrice did not believe a word of it. "No one can do that."

"Rella can," Anastasia insisted.

"What difference does it make? Mrs. Griffin is going to tell everybody what Rella said today. She cannot keep anything to herself. Especially if she feels any emotion about whatever it is, and she feels emotional about this. The whole village will know by dinnertime. Then what shall we do? Mama will hear sooner or later."

"Let us hope it is later," Anastasia said, "much later."

Chapter 5

Beatrice did, of course, tell Lady Evelyn all about the cherries, the two village boys, and Val.

Lady Evelyn listened quietly until Beatrice finished her tale, and then she took Anastasia into the library.

Anastasia learned all kinds of things about men that she did not know before. Lady Evelyn warned her to stay away from Val. Common men did not act with honor. Lady Evelyn told her she was never allowed near men and certainly not close enough to tell if they had regular intentions, let alone evil ones. She noticed her mother failed to mention anything about the reactions Anastasia experienced. Surely a proper talk should also address the weakness in her legs, the fluttering in her stomach, and how hard it was to breathe when Val held her in his arms, shouldn't it? Anastasia sighed.

Girls her age were generally betrothed and sometimes married. She supposed most girls her age were experienced with men and their intentions. She had never been near one until Val caught her in his arms, and she had to fall off a roof for that to happen! *I wonder what I shall have to do to get married,* Anastasia thought with a grin. Beatrice was not betrothed either, so really, she had no reason to complain. Papa brushed the subject aside whenever Mama mentioned it, saying they still had plenty of time.

Well, apparently not as much time as they planned. Things did not always work out the way they should.

Lady Evelyn heard some of the whispering of the villagers, and promptly moved Rella back upstairs to her own chamber. "I cannot have everyone thinking you are a burden, dearest. And although I appreciate your willingness to sacrifice your personal comfort and sleep downstairs. It simply will not do. We will have to work a little harder, and I believe it will all work out."

****

The Spring Festival would soon begin, and the whole village was excited. The festival was a time of joy and fun after the long dark days of winter. There would be games, food, and entertainment for everyone.

Lady Evelyn and Cook got together and decided to sell sweet tarts at the festival. The money would see them through until the orchards and gardens started to produce. It was a very busy time.

Anastasia tended the stall in town today. Lady Evelyn sent Beatrice to help Cook in the kitchens making tarts. Rella should be helping Anastasia, but as usual, she was nowhere in sight. The day was unusually hot, and the customers were especially hard to please. Rella left on the pretense of getting more water to drink, but that was several hours ago. Anastasia blew a wisp of hair out of her eyes. *Where is Rella?*

Several customers approached the booth at once and Anastasia did her best dealing with all of them.

Suddenly, Rella appeared by her side and, with a quick hard shove, she knocked Anastasia out of her way and to the ground. Anastasia landed with a thump; the breath knocked out of her lungs. She laid there for a minute trying to decide what happened.

Mrs. Griffin's nasal voice reached her. "Oh, my dear girl! Here you are again, left alone tending the booth. Where is that worthless sister of yours anyway?"

"Why I have not seen her all morning, Mrs. Griffin, and there have been so many customers I have not even had a chance to sit down. I have been on my feet all day in this hot sun. Anastasia said she would get some water earlier this morning, but I have not seen her since."

Anastasia could not believe what she was hearing; she struggled to her feet, mad as a drowned cat. Rella was the one who had been gone!

Anastasia glared at Rella and opened her mouth to dispute her lies when Rella said, "Anastasia is constantly mad at me, too, and I do not know what I have done to deserve her anger." Rella innocently glanced at Anastasia then. "Oh, here she is," Rella said as if barely becoming aware of Anastasia's presence.

Mrs. Griffin glanced at Anastasia who appeared next to Rella. "You should be ashamed of yourself, Anastasia Covington, to make your poor sister stand here all day in the sun while you…What were you doing down there? Having a nap while your sister did all the work? You are a lazy girl, and your dear mother should see to it you are taught better than to treat your sister with so much disregard. Come, Rella, you can rest in my shop while Anastasia tends the booth for a while."

Mrs. Griffin wagged her long thin finger at Anastasia. "It will do you well to tend the booth all by yourself. Then maybe you will be kinder to your sister. Come along, Rella, dear; let us get some cold tea to drink."

Rella turned and smirked at Anastasia as she let Mrs. Griffin lead her away.

Anastasia sighed. Was it possible for this day to get any worse? The long sleeves on her dress made her hotter, and she wished she dared bare her arms to the elbow, but that was out of the question. The hideous scarring on her right forearm was a sight few people could bear to look upon. Stylish or not, long sleeves were what she wore.

Anastasia was so thirsty she did not think she could swallow anymore, and it was impossible to leave the booth to fetch some water. She was stuck here again. Her mind went to Rella and Mrs. Griffin. How was she going to explain to anybody that Rella lied and twisted the truth so cleverly, it appeared precisely the way Rella wanted it to? Rella was right, she was mad, but not for the reason Rella gave Mrs. Griffin. It was useless to try to defend herself.

Lady Darling's maid approached her booth. As Anastasia helped the woman, she placed her pouch of coins on the counter to give the woman her change. The same two unattended boys who took the cherry basket ran by and grabbed the pouch of coins off the counter.

"No!" Anastasia lunged for the pouch, but she missed, and several coins flew into the air. She ran around the counter, but the boys were gone. They were nowhere in sight. The maid took her purchase and walked away with a, "Good day, miss."

Anastasia was so upset. She wanted to stomp her foot and curse. Ladies did not do that sort of thing, of course, so she smacked her palm on the wooden counter instead. How was she going to explain this to Mama when she got home? Maybe if Rella had been here at the booth helping, the boys would not have gotten the pouch of coins. Anastasia spied the glimmer of a coin in the dirt and bent to pick it up. She was so intent on getting the coin, that she missed seeing the man who bent to pick up the same coin at the same time. She hit her head against his and would have toppled over but the man grabbed her arm to steady her. Her surprised eyes gazed into his amused ones.

"It appears that we have bumped into each other again."

It was the man named Val; a smile tugged at the corner of his well-shaped mouth.

"So it would seem," Anastasia agreed breathlessly.

His hands caressed her arms where he held her. His hot gaze traveled boldly over her from head to toe. Her stomach tightened in response. She was branded by the heat of his touch.

"I am beginning to think I should put on my armor before I approach you, little one," he teased. His eyes continued taking inventory. The heat in his gaze did crazy things to her breathing.

"That might be a good idea," Anastasia agreed. She had no idea what they were talking about. She drowned in the heat surrounding him.

Val's gaze traveled over her face. He frowned. "You are well today, yes?" Val inquired.

Tears pricked her eyes at the gentleness in his voice. It had been a horrible day, with Rella disappearing and the loss of her coins. Now, this incredibly handsome man was being gentle and kind.

"Yes." Anastasia swallowed the lump that formed in her throat at his question. When was the last time someone asked after her health? Anastasia did not know. Val was kind, gentle and seemed to truly care about her answer. His hands rubbed slow heated paths up and down both her arms. She wanted to soak in the warmth that radiated from him. Anastasia took a quick step backward, away from temptation. Her foot caught in her long skirt, and she would have fallen, but Val tugged at her and caught her against his broad chest. His arms held her close to him.

"You must be more careful, little one, or you will fall," he said gently.

Damn. Why am I not graceful and clever? Anastasia dropped her gaze. *Why must I trip and fall so much when he is around? He must think me a complete oaf.* Her eyes filled with tears. *Hell and Damnation!* She never cried. Blinking rapidly, Anastasia turned away, but he caught her chin and lifted her face to study it. She could not bring herself to meet his gaze, so she stared at his chin.

Very gently his hands cupped her face. Carefully he wiped away the lone tear that escaped with the pad of his thumb. "Anastasia." His voice was gentle.

So, he remembers my name! She looked into his eyes, caught by the heat radiating there. Anastasia grabbed the front of his tunic to steady herself.

"Do you cry because of my jest?" he asked softly, placing his large warm hands over hers.

She shook her head.

"Then why? Tell me, little one, and I will solve this problem of yours."

Anastasia took a deep breath to steady the racing of her heart. Why did this man unsettle her with one look into his eyes? "You do not want me to tell you about my problems." Anastasia began to turn away, but Val stopped her again.

He tipped her face up to his and placed a gentle kiss against her lips. "Oh, but I do," he whispered into her ear. "I want to learn all about you. Every one of your secrets, your thoughts, your feelings, I want to hear. And your problems? These especially do I want to hear. I cannot solve problems I do not know about, can I?" He whispered his words a breath above her lips.

She shivered all the way down to the soles of her feet.

"So tell me, little one, tell me this problem that has you shedding tears, and I will solve it." His warm eyes were hypnotic and the heat from his hands warmed her through.

Anastasia found herself telling him about her problems. "I have not had much business today," she started and at his nod and the gentle squeeze of his hands it all came rushing out. "I have been here alone all day. My sister is supposed to be helping me, but she has not been here. She left with the dressmaker a little bit ago, and I was alone again. I was helping a customer and had my bag of coins on the counter, two boys came by, and now the coins are gone."

Her eyes filled with tears again, and she shook her head. She would not cry in front of him. "Mama is going to be so disappointed in me. How can I let her down like this? She is counting on me to sell our goods and bring the coins home. But now, the ones I had are gone, and I have nothing to show for sitting in the booth all day. It seems I am a disappointment to her more and more. No matter how hard I try not to be. I do not know what to do."

His gaze captured her soul. Anastasia normally did

not talk about herself, and here she was telling him all about her feelings as if she did it every day.

He seemed to genuinely care. He bent his head toward her as he listened. His hand still held hers against his chest and his eyes looked warmly into hers. It was a wonderful feeling, and it melted all the cold places in her heart. She was unable to remember a time when she was able to express herself so freely to someone who really listened.

"It was the same two boys who took your basket, who took your coins, yes?"

She nodded.

"This I can fix." He glanced at Vroknar, a tall muscular man with dark hair and a dark bushy mustache standing somewhat behind him. "I would like some tomatoes with my dinner tonight, Vroknar." Val let go of Anastasia's hand and winked at her.

Vroknar dutifully stepped forward and took the basket of tomatoes, placing coins on the counter as he did so.

Anastasia blushed. "Oh! I did not mean…forgive me, sir…" she began. She wrung her hands in consternation and embarrassment, but Val waved his hand to stop her.

"Do not worry, little one. I like tomatoes and was coming to purchase them for my dinner." He paused. "Now, you have coins for your mama, and I have tomatoes," Val paused as he studied her face. He focused on her mouth. "You have what you want, yes? But me, I am far from satisfied." His gaze traveled over her slight form making a heated path from her mouth to her breasts, her hips and then back to her mouth. His eyelids dropped over his eyes. His gaze that of a hungry predator.

Anastasia's mouth went dry. She took a step backward. "Thank you," she managed to say. "You are very kind."

"It was not kindness, *Dorogaya,* it was my need to see your smile," Val said. His hand reached for hers.

She tried to hide them behind her back. Thank God her long sleeves hid her scarred forearm from his sight. She was not fast enough. He caught her hand, turning it over in his much larger one. The pad of his thumb explored each callous, one finger at a time.

Anastasia could not breathe. The air left her lungs. Dizziness washed over her, and she thought she might swoon. Her heart beat loudly in her ears. Her knees began buckling. His eyes met hers as he slowly lifted her hand to his lips. She closed her eyes. *Oh God!* She was going to die, right here, right now, in the middle of the village, where everyone could see.

He placed his hot mouth on the palm of her hand and kissed her there. His lips were warm and firm. She opened her eyes at the contact, and his eyes looked deeply into hers as his lips moved over the palm of her hand.

She felt the tip of his tongue lick the center of her palm and she started to shake. White heat flooded her veins like wildfire. It was the most erotic thing Anastasia ever felt. She shook so violently, she was sure he could tell. Hell, the whole village could probably tell.

Then it was over. His eyelids dropped over his beautiful eyes and he let go of her hand. Val bowed slightly at the waist and said, "Good day, Anastasia," and then he was gone.

She blinked hard and leaned weakly against the counter. Did she affect him the way he affected her? It did not appear so. She shook like a newborn calf in a blizzard, unable to stand on her own two wobbling legs, while he moved swiftly, disappearing in seconds.

How did he move so fast and so silently? He was like a wolf, there one minute and gone a second later, without a sound. A sudden thought entered her mind. Had Val's kiss in the palm of her hand been an intention? She trembled again and closed her hand to keep the memory from escaping.

Then Anastasia shook her head. Mama would be waiting for her. She needed to gather their baskets and go home. Anastasia saw the coins Vroknar left on the counter and picked them up before they disappeared, too. She counted them and nearly choked. She counted again to be sure. She held one hundred ducats of gold in her hand!

Good Lord! How am I going to explain this?

She tucked the gold hastily into her waistband and gathered up the empty baskets to take home. Anastasia's mind was on Val as she walked through the narrow streets toward the road. He was a dangerous man. She turned into a complete idiot whenever he was close, and she knew it. Every part of her quit working the way it was supposed to with one look at him. She thought of the way his lips moved over the palm of her hand and clenched her hand tightly. She wondered what his lips would feel like moving against hers that same way. The soft quick kiss he gave her earlier was nothing like the one he placed in the palm of her hand. She could still feel the tip of his tongue as he licked her. A shiver went down her spine and she tripped. That was another thing. *Why do I have to be so clumsy?* She wanted to be one of those beautiful ladies that floated everywhere they walked, their hair hanging in soft beautiful curls behind their backs, with beautiful gowns and soft hands. She glanced at her own work-stained hands with callouses and chipped fingernails. Val had not minded the callouses or the stains on her hands. He stroked them as if, as if what? As if they were beautiful to him.

Anastasia stopped dead at the thought.

This was going nowhere. It went nowhere because it could not go somewhere. She was a lady and truthfully, she knew next to nothing about him. And…And, who was she kidding? A beautiful man like Val could have any woman he wanted. She was severely scarred and a disappointment. She shook her head to get rid of the fantasies that lived there. It took her several tries because there were a lot of fantasies in her head that involved that man. She needed to focus on helping Mama. Anastasia was so lost in her thoughts, she did not see the dark-haired man who stood in the shadows watching, a cigar in his mouth.

Rella appeared as she turned to walk up the long driveway toward the house. She hummed to herself as she caught up with Anastasia. That meant Rella had been up to her usual mischief.

"Did you have a nice day?" Anastasia asked caustically.

"Oh! I had the best day." Rella smiled sweetly at her. She ran ahead of Anastasia to the kitchen door. As soon as the girls entered the house, Rella started to moan and hold her stomach.

Immediately concerned, Lady Evelyn hurried to

Rella to put her arms around her. Rella launched into a sad tale of how Anastasia disappeared, and how Rella stood in the sun all day selling the goods alone. Rella told Lady Evelyn that Anastasia ate all the lunch, refusing to share. She claimed Anastasia would not let her have any of the water to drink. Rella asked permission to go lie down, exclaiming she was sick from the sun and weary from standing all day in the heat.

With an exclamation of dismay, Lady Evelyn helped Rella to her chamber.

Anastasia put the baskets away and started her nightly chores, knowing what would come next.

Lady Evelyn returned after a time and stood looking at Anastasia before the words began to pour out. She was so disappointed in her. Lady Evelyn did not know how she raised such a daughter. The talk went on and on.

Anastasia listened and waited for her mother to finish. She knew better than to defend herself. Rella always had an answer for everything. She twisted and turned the truth to make Anastasia appear as the most hateful sister there was.

Yes, she would be more kind.

No, she did not know what had come over her.

Yes, she would be more helpful and learn to share.

No, she did not wish to disappoint her mama.

Yes, she would take better care of her sister.

No, she did not deserve to hunger and thirst.

Yes, she would try to behave as a true lady would.

When Lady Evelyn was finally done, Anastasia wearily took the coins from her waistband, put them in Lady Evelyn's hand. She turned to leave but Lady

Evelyn stopped her.

"Where did you get this?"

"From the market, Mama." With that, Anastasia turned and left the room. Let Mama figure it out, she was too tired to explain.

Chapter 6

Lady Evelyn sent her back to the market the next day. Rella did not come because she was far too sick from her ordeal the previous day to climb out of bed. She claimed a massive headache and fatigue.

Anastasia had to bring Rella her breakfast, and then wait for her to finish so she could remove the dishes. Because of that, Anastasia was later than usual starting for town. Lady Evelyn wanted her to learn her lesson about being kind to her sister. So, Anastasia would tend the market alone today, since it was her fault Rella was sick. Now Rella was home, in her bed, all tucked in with Mamma fussing over her. *That is fine with me,* Anastasia said to herself. She relished a day without the drama Rella created in her wake. Anastasia rode along beside Henry. The daily quantity of vegetables was loaded in the wagon behind them. The basket of eggs, she held on her lap. She sat on the wooden bench enjoying the quiet of the morning. The air was cool. The breeze smelled of spring blossoms and fresh new grass. Birds sang to each other and flew from tree to tree. She took in another deep breath.

Anastasia relived the kiss Val placed in her palm at least a hundred times before she finally fell asleep the previous night. What would it be like, she wondered, to be loved by a man like Val? What would it feel like to be the object of his intentions? A shiver went through her at the thought, and her knees wobbled. Better not think about that, she decided. Thoughts of Val would not help her sell the vegetables and bring money home to Mama. Anastasia sincerely hoped today went better than yesterday. It hurt to think Mama was disappointed in her, but if Rella continued to tell untruths about her, Anastasia did not know what she could do about it.

"You are very quiet, Miss Anastasia," Henry said.

"I am enjoying the morning, Henry."

He was silent for a minute and then said. "Do not let the goings on with Miss Rella upset you, Miss Anastasia."

Anastasia blinked in surprise.

"I see more than you think I do. I have been in service to Lord Robert since before Miss Rella was born, and I understand how she is."

Anastasia did not know what to say, so she only nodded.

"Lady Evelyn is a smart woman, and she will soon see the truth. You keep being the sweet girl that you are. Do not let Miss Rella beat you down."

"You know?"

Henry nodded. "I know."

Anastasia sighed. That was the very thing she needed to perk herself up today. If somebody else understood what Rella was doing, it might turn out all right, after all. Today was already better than yesterday. It was wonderful Henry saw through the façade Rella projected. *If only Mama could, too.*

Henry put a hand on her knee. "You cannot hide the good that is in you, and she cannot hide that which is in her, not for long anyway."

His words of wisdom wrapped themselves around

Anastasia's heart and she found herself smiling.

They reached the village and pulled into the market. Henry unloaded the baskets from the back, and Anastasia carefully carried the basket of eggs to the counter. When he was finished, he touched his cap. "See ye later, miss. Keep your chin up."

"Goodbye, Henry. Thank you."

He clucked to the old mare and turned the wagon toward home.

The hours went by. The customers came more frequently. Not because they wanted to talk to Anastasia, but because they were all getting ready for the festival and needed the goods she had for their own preparations. Finally, she sold the last of what she brought for the day. Anastasia sighed wearily and began to gather up her empty baskets in preparation for the long walk home. The sun dipped low as evening approached. It was later than usual when she started for home. She'd hoped if she sold everything, that Mama would be pleased with her, for once.

As she walked down the narrow streets, she realized how empty they were. The villagers had all gone to their own homes, leaving the streets pretty much deserted. Anastasia decided she better hurry. As she walked along, she became aware of heavy footfalls behind her. Who was following? Was it a man? The sounds were too heavy to belong to a woman or a child. Anastasia hurried faster. The footfalls behind matched her speed. Anastasia crossed the road and quickened her pace. She heard the footfalls cross the street, also. Her breathing became fast and erratic. Fear caused her to trip. She caught herself against a building and stiffened as the footfalls came closer. *Oh God!* She started to run and as she ran past a narrow alley, she was caught about the waist. A man's strong arm pulled her around the corner. Anastasia let go of her baskets and hit the man with her fists. The man was very large, and her puny attempts to fend him off had no effect. The man pulled her tightly into his chest, wrapped both his massive arms around her slight form, and covered her mouth with his!

She breathed in deeply preparing herself to fight, and suddenly, she knew who was kissing her. Val! His wonderful scent was all around her, his arms holding her close. She was pressed against the heat of him from chest to knee. He tipped her head a little to the side and licked at her lips. She gasped in surprise, and he thrust his tongue into her mouth. His tongue began to stroke her tongue and to explore her mouth. She trembled with emotion and sensations such as she had never known before. Fear heightened her senses and now she was keenly aware of his scent, his strength, his warmth, and his mouth. Anastasia wrapped her arms around his waist and pressed herself closer to him. Somehow despite the assault he unleashed on her senses, she knew she was safe. She knew he would protect her and keep her from harm. He plundered her mouth with his tongue repeatedly. Liquid heat poured into her stomach and she quivered with excitement. Tentatively, she touched her tongue to his and began to imitate the stroking motions. Val groaned low in his throat and cupped the back of her head with his large hand.

****

God, she is sweet. He needed more. He drank from her mouth, his tongue stroking and mating with hers until he shuddered against her with need. He lifted his head and dragged in a deep breath. He forced his breathing to slow while he stroked her back with his other hand. Val pressed her head into his chest and listened. The man who followed her was still nearby. He could hear the man shuffle his feet. He could smell the man's cigar. Val continued to stroke Anastasia's back with unhurried caresses while he whispered in her ear, "Do not make a sound, *Dorogaya*, the man is still waiting, listening. We will make him think we are lovers meeting in the dark and that he has lost his quarry."

****

Then his lips settled on hers once more. His mouth was hard, demanding, his touch arousing. His tongue swept inside her mouth. It was the most amazing thing she had ever experienced. It was much, much better than she ever imagined. His hands came up to cup her face and he stroked her cheek softly while he plundered her mouth. He stroked her tongue with his, holding her slim body tight against his.

She whimpered into his mouth, liquid heat pouring into her stomach and she wrapped her arms around his neck, pressing herself closer to the heat of him.

"*Dorogaya*, you taste so sweet, so much better than I imagined."

His mouth found hers repeatedly, his tongue stroking and tasting, and stroking and tasting. Anastasia was caught in a whirlwind of sensations. She never imagined it was possible to feel so many things at one time. His mouth was hot, wet, and tasted of pure male. It was a taste she would never have enough of, she realized. His body was hard, warm, and pressed intimately against her. He was so big; he blocked everything and everyone out. There was only him and the erotic sensations he created inside her with his mouth. Blood pounded in her ears. Heat inside her stomach pooled into the juncture of her legs. She was not certain what was happening to her, but she did not want it to stop.

****

He could not seem to get enough of her, the second his mouth settled on hers he had been lost. He wanted more, so he angled her head to savor and explore her mouth fully. Once he knew the honeyed sweetness there, he could not stop himself from drinking his fill. His hands reached for her full breasts, and he cupped them through the cotton fabric of her dress. His thumbs found her nipples. He rubbed them back and forth, until she cried out and arched her body against his. Her nipples hardened and pressed against the fabric of her chemise.

She whimpered with what sounded like pleasure and pressed herself closer for more. She made the most arousing sounds at the back of her throat, and damn if she was not kissing him back. Her arms wound around his neck, and she pressed her beautiful body into his, her legs restless against his own. Her tongue stroked his, tasting, then sucking, and then tasting again. He groaned aloud. She was a fast learner. She seemed timid at first, but now she aggressively kissed him back. She tormented him with her mouth, with her tongue, following his lead as if her life depended on it. *God, she is on fire.* He wanted more, so much more. Images of their naked bodies writhing together on sweat-soaked sheets danced across his mind and he throbbed with need. He realized then, if he did not stop, he would not be able to do so. He dragged in a heavy breath and rested his forehead against hers. For several minutes, they stayed that way, his hand stroking up and down her back, as if to soothe her.

Then he looked at Anastasia in the moonlight. Her face was flushed, and her eyes were glistening with emotion. She looked bemused and so damn beautiful he wanted to drink from her again. Her beautiful soft lips were swollen, and her chest heaved with every breath. He felt her quiver against him. He pulled her back into his chest and held her tight, giving them both time to control their breathing. It was then, he realized, he was shaking too. When had he become so lacking in the self-restraint with which he prided himself? Damn! He needed to get himself under control! What was it about this woman that caused him to lose his self-discipline? Why did this woman occupy his thoughts the way she did? What was it about her that fascinated him?

He really did not know. He had been with many women that were more beautiful than she, women far more sophisticated than she could ever be, and women who were more graceful, and yet he could not seem to get Anastasia out of his mind. He wanted to toss her skirt up, wrap her long legs around his waist and plunge himself into her heat, but something held him back. He wanted his first time with her to be in a soft bed, in a quiet place where he could drink his fill. He wanted her all to himself.

****

Anastasia lifted her head and looked up into Val's eyes. He was the most handsome man she had ever seen. Never in her wildest dreams had she considered the things he did to her would cause such intense pleasure. She wanted more. She wanted him to kiss her and touch her. She wanted him to show her more. She wanted him to show her everything and it surprised her. She should be embarrassed, she should be shy even, but she was not. When she was with him, she was not a disappointment.

Val studied the corner in front of them.

"Is the man still there?"

Val glanced at her face. "Nay."

Anastasia let out a long shaky breath. "How did you know I was here? How did you know I was being followed?"

"I had business in the village and watched you leave the market. I noticed the man following you. I thought to overtake you and walk with you, but the man was gaining on you, so I removed you from his path."

She pulled back from his arms. "What if he had followed me around the corner when you caught me?"

"It would have been the last decision he ever made."

"Why the last one?"

He lifted her chin so he could look into her eyes. "Because he would be dead."

"You would have killed him?"

"Aye, for daring to threaten you, he would pay with his life."

She was not frightened at the intensity with which he made the statement; she was instead comforted. This man had rescued her once more. He would not let anyone hurt her. He was so big, so powerful, he could crush her bones without any effort, and yet he held her so gently when he kissed her. He was a contradiction. Anastasia stared at his mouth as she thought about that kiss and wanted him to kiss her again.

****

He became aware of her looking at his mouth, and he knew he needed to get her home before he gave into the temptation her sweet mouth posed. "Which way is your home, little one?"

She walked with him to the street outside the alley and was turning to point toward home, when she spotted Henry and the wagon headed their way. "It looks as though Henry has come for me." She pointed to the wagon. "Thank you, sir, for rescuing me once again." Anastasia smiled at him as she curtsied, and then she ran toward the wagon.

Val stepped back into the alley. He wanted to watch and see for himself who crept around in the shadows. He wanted to see where this man went, who followed his Anastasia.

My Anastasia? Val shook his head. *Since when had she become his Anastasia? Well, no matter, the man would die for frightening her.*

Val considered who the man might be. *What if the man follows her because of me?* He thought of that for a minute. No one knew Val was here, so it could not be that. *Then why was the man following her? Was he a common thief who thought to take the coins Anastasia had earned this day? Or was there some other reason?* Val frowned as he thought. There had been a lady murdered in the alley. *What was her name? Ah, yes, Lady Remington.* Was there a villain about who preyed on females, especially ones out on the road alone? If so, he must warn his Anastasia to take more precautions. He would not always be here to keep her safe.

Things were getting complicated. He still had no

idea who Anastasia was. He had no idea who this Henry was, either, but he was going to find out. The girl was such a puzzle, he mused.

Val thought at first that she was from the village. She had the callouses of a servant, but then she had the speech of an aristocrat. Her dress was poor, but not the coarse wool the villagers or the servants wore. Her shoes were plain but well made. She carried herself with the grace of a queen but sold vegetables and eggs in the village market. And, she kissed with the innocence of a virgin, but went home with a man named Henry.

He shook his head. None of what he knew about her made any sense. If she were a lady, she would have a lady's maid trailing her everywhere she went. *And I would not have gotten the opportunity to take her in my arms and taste her sweet lips*, he reminded himself.

Val thought about that kiss. He could swear he was the first man to ever kiss her. Her response to him had been too innocent for it to be otherwise. The girl was a puzzle. He liked puzzles. He also liked the girl, and he was going to find out all her secrets. Protocol and tradition be damned, the girl would be his one way or another. The thought cheered him up considerably as he got on his stallion and rode toward camp.

****

Son-of-a-bitch.

The man stepped out of the shadows and hit the side of the building with his fist. He missed his opportunity. He had the girl right where he wanted her, when she so willingly obliged him by turning down the alley. That was exactly where she was going to end up anyway, and he nearly laughed out loud when she ran right into it. It was a little like a chicken putting its head on the block for you, so you could cut it off. He was moving into position to grab the girl when he first saw the big bastard. He recognized him from the other day in the marketplace. He and his man had been at the girl's stall and left with a basket of her produce.

Something kept bothering him about the man. He had seen him somewhere before. The bastard could fight; he remembered that. There was a battle somewhere in the back of his mind. Five soldiers came at the big bastard. He snapped their necks and spines in minutes and walked away without breaking a sweat. That was a sight he could not forget. He simply could not remember who the man was, or where he saw the fight.

When he looked at the big bastard with the girl in his arms, he decided to make himself scarce. He was a good fighter, but he would have to be demented to take on that demon by himself. So, he stepped into the tavern and out the back door into the alley, where he witnessed the scene play out between the man and the girl. It had been interesting, productive, too. Not as productive as he hoped, but his employer still paid good coin for information on the girl. With what he saw tonight, the pay should be enough to get him a wench for the next week.

He was going to find out who the man was, so he knew what they were dealing with. The bastard wanted the girl, that much was evident. Maybe that could be used to his advantage somehow. The man grinned. Now all he had to do was report what he had seen and collect his money. He stomped on the end of his cigar and wandered off down the street.

Chapter 7

Anastasia rose at dawn, again. The festival started today, and they needed to set up their booth early with the trays of tarts Cook made. Anastasia's feet were running before they hit the floor. Lady Evelyn anxiously barked out orders like a knight before a big battle. At one point, Anastasia stopped to catch her breath and Lady Evelyn caught her.

"Where is Rella?"

Anastasia was so busy she had not taken the time to see if Rella was up or not.

"Go to her room and see if she is well. If she is, tell her we need her help and to come at once," Lady Evelyn instructed.

Anastasia ran up the stairs to Rella's room and went inside. Rella lie on her bed, propped up on a mountain of feather pillows.

"Where is my breakfast?" the girl demanded.

"Well, good morning to you, too," Anastasia replied coming to a stop inside the door. "Mama wants you downstairs as quick as you can."

"I will not be going to help today," Rella replied, settling herself further into her pillows.

"Are you ill?"

"No, I am done helping. I am done being a servant in my own house. I am done being told what to do and done being ordered about. I am never doing dishes or laundry again; do you understand me? All that work is ruining my hands. They are perfect, soft, and beautiful. They are going to stay that way. God forbid, they become calloused and dirty like yours." Rella gave a little shudder. "I am a lady, and not simply any lady. I am the lady of this house. You will treat me with the respect I deserve. You can start by attending to my every need."

Anastasia's mouth fell open. This was bold, even for Rella. "I do not think I will be waiting on you. There are too many things for me to do, but I will be sure to give Mama your answer."

Anastasia started to leave when Rella called after her, "Be sure to tell your mother the reason why you were so late last evening, as well."

Anastasia turned back. "What reason would that be?"

A crafty smile curved Rella's full lips. "Why, the fact that you were having a little interlude with a certain man in a dark alley in town, all alone. I believe him to be the same man Lady Evelyn told you to avoid. I wonder what she will say when she knows you two were seen passionately embracing, and kissing, perhaps more, who can tell? I hear the man had his hands all over you. I am curious as to what your mother would think of that?"

The blood drained from Anastasia's face. *Oh God! How did Rella find out?*

"I do not understand why a man would look at a deformed creature like you. Perhaps he is as ugly as you are and does not mind. Or did he even see your arm? Maybe he was so busy tossing your skirts he did not notice? I imagine Lady Evelyn will be terribly upset at the news."

Panic rose in Anastasia and she hastily pushed it back down. She did not have time to worry about what Rella intended to do with the information. Thinking quickly, Anastasia made up her mind. She would play along for now, Mama would be furious if she was late.

"What do you want me to do?"

A victorious smile curved Rella's mouth. "I would like a bath."

"A bath? Are you mad? Mama wants to be on the way to the festival within the hour. I do not have time to haul a tub, and water up to your room!" Anastasia waved her arms about, emphasizing her point.

"Then tell Lady Evelyn I require her attendance, at once," Rella answered.

Anastasia took a deep calming breath. "I shall be happy to help you with a bath this evening, and I will keep the water warm for you as long as you like, if you get up now so we can go."

Rella considered this for a minute. "As long as I like?"

"Yes."

"Then fetch me a gown. I want the one in my wardrobe that is still in paper, the new one."

Anastasia faltered. The *new* one? No one had a new gown since Papa died. They all still wore last year's clothing. Anastasia pulled the gown from the wardrobe and removed the paper. She gasped. The gown was utterly splendid. It was made of light lavender silk with a white lace insert in the small bodice. It had tight little sleeves, with several inches of lace adorning the bottom. A lavender sash, slightly darker in color, wrapped about the tiny waist. The sides of the full skirt were caught up with sprays of lilacs, and orchids the exact color of the sash. It was breathtaking. Anastasia had not seen a gown this intricate, and beautiful, since—well, before Papa died.

"Hurry up, you stupid girl. I am waiting," Rella commanded.

Stupid girl? She took this lady of the house thing a bit too far. Anastasia raised an eyebrow at her. Rella merely stood up and held out her arms so Anastasia could remove her night rail. Working furiously, Anastasia helped Rella dress, and arranged her hair. All the while, she listened to a constant stream of criticism, and verbal abuse from Rella. When Anastasia finished, Rella left the room with a, "Now, straighten my chamber," over her shoulder and went down the stairs. Anastasia hurried to comply and practically ran all the way downstairs. Rella's voice floated up to her as Anastasia came down.

"...told me to put it on. I have no idea where it came from. I am quite confused on how it even got into my room, but she would not let me leave until I put this dress on and did my hair up this way. Anastasia was so mean to me about it; I did not dare refuse. I am all dressed up as if I were going to a dinner or a ball. This dress is far too expensive to work in. I cannot think what Anastasia planned that she wants me dressed this way. I did not want to fight with her, so I put the dress on like she said. Perhaps she wants you to be disappointed in me, and I think she wants it to appear as though I am selfish, vain, and not willing to help you. I am truly sorry, Lady Evelyn. It is the greatest desire of my heart to be a help and a comfort to you. I shall go change at once."

Anastasia could not believe her ears. She walked toward the kitchen, fuming mad.

"There is no time now, dear," Lady Evelyn said. "We really must go."

"It frightens me when Anastasia is mad. I do not know what to do so I simply do as she says." Rella clung to Lady Evelyn as she made the statement.

Lady Evelyn turned as Anastasia entered the room and frowned over the anger on Anastasia's face. "Well dear, since you cruelly decided to belittle your sister, I shall let you have your way." She looked at Anastasia, disappointment in her gaze. "What would Papa think if he were here today? Rella works as hard as anyone here, and I have decided to give her the day off. She cannot work in the dress you forced her to wear, and though you seek to make sport of her, it is you that shall do her part. You are dressed for work, and she is not, so work you shall. You will tend the booth alone today. The rest of us will sit in the stands and enjoy the games. You shall miss every event. Perhaps this will serve as a lesson for the next time you decide to be cruel to your sister."

Anastasia's spirits plummeted. The games were the very reason she worked so hard. She hoped that Val would participate in the games. His body was pure muscle, lean and fit. He would win every event he entered, and it would be so wonderful to watch. Anastasia sighed. It did not help when Rella gave her a self-satisfied smirk behind Mama's back. It was not fair but arguing would do no good.

"Yes, Mama," she said, and went to ride on the wagon with Henry, while Lady Evelyn, Beatrice, and Rella climbed into their carriage. Grigori, the gardener, doubled as coachman today. He clucked to the old mare as they started off. Henry hitched the mule to the wagon, and he and Anastasia rumbled along in the dust behind the carriage. The trays and trays of tarts in the back of the wagon were covered with cloth to keep the dust out. They drove slowly to town and unloaded the wagon at the booth they rented. Henry smiled and chucked her on the chin the way he used to when she was a child.

"One thing is sure, Miss Anastasia, everything is always changing. Do not let Rella upset you. It is what she wants, to make you all upset and afraid."

Anastasia nodded. Henry was right. There was something different, though. Ever since Papa died, Rella seemed to be spending every waking minute making Anastasia's life hell. It was as if lying to Lady Evelyn and watching the pain Anastasia experienced by being a constant disappointment to her mother, was not enough anymore. Her schemes and lies only got bigger, and grander. Now, Rella was drawing the people from the village into her game of lies and deceit.

Anastasia spent long hours at the booth. She could hear the cheering and excitement from the stands where the games were held. She wanted to sneak over and peek, but she did not dare. Somebody was watching everything she did and telling Rella. *But who?* It could be anybody really, she decided. So many of the villagers she thought she knew and counted as friends, refused to speak to her. Most of them refused to even acknowledge her presence. They all heard how 'unkind' Anastasia was to Rella. Anastasia always walked up at the wrong time, or did something right at the right moment, and Rella twisted it around. Anastasia did not know how the people in the village could be so unkind, when she had known them for the last five years. Rella had such a way of twisting the truth with little lies. It was difficult to discern what the truth was, and what was a lie.

So, it should come as no surprise they told Rella what she did and where she went. Even Lady Evelyn believed everything Rella said. Anastasia sighed. Only Papa listened to her. Rella did not seem as bad then, but the more she thought about it, the more she realized, it was probably because of Papa. Every time when they were growing up something like this happened, if Papa where home, he would take Anastasia for a walk, the two of them, and ask her what happened. *Maybe he understood about Rella?* She considered that thought for a minute. He must know because he never acted on what Rella said alone. He always asked her for her side of the story. Emptiness crept over Anastasia, and she wished with all her heart, he was here now. Papa would know what to do. Anastasia's eyes filled with tears.

Stop that! She commanded herself. *It is exactly what Rella wants.* She wanted Anastasia upset. She wanted her to cry, to make her suffer. It all made Rella so happy, when she thought she succeeded in hurting her. Anastasia angrily rubbed her cheeks and wiped the tears away. She would be damned if she gave Rella what she wanted. She may have to wait on her, and jump when Rella said jump, but she was not going to show Rella how badly she hurt. Anastasia had never been so alone.

"*Dorogaya.*"

She jumped. *Oh Lord, where did he come from?* She looked around frantically and spied Val leaning against a tree a few feet away. "What are you doing here?" she cried.

A frown darkened his face. "You are not happy to see me?"

"Of course I am!" She walked toward him and pulled him around behind the tree.

"This is better." He grinned at her and settled his mouth on hers. His tongue plundered her mouth, while his hands pulled her hard against him. He reached up and cupped the back of her neck with his hand, angling her head so he could gain deeper access to her mouth. His hands found her buttocks and he pulled her intimately against his throbbing arousal.

She blushed at his boldness, and half-heartedly pushed him away. She did not feel like a disappointment when Val held her like this. She felt alive and wanted. Anastasia sighed, and gave into the erotic pleasure of his tongue mating with hers. Soon, she had her arms wound tightly around his neck. She returned stroke for stroke, whimpering in the back of her throat when at last, he lifted his head.

Val pressed her against the tree and drank until he shook with desire. He lifted his head and tucked hers beneath his chin, while he fought to regain control. "You make me forget myself, little one."

She tilted her head back and noted his deep breathing. She smiled. So he was affected by their kisses as much as she was. Somehow the day seemed a little brighter. "You make me forget, also." She remembered Rella and pushed against his shoulders.

He stepped back frowning, as she hurriedly smoothed her hair and skirts.

"Someone knows about last night, and I am in

trouble. I do not know how they found out, or who saw us, but it is known we were in the alley and that we were....kissing." Anastasia blushed at this.

The frown immediately deepened. "Who spoke of this?"

"My sister Rella."

"The one with the black hair like you or the one with the yellow hair?"

"The yellow hair," she paused. "I am sorry. I do not know who told her." Anastasia asked. "Do you think it was the man chasing me?"

Val considered this. "No, if he chased you to do you harm, why would he confess to this, and tell your sister he saw you?"

Anastasia shook her head. It was too confusing. She looked at him and asked, "Why are you here? Are you to participate in the games?"

"No, *Dorogaya*, I come to tell you I must leave for a little while, and that you must be careful. Do not be out alone as you were last night. I will not be here to keep you safe. I believe the man who followed you last night was but a visitor, coming to the festival. We followed his footprints out of the village. Still, it is not safe for you to be out alone."

"Are you sure the man has gone?"

"I would not leave if you were in danger." He brushed a strand of hair from her cheek, and she shivered at his touch. "Even so, you are not to take any chances. I do not want harm to come to you while I am away. I am leaving Darok to keep an eye on you."

"Who is Darok?"

"He is a trusted...friend. He will not let anyone hurt you. If you are afraid, call out, he will be nearby until I return."

"Can I meet him?"

Val smiled, "It is best if he stays hidden. Do you trust me?"

It was a good question. She gazed into his deep blue eyes and knew that she did. Miraculously, she trusted him with her life. She trusted him since the moment he caught her in his arms. "Yes," Anastasia whispered.

His smile widened. "I want to kiss your sweet mouth, *Dorogaya,* very, very, badly but I dare not. I have not been able to stop thinking about you, or about the kisses we shared last night. You are a drug to me and if I kiss you, again, I might not be able to stop, until I taste all of you."

All of me? Dear God! Her knees shook at the mere thought. She drew in a very shaky breath, her eyes wide at the pictures his words evoked. Anastasia felt the blush cover her cheeks. It was wonderful to hear he thought about her, too.

Val held out his hand. She placed her hand in his. The breath left her lungs at the contact, but he simply placed a quick kiss on her knuckles and said, "Goodbye, *Dorogaya.*" Then he disappeared.

She blinked. He did it, again. How did such a large man move so swiftly and so silently? She glanced down at the pouch he left in her hand. *How did that get there?* Anastasia opened it and peered inside. Five hundred ducats of gold! Anastasia counted again, her mind reeling. Where did Val get so much gold? Why would he give it to her? He knew she sold vegetables for money, maybe he thought to help. It was very sweet and very generous of him. She tucked it carefully into her waistband. Here was something else Mama would not understand.

At last, evening came. The games were over for the day, and all her tarts had sold. Anastasia was bone weary. Her head swam from sitting in the heat all day. She was grateful when Lady Evelyn walked toward her after the last game.

"How did the tarts do?" Lady Evelyn asked as she glanced quickly around the booth.

"All sold." Anastasia handed Lady Evelyn the pouch containing the coins she made selling the tarts and began to stack the trays.

"I am sorry I had to be so firm with you today, Anastasia, but you must start acting like the lady I taught you to be. You have been acting so out of character lately, and I need not tell you of the disappointment I feel in you."

Anastasia simply nodded her head.

"Mrs. Griffin approached me today at the games. It seems we owe her money for the new gown you ordered for Rella."

She looked at Lady Evelyn in surprise, "New gown?"

Irritation and something else flashed in Lady Evelyn's eyes. "The new gown Rella wore today. Mrs. Griffin says you are the one that ordered it." Lady Evelyn watched Anastasia's face and frowned. "I am wondering how you intend to pay for it."

"Would you believe I did not order the dress and that I had nothing to do with Rella wearing it today?"

Lady Evelyn shook her head, "Do not disappoint me further by lying to me. Mrs. Griffin would not lie. I do not understand what is happening to you! You were such a sweet and loving girl when your papa was alive. I cannot help but think of his disappointment in you if he could see you here today!"

Even if Mama did not believe her, they still needed to pay Mrs. Griffin for the dress.

"How much is the dress?"

Lady Evelyn sighed, "Two hundred ducats of gold, and Mrs. Griffin says she discounted it. That is the price for the fabric and lace only. She wanted to donate her sewing to the poor girl."

Mama was weary, too. Anastasia saw the sadness in her eyes. She did not like being at odds with her but there was nothing she could do if Mama would not listen to her side of the story. Anastasia reached into her waistband and withdrew two hundred ducats of gold. As she placed them in Lady Evelyn's surprised hand she said, "I have not lied to you, Mama. I am the same girl I have always been. I believe if Papa were here, he would listen to my side of the story. I am trying to be the lady you raised me to be, whether you believe that or not. I love you, Mama, and I would never hurt you in any way."

Anastasia hurried from the booth before Mama could ask too many questions about the gold she held in her hand.

Chapter 8

Rella returned home in the early hours of the morning. Lady Evelyn allowed her to stay at the festival with Lord Durst and his family. Lord Durst was an old acquaintance of Lord Covington's and promised Lady Evelyn he would look after Rella.

Anastasia promised Rella a bath and so she waited in Rella's room until the girl finally staggered in, and she did stagger. She drank way too much wine and could hardly keep herself upright. A young man held Rella about the waist and helped her into her chamber.

Anastasia was shocked. "Rella, what are you doing? You cannot bring a man into this house unchaperoned, and you certainly cannot bring one to your chamber!"

"Why not?" Rella asked, leaning heavily on the young man.

"Well, for one thing, there is your reputation and honor to consider, and for another, Mama will not like it at all!"

"An whoz goin' tell 'er? You?" Rella went into peals of laughter, which turned to coughing and then to retching.

Anastasia grabbed a bucket she brought up to Rella's room in preparation for her bath and held it under Rella's head as the retching started. "Who is this man, Rella, and why have you brought him here?"

Anastasia asked. Her mind whirled with the impropriety of it all.

"He's my friend," Rella said smiling widely at the coarsely dressed young man.

The man laid Rella on her bed. Rella started laughing again. She waved a hand at the man and at Anastasia. "Eric, my maid, maid, Eric." Anastasia supposed that constituted some sort of introduction.

"Eric, or whoever you are," she began, "you really must leave. Thank you for helping Lady Rella home but this is simply not done. It is very inappropriate and definitely not proper, and you need to go, *now!*"

Rella sat up and pointed a finger at Anastasia. "He'z not goin' anywhere. You are. Go! Now!" Then she turned to Eric. "I nee' you!"

Eric moved toward the bed and started to remove his coarse woolen jacket.

Anastasia stood still, frozen to the spot. It dawned on her that Rella meant to share her bed with this man. "Rella, you cannot mean to do this! You," Anastasia pointed at the coarse young man, "get out now before I call for help and have you thrown out!"

Rella's eyes turned mean. "Who you thin' you are? This is my house and I say who comes and who goes! Besides, who will come if you call? Henryth?" She burst into laughter. "Get Out! Or I will call Ladyth Eve…Evelyn," she yelled at Anastasia and then she started to remove her dress. "Hurry Eric! I neeth you!"

Anastasia ran from the room and shut the door. She needed help.

She ran downstairs to find Henry. He was in the red salon, banking the fire for the night. Anastasia began to pace; she wrung her hands in consternation.

93

"Henry, Miss Rella finally came home, and I believe she is drunk! And not only that but there is a man in her room, and I do not know what to do! After today and the things she told Mama about that dress I am afraid of what she will say! I am afraid that this will be my fault somehow and what Mama will think. She will tell Mama I brought the man in or some such thing. What should I do?"

****

Henry turned and looked at the girl. Anastasia paced while she talked. She was so upset. He sighed. If only Lord Robert where still alive. He would know how to solve this situation. Lady Rella was out of control and his concern was that Lady Evelyn would not see the truth before it was too late.

"There isn't anything you can do, Miss Anastasia. Don't you worry and fret. Miss Rella has done this before, and she kept it all a secret. I don't rightly know why she is dragging you into her evil doings, but I will speak with Lady Evelyn if Miss Rella tries to blame you. You are tired from your long day, and it will be another long day tomorrow, so off to bed with you. I will keep watch over Miss Rella. I've been doing it for Lord Robert for seventeen years, and I am not about to stop now." He glanced at Anastasia's pale face. "I have been here for many years, Miss Anastasia, and I have seen a lot of things. I tend to my work, and I keep my mouth shut. It is healthier for you that way, if you understand my meaning?"

Anastasia nodded.

Henry watched her walk away slowly. He knew Lady Rella upset Miss Anastasia with her lack of propriety. No young lady did the things Miss Rella did.

He doubted Miss Rella could shock or surprise him anymore with her antics. Ever since she was born, she thumbed her nose at authority and tradition. Lord Robert was the only one who seemed to have any influence with the girl. With him gone, who knew what lengths Miss Rella would go to? With a weary sigh, Henry turned his attention back to his evening duties.

****

Anastasia slowly made her way up the stairs to bed. She was relieved but at the same time deeply shocked. Rella had men stay in her chamber before? And Henry knew? Apparently, there were a lot of things going on Anastasia did not know about. She wished it stayed that way. She doubted she would ever look at Rella the same way again. Who risked their innocence and reputation the way Rella did? It horrified Anastasia. It took a long time for her to go to sleep. Her mind replayed the scene in Rella's chamber, over and over. As the first light of the sun lit the dark sky, Anastasia fell into a deep sleep, tortured with images of Eric leaning over Rella's bed and Henry telling her not to worry.

The next morning, Anastasia dragged herself out of bed and began to get ready for the day. Suddenly she remembered Rella and Eric. She hastily left her chamber and ran all the way to Rella's. *What if I am too late and Mama already knows? Rella will blame me!* Anastasia knocked quietly on the door. When there was no answer, she let herself inside. Rella still slept, and she was alone. Anastasia let out a relieved breath. *Thank God for that, at least!* She tiptoed out of the room and ran down to the kitchens.

Lady Evelyn was there giving her commands, as

usual. She stopped when she saw Anastasia. "You are rather late this morning. Is there some reason for your tardiness?"

"No, Mama, I am sorry."

Anastasia hurried about helping as best she could. She caught Henry's eye, and he winked at her. She grinned and whispered, "Thank you, Henry."

He nodded.

"You will ride in the carriage with me today, Anastasia, there is something I would like to speak with you about. Beatrice, you will go with Henry. Rella is feeling too ill today to leave her chamber I am told, so it will only be you and I, Anastasia."

Anastasia sighed. *So much for thinking it will get any better.* "Yes Mama."

They set off and Lady Evelyn was quiet for a minute, and then she began. "You told me yesterday that you do not lie to me. You also told me that Papa would have asked for your side of the story. I have reflected on your comments to me, and I have decided that Papa would have listened to your side of the story, as you say. And so, I would like to hear your side of the story about the gold you placed in my hand last night. Where did you get it, Anastasia?"

"A man gave it to me at the festival yesterday."

Lady Evelyn frowned. This was not what she expected. "What man?"

"A man who came to our booth during the games."

"What did this man receive for such an amount of gold?"

"Nothing, Mama."

Lady Evelyn began to get irritated again. "I am trying to trust you, Anastasia, to speak to you as Papa would, but you are making this difficult for me. You tell me that you do not lie, so help me to understand why a man would simply give you so much gold?"

Anastasia shrugged her shoulders. "We only spoke for a minute about the festival and then he left. After he left, I noticed the gold."

Lady Evelyn's brow wrinkled. "Perhaps he left it by mistake." Lady Evelyn sat in silence, considering the situation. "Perhaps we should keep it safe for him. He may come back today looking for it." Her mind made up Lady Evelyn announced. "Beatrice will help you in the booth today. We will take turns between the booth and the games, but you will stay in the booth again today. I do not want you alone in the booth, or alone in town anymore. Is that understood? I cannot fathom why any man would give you gold and for nothing. Something is off about all of this, and I cannot leave you alone. I have yet to see that you are, indeed, telling the truth. I am not ready to trust you yet."

"Yes, Mama."

So, it went for the entire week of the festival. Anastasia stayed in the booth selling tarts. She was not allowed to attend the games at all. Lady Evelyn and Beatrice traded back and forth between the booth and the games, so she was never alone. Rella would sleep until afternoon, every day, claiming illness in the mornings. She would then attend the games in the afternoon, and Lady Evelyn would let her stay after they went home. Rella would stumble in with a different man every night, and Henry would nod to Anastasia and send her up to bed. The man never came back for the gold; Val left it there on purpose. On the last day of the festival, Lady Evelyn paid Mrs. Griffin the two hundred ducats for Rella's new dress. They sold all the tarts Cook could make. Lady Evelyn was quite pleased with the coins they gathered in. She declared the festival, a success.

Later that night while they were at dinner, a royal messenger arrived from the palace. Henry placed the invitation on the table beside Lady Evelyn.

She broke the seal and read, "His Royal Highness, King Alexander Kazimir Augustine, requests your presence at his annual spring ball following the spring festivals in all the provinces. The ball shall take place in the Royal Palace in Larenia in two months' time. It shall be a masquerade ball, so a mask is required for attendance. Lady Evelyn Covington, Lady Beatrice Covington, Lady Anastasia Covington, and Lady Rella Covington will please attend."

Silence greeted the announcement.

Beatrice spoke first. "But how shall we go, Mama? We would need new gowns for the ball."

"And masks," Anastasia whispered. Her mind whirled with the news.

Lady Evelyn sat silently for a minute and then she said. "I have a note from the overseer. There is a large amount of brandy that is now aged enough to sell. He requested that I come to the distillery and go over the count with him to approve the brandy shipment with Papa's seal. I had not thought to go quite yet, for the sales from the festival helped quite nicely. Now with the ball coming up, the brandy must be sold."

"A ball, Mama, a real ball. I cannot believe I shall be at a real ball." Beatrice breathed, a dreamy expression on her face. Rella looked from one to another, her gaze thoughtful. Anastasia felt the familiar tightening in her stomach. Rella was busy plotting something.

"You all shall," Lady Evelyn smiled at the three girls. Her mind made up. It would be the perfect opportunity to alleviate another worry she had been minding. "We shall order the most wonderful gowns and perhaps we can attract a suitor or two while we are there."

A suitor? Or two? Anastasia lowered her gaze to the table, so no one could read her expression. Dread filled her. *What is wrong with me?* Anastasia wondered. *I should be excited like Beatrice, but I am not.* She realized then that she did not want a suitor. She wanted Val. Every man paled in comparison to him, and it was doubtful that he would even be invited. She did not know who he was or what he did, but she was pretty sure he did not come from nobility. Therefore, he would not be at the ball. She did not want another man to hold her in his arms. She did not want another man to look into her eyes or kiss her lips. She simply wanted Val. It was him she dreamed about when she closed her eyes at night.

Rella asked to be excused saying she was going to her room. Anastasia knew better for she had seen the cape and shoes waiting by the kitchen door. Rella was going out again.

****

Sometime later, Anastasia was awakened by Lady Evelyn shaking her shoulder gently. It was still dark outside.

"Wake up, dear. I need you to dress and come to the kitchens. I shall be waiting for you."

Oh Lord, now what? Anastasia hurried to dress

herself, plait her hair, and straighten her chamber.

Lady Evelyn sat drinking a cup of tea, when she entered the kitchen. "I do not know what has happened, but Rella fell ill in the night. She has been retching, and I am concerned about all her recent illnesses. I do not dare to leave her, and so I cannot make the journey to the distillery, as I had hoped. I must stay and tend to the dear girl."

Lady Evelyn was tired. She handed Anastasia a bundle with Papa's seal and said. "I have decided to trust you, Anastasia, to go to the distillery for me. Make an accurate count and be sure to fix Papa's seal to the document. Make sure the numbers of barrels are correctly recorded before you sign your name and bring me a copy of the count. I cannot send Beatrice, she has no head for numbers, and so I am entrusting you with this important errand. Do not fail me, Anastasia; I do not need to tell you how important this errand is."

Anastasia was relieved. *Well, if that is all Mama wants that is fine with me. I will go on this errand to the distillery and enjoy the time to myself.* She nodded her head at Lady Evelyn and said, "Yes, Mama. I will go and take special care to make an accurate count. When do I leave?"

"You will leave immediately. It is a long journey and will take you until midday to get there. Do not stay overly long. You must travel back quickly so you are not caught traveling in the dark. I shall be looking for your return by dinnertime."

Chapter 9

"Drat," Anastasia muttered to nobody in particular. Marigold wandered off again. The old slump back mare remained the only horse left in the Covington stables. The other horses were either sold or bartered off. Anastasia pulled on the reins with all her strength. She leaned to the right as she pulled hoping the mare would quit veering to the left and stay on the path. The old dappled mare paid no attention to the girl on her back. She continued off the path and stopped by a fallen tree. *Apparently, the grass there tastes delicious.* Anastasia pulled the reins again and nudged the horse with her heels. Nothing happened. Marigold continued to graze at her leisure.

"Come on Marigold, we are late enough as it is!"

The mare did not even lift her head up. Anastasia slid off the horse and sat on the fallen tree. *What a day! Lord, am I tired!* It seemed a simple enough errand, traveling to the distillery and back. She made good time, and the trip there went well enough. She met the overseer, counted the barrels, recorded the correct number, and signed the count sheet. She fixed Papa's seal to the count sheet she left with the overseer, and recorded a second count sheet, precisely as Mamma asked. Anastasia ate her lunch seated on a keg of brandy, before mounting Marigold, and turning toward home. Marigold, however, decided to explore on the way home. She stopped now for the third time. Anastasia's arms ached from pulling on the reins and trying to make Marigold change her mind. Marigold was the most stubborn horse Anastasia ever met.

Anastasia pulled a blade of grass and chewed on the end. As usual, Val's face appeared whenever she closed her eyes, or held still and tried to think. He lived in her mind and thoughts. She could see his face, his beautiful eyes, and his mouth. *O Lord, his mouth!* She relived every minute of the kisses they shared in minute detail. She thought about them at night, when she tried to sleep. Her stomach still got all fluttery, and her breathing ragged, every time she thought of his lips and how they moved over her own.

Anastasia thought about the ball. She pulled up another blade of grass. *What if Mama finds a suitor for me at the ball?* Anastasia did not want to think about it, so she pushed the thought aside. She did not want a suitor. She wanted Val. She knew Val liked her, a least a little. He kissed her, after all, and at the festival he claimed he wanted to again. But did he like her enough to want to marry her? Was he the kind of man Mama would let her marry? Val was not a poor man, because he had gold. He gave her far more than was proper on both occasions. So, the question was, how much gold did Val have, and where did he get it from? Could he be a mercenary of some kind? Anastasia considered the possibility for a minute, and then tossed it aside. Val was no mercenary. He was too kind, and gentle. He was not the kind of man that killed for money. He was used to physical labor for Lord, was he fit. There was not one ounce of fat on the man anywhere. So, whatever it was he did, it required physical strength. One did not become as fit and lean as Val by sitting around. The man was all muscle and he wore his strength easily. His arms were like roped steel when she caressed them.

Anastasia shook her head to clear her thoughts. She daydreamed long enough. Mama said to hurry. Anastasia stood up and stretched.

"All right Marigold that is enough. It is time to go."

She climbed into the saddle and adjusted her skirts. When she nudged Marigold, wonder of wonders, the horse began to move. After a bit, they came to a stream. Anastasia thought she detected movement out of the corner of her eye. She pulled hard on the reins, and Marigold stopped. Anastasia patted the mare's neck in approval. She studied the forest around her on both sides but saw nothing but trees. The hair on the back of her neck stood on end, and a shiver went down her spine. Someone was watching her! She knew it. Fear zinged through her, and she realized, she was all alone, deep in the woods. Perspiration broke out on her brow. *Wait. Val said Darok would be close by, but where?* If she called out, would he be close enough to help her, as Val said? If she had to run, she would be in deep trouble. Marigold only walked unless food, or her stall in the barn, appeared before her. Darok would be her only chance, if he were nearby. Without him, she had no chance to defend herself or escape.

Thoughts of Lady Remington dying alone behind the inn in town crept into her mind. *Now where did that come from?* Anastasia thought about the man who followed her in the village. *What if he is following me, now?* Val only mentioned the man left town, not which direction he went. She did not tell Mama about the man who followed her, her mother worried enough already. Now she wished she had. Only Val knew about the man, and Val was nowhere around. *Gather your wits about you,* she told herself.

Marigold whinnied and sidestepped, tossing her head. She picked up on the girl's fear.

We need to move, Anastasia told herself. She nudged Marigold with her knees, and the horse stepped gingerly into the stream. Half-way across, Anastasia heard a strange whistling sound by her ear, and fire burned her shoulder. Everything happened at once. The force of the object knocked her off her horse into the stream. Marigold reared and screamed with fright. She plunged through the stream to the path on the other side, galloping furiously away, the reigns flapping behind her.

Anastasia opened her mouth to scream as she fell, but her mouth filled with water. She started coughing, scrambling frantically to get her head above water. The strong current caught Anastasia, sending her tumbling this way and that, as it carried her effortlessly away.

****

Sometime later, Anastasia realized she was still alive, or so it seemed. *Everything hurts, so I must be alive,* she reasoned. Cautiously, she moved her head. She discovered she lay face down in the mud, one arm hanging over a tree branch of some sort. Anastasia groaned. Wet and freezing with cold, she tried to shake the haze from her mind. When had she gone swimming? This did not look like the lake at home. So, where in thunder was she? Anastasia moved her arm off the tree branch and tried to push herself up. Pain raced up her right shoulder, causing her to cry out. That is when she discovered the blood. The shoulder of her gown was soaked with it, and blood ran freely down her arm. Sitting up gingerly, she ripped the shoulder of her gown to inspect the wound. Dizziness hit her hard. She leaned her head against her bent knees until her head quit spinning. Then, she examined her wound. A furrow cut across the top of her shoulder where an arrow sliced a neat path through her flesh. Blood seeped from the wound, running everywhere. *Where am I? Why have I been shot?* Then she remembered her trip to the brandy distillery for Mama, and the stubborn horse. *Marigold?* Anastasia looked about her but saw no sign of the mare. *Where is this Darok? Did not Val say this man could be trusted? That he would be nearby?*

She tried to stand up but fell back, crying out with pain when she moved her arm. Fresh blood poured out of the wound.

Dizziness washed over her. Her last thought was that she needed to tie up the wound, and hurry home before Mama started to worry.

****

When she awoke again, she was warm. Soft wool rubbed against her cheek and she pulled it a little closer. She could hear the fire crackling nearby and the murmur of voices.

Men's voices.

Her eyes popped open. *Where am I, and where did the fire and blankets come from? Whose voices are those? And why am I here? Have I been rescued? Or captured?* Someone shot an arrow at her and she had no idea who would want her dead. She listened to the sound of the voices. Maybe if she could make out what they said, she could decide if she should be thanking

105

them for finding her or trying to get away. She tested her shoulder. It was bandaged tightly. *So, whoever found me, cared for my wound?* Anastasia tried to move her legs. She felt wool. *Oh Lord, I am naked! Wait. No, I still have my chemise. Thank God for that! But where are my clothes? And where am I?* Suddenly, a familiar face came into sight. Val!

Anastasia tugged the blanket closer, making sure her right forearm remained covered. She did not want Val to catch sight of it, ever! Anastasia smiled up at him. She was so happy to see him; she almost started to cry. She needed his strength, his warmth, and his gentleness. She had been so frightened, and now it would be all right. Anastasia closed her eyes and breathed in deeply. His scent filled her lungs. She really hoped she was not dreaming.

"Anastasia."

She opened one eye. His face was still there. She opened the other eye.

"Are you awake?" he asked.

"I am not sure."

Val smiled. "Why?"

"I think, perhaps, I may be dreaming, because you are gone, so you could not really be here. Although, if I am not dreaming, and you are here, then it would mean you found me, and I am safe. 'Tis the truth; I hope I am not dreaming and that you truly are here, because I am frightened, and I believe someone shot an arrow at me. But then I thought, why would anyone want to shoot an arrow at me? It can only be a horrible dream I am having. So, I am not certain, whether I am awake or not."

Val frowned, confused. "I am here, little one, and

you are safe."

Anastasia glanced up at him. "Then I have only one concern."

"And what is that?"

"Where is here?"

"We are several miles from the village, on the bank of a stream, deep in the woods."

"Why?"

"Why what?"

"Why are we several miles from the village, on the bank of a stream, deep in the woods?"

He chuckled. "This is where we found you."

It all came back with a rush. The errand, Marigold, the stream, she flexed her shoulder and pain raced up her arm. Anastasia grimaced. "There is a bandage on my shoulder."

He glanced at her. "Aye."

"Who bandaged me?"

He pointed behind him. "Darok"

Oh yes, Darok. "Where was he? I did not see him anywhere. I hoped he was close, as you said. I did think about calling out to him, but then something burned hot on my shoulder, and I fell. The water came over my head, and I was so frightened. I tried to scream, and almost drowned. I was all alone, and when I woke up, my shoulder was bleeding, and my face was in the mud. I could not breathe, and then I think I swooned again, because I cannot remember much after that, except the cold. I was so cold." She was babbling she knew, but she did not care. She was so happy to see Val that her mouth kept talking, to cover her nervousness.

Val sat down next to her and asked, "Are you cold, still?"

"Nay."

Val threw his arm around her shoulders and pulled her in close to his side. "Darok did not know you were leaving so early. He caught your tracks about sunup and followed you to the distillery. He circled around and caught sight of the shooter right as you crossed the stream. He shot at the shooter as he took aim, causing him to miss his mark. Otherwise you would be dead. Whoever this man is, he is a very skillful marksman."

Anastasia drew a deep breath. It sobered her to think that if Darok had not been following her, she would be dead.

"After you fell into the stream, the current washed you quite a way downstream. Darok found you in the mud, and carried you here, where we could tend to your wound."

"Do you think this man meant to shoot me? That he wanted to kill me?" It frightened her to consider that someone might want her dead.

"I do not know, *Dorogaya*, whether he meant to kill you, or he intended on robbing a traveler, and you came across his path."

"If this man was waiting to shoot at me, do you think...do you suppose, it might be the man that followed me in the village?"

"This I do not know, either. The thing I do know for certain is, he is a dead man for daring to shoot at you." Val's tone softened as he said the words, and Anastasia shivered. "We will find this man who hides like a coward, and shoots at women. I will kill him. Such a man does not deserve to live." Danger emanated from him as he said the words.

Anastasia shivered again.

He scooped her up into his arms, blanket, and all. "You are still cold. We will go closer to the fire." Val stood smoothly and carried her to the fire. He found a fallen tree and sat with her cradled in his arms. He carried her as easily as if she were a child.

"Would you like some soup, miss?"

Anastasia peered out of her blanket cocoon toward a short little man with blond hair and a scruffy beard.

"This is Darok," Val whispered into her ear.

Anastasia pushed the blanket away from her face and smiled at the man. "Yes, I would, thank you, Darok. I would also like to thank you for following me, for bandaging my wound and for saving my life."

The little man blushed. "It was my pleasure," Darok said, smoothing the front of his tunic. "Do you need some help with the soup? I would be more than glad to help you; your shoulder being wounded and all."

"No, you won't "Val glared at Darok as he took the soup from him, growling low in his throat. Val took the spoon and holding Anastasia crossways on his lap, he spooned the soup into her mouth. He was so close; she could see the pulse beating in the side of his neck and count the whisker stubble on his chin. His scent floated all around her, so clean, so warm, and so male.

She glanced up at him and nearly missed the spoon. His hypnotic gaze centered directly on her. A drop of soup spilled on her lips. She licked it away and looked back up at him. He stared at her mouth with the same intensity as before, his eyes dark with desire. Their gazes locked, and she drowned for the second time that day. Val leaned a little closer, his gaze focused on her mouth, again. Anastasia forgot to breathe. She wanted, no, she *needed* his kiss. She stared at his lips, so close to hers and quivered against him.

He touched his mouth to hers, once, twice, three times. Gentle searching kisses, as if he were afraid to hurt her. Anastasia wanted him to kiss her like he did that night in the village.

She moved her arm so she could pull him closer. The rasp of wool against her bare skin reminded her of her lack of clothing. "Where are my clothes?"

Val nibbled at the side of her neck. "They are drying by the fire."

She sat silent for a minute and then asked. "Who...um...who removed them?" she whispered the question, but he heard. Val lifted his head.

He studied her face as he answered, "I did."

"I see." A blush started from the soles of her feet and worked itself to the top of her head. She ducked her head so he could not see that her face flamed red. This beautiful, beautiful man removed her clothing. He must have seen her arm. He could not have missed it. She would not be able to look into his eyes ever again. He must have seen many beautiful women without their clothing, and now he saw her body too, with all its flaws. Her breasts were too big and her waist too small, as Rella often pointed out. Most importantly, he saw her arm.

****

Val watched the emotions chasing themselves across her face and wondered what she thought. She was embarrassed, of that he was certain, but she did not need to be. Her body was perfect. "You have nothing to be ashamed of, *Dorogaya*, you are very beautiful."

Anastasia looked at him in surprise. "How can you

110

say that? What I am is not beautiful, I am hideous."

He knew instantly of what she spoke. Val reached for her right arm and pulled it slowly from the blanket. She tried to resist but the blanket started to slip from her shoulders. She quit struggling and waited, dropping her gaze. "Look at me, Anastasia." Val could feel her tense against him.

She squeezed her eyes shut as if waiting for a blow. Whatever caused the massive scarring on her right forearm had been extremely traumatic and emotional.

Val rubbed his thumb over the scarring, searching her face. Anastasia jumped at the contact and tried to pull away in a defensive gesture, but Val held her still. Then, he bent his head. When his lips touched her arm, her eyes popped open in surprise.

Her head came up. She tried to pull her arm away again, but he would not let her.

He outlined the pattern of scarring with his tongue and his lips, until he traced over every single one. He watched her face intently, the whole time. She was frightened. He read it in her expression. "Will you believe me when I tell you, you are beautiful to me? Scars such as these are marks of valor and strength; they are not to be hidden away in shame."

****

Anastasia ducked her head once more. Tears sprang to her eyes and she tried to swallow the lump in her throat. *How can he say such a thing?* "They are hideous," Anastasia stated.

"I disagree."

Nobody ever looked at her arm with anything other than horror since the beast tore her flesh with his teeth. Slowly, Val bent his head, and kissed her arm once more. *How can he think it beautiful?*

"Is it man or beast I kill for hurting you, thus?" he enquired. "You must have been in terrible pain. I will kill whoever did this to you."

"It was a beast," she answered with a shiver and pulled her arm away. She tucked it back inside the blanket out of sight.

"Will you tell me what happened?"

Anastasia shook her head. She could not talk about it. It was all still raw inside.

Val frowned at her denial but did not argue. "Someday soon, *Dorogaya*, I will know all your secrets," Val promised, "but this one I will let you keep until you want to tell me about this beast. "

"Did anyone else see my arm?" she asked quietly.

"No."

She looked up at him then and met the heated look in his eyes. Her breath caught at the need she read in their depth.

"I am the one who removed your clothing. You were freezing from the dunking in the stream. The sun was going down. I needed to get you warm. Your body is for my eyes alone. No other shall look at you; I will not allow it. Do you understand?"

She nodded her head and wearily leaned against his chest.

****

Val wrapped his arms around her and held her close. She still shook, whether from cold or from memories of the beast who scarred her arm, he did not know. He ran his hands up and down her back as he thought about their conversation, and the way his men found her earlier, unconscious, bloody, and covered in

112

mud. This girl needed protecting. Val was still angry over the way his men all stepped forward, volunteering to be the one to remove Anastasia's wet clothes, and warm her by the fire. He recognized the look in their eyes. Anastasia was a very beautiful woman, but she belonged to him, and by the gods, he meant to keep her. He did not realize he felt that way until he witnessed his men scrambling to help her, then, he wanted to run them through for thinking about it.

****

Heat and safety radiated from him and Anastasia leaned into him to soak some of it up. It was wonderful.

"How is your head?" His hands eased under her hair, and strong fingers caressed her scalp looking for any bumps he missed.

Anastasia shivered in response. His gaze turned warm and his hands slid to the back of her neck. He massaged her there, his fingers probing the softness of her skin. Waves of pleasure washed over her.

"Is she awake, Val?"

His hands stilled and Val glanced back over his shoulder. "Aye."

Several more men came into view. Val scooped her off his lap, leaning her back against the tree for support, and stood up.

"We found the spot where the man ambushed the girl," the one named Vroknar said. "You were right. There was one shooter. We looked around for any sign to identify him but found nothing. We did find the arrow some distance away. It bore no markings that we could identify. It would have been a clean shot if Darok had not stopped him. We could see where the bastard waited in the trees since early morning as you thought.

He knew she would be along and so he hid and waited. The horse spooked when she was shot and dumped the girl in the stream. The horse went off down the trail. It is probably safe at home in its stable eating hay by this time."

If Marigold made it home, Lady Evelyn was probably worried. Anastasia tried to stand but realized that her legs would not hold her up. At the same time, she remembered she wore only her chemise. "Do you suppose my clothes are dry?" she asked Val's back. "I really must get home; my mother will be worrying about me." She quickly sat back down. *Lord, I ache all over.*

Val turned to her. His eyes were gentle. "You are not going anywhere until we find out who is trying to kill you." Grim determination was very evident in his voice.

Chapter 10

They sat around the fire. The men pulled a log close to the heat for Anastasia. She was dressed once more, but held the wool blanket tight around her. She still shivered with cold. The blanket smelled like Val, so she held it close to her face and breathed his scent in. He came over to the log and sat down beside her. She felt the heat of his body next to hers and scooted a little closer.

"We need to find out who this man is, that would shoot at you and in order for us to do that, we need to ask you some questions," Val began.

She nodded her head. She had questions too.

"What is your given name, little one? And the name of your family?"

"I am Lady Anastasia Covington, daughter of Lord Robert Covington and Lady Evelyn Dunbar Covington."

****

Val stiffened in surprise. *So, she is a lady, and Lord Covington's daughter*. He was not expecting that answer.

She had their undivided attention.

That explained a lot and at the same time complicated the situation. For now, there could be several reasons why someone would shoot at Anastasia. Val had a lot more questions to ask. *How did she come*

by the terrible wound on her arm if she is gently bred?
Why does she travel alone? Where is her lady's maid?
The daughter of the king's favorite diplomat should be
well protected, not traveling about without protection.

"Why were you alone in the woods, my lady?"
Vroknar asked.

A blush showed on her face, and Anastasia stared
down at the ground.

"Where is your escort?" Val asked her gently. He
could see their questions upset her. He watched her
blush and misunderstood the reason for it. Jealousy
filled him with rage. *Had she been with Henry?* He
assumed so, because of her blush. *By God! He would
hunt the bastard down and kill him if he so much as
touched his Dorogaya!*

"I did not have an escort," Anastasia confessed.

"Why not?"

"Things have been…difficult since Papa died," she
began. "We have not had the wages paid to him by the
king. With no coin to pay for an escort, we have done
without. Mama let everyone go but Henry, our butler,
Grigori, our gardener, and our cook."

Val nodded his head. The anger died within him as
quickly as it came. Henry was merely a servant looking
out for her. Her answer also explained why Anastasia
was in the village selling vegetables and eggs. "Why
were you in the woods alone? Why did your family not
journey with you?" he repeated.

"Mama received a note from the overseer. We
finally had enough aged brandy to ship but he needed a
count and a signature. Mama was tending to Rella who
is ill, and Beatrice has no patience for numbers or
traveling."

"So, your mother sent you," Val finished for her.

"Yes."

"With a horse."

"Yes, and she is the most stubborn headstrong mare that ever lived. I would have been home hours ago, but Marigold kept stopping to graze, and I could not make her go any faster."

"We are aware this is difficult for you, my lady, but we must ask if Lord Covington received any threats toward himself or your family that you are aware of."

She shook her head. "Nay."

"Has anyone threatened you? Does anyone have reason to shoot at you?" Val kept his voice soft.

She shook her head again, a tiny voice whispered doubt. "Only the man that followed me in the village," she said and shivered.

Val pulled her into his arms and tucked the blanket around her. He noted the shiver and hugged her against him. He watched the emotions that came and went in her eyes. The assassin waited for hours for her to appear. It was doubtful that she would have made it home at all if she traveled any faster. Darok would not have reached her in time to shoot at the man, sending the assassin's arrow skittering higher than its intended mark. He would not have found her for he would have been too late. That thought settled in Val's mind like a stone, tightness squeezed at his chest, so he pulled her a little closer.

Anastasia looked into his eyes, hers wide with fear. "I have no idea who would do this. I do not think Papa has any enemies. Everyone loved Papa. He was the kindest most loving man anywhere. No one has threatened him or our family. I do not know why anyone would wish to shoot at me."

"Did you notice anything, hear anything?"

"No," she said thoughtfully. "There was only a feeling that something was wrong."

"Sir, do you think it might be…"

Val shook his head at the man. Anastasia was frightened. He could feel her shaking against him. He did not want it mentioned that they never found Lord Covington's killer. Nor did he want it mentioned that they suspected Lichtenburg. *Perhaps one of their spies followed her. But, why only her? Why not the older sister? Or the blonde girl? That one wandered off alone all the time and often late at night with the most unsavory of characters.*

"We need to get you home to your mother." Val gave her a little squeeze, to comfort her. He wanted to kiss her and caress her until she lost all thought but him and what he was doing to her, but he could not with all his men watching. She was a lady after all. He frowned, that complicated things.

Anastasia must have thought the same thing, because she said. "No one can know I was alone in the woods with you without a chaperon. If someone were to see the tear in my dress and realize I was here with you, I would be ruined." Panic edged her voice.

Anastasia was right. With her dress ripped that way it appeared as though she had been attacked. Val looked into her eyes; his hands rubbed her back through the blanket to soothe her.

"We will take you home, Lady Anastasia. We will cover you with a cloak and no one will know a thing," Vroknar assured her.

"Not even Mama," Anastasia said, "She would not

understand."

She did not say that she did not want *anyone* in the house to know of her night in the woods and her ripped dress, but Val understood. "It shall be all right, little one, your sister will not know. We will take you to the edge of the woods by your home, and if you feel strong enough, you can walk from there. We will stay close by until you are safely inside your gates."

"That would be most helpful."

"They will only know what you tell them, Lady Anastasia."

She smiled at Val then.

"Anastasia."

She looked at him again.

"I will find this man, whoever he is, and I will kill him."

She believed him. The look in his eyes sent a shiver down her spine.

****

Anastasia walked in the front door as the sun came up. Her legs shook so hard, she sat abruptly on a chair in the entry hall, as she could walk no farther. Lady Evelyn came running from upstairs, tears evident on her pale cheeks. She hugged Anastasia then questioned, prodded and fed her. Lastly, she ordered Anastasia to bed to rest.

Rella wandered downstairs, only mildly interested in the fuss being made over Anastasia's return, her illness miraculously gone.

Marigold showed up riderless about sundown the night before. She went to her stall and lay down as though nothing was amiss.

Lady Evelyn sent word to the vicar that Anastasia

was missing, and he organized a search party. They were leaving at first light. Everyone was glad she returned home and exclaimed over the wound on her shoulder. Only her mother knew the wound came from an arrow.

"I am to blame," Lady Evelyn said. "I should never have sent you out alone."

"Who could it be, Mama? Why would somebody want to shoot me?"

Lady Evelyn seemed convinced it was merely a scoundrel who followed her from the cellars thinking to rob her of any gold coins she carried.

Anastasia was not so sure. She had a heavy feeling in her stomach.

****

The tavern was dark in the corners, exactly the way Blackjack Kelly liked it. It kept people out of his business. He took another drink of the watered-down ale and puffed on his cigar. He was only waiting ten more minutes, and then he was leaving. The door opened and a figure entered the tavern covered in a black cape from head to toe. *At last.* Jack stubbed out his cigar and leaned back in his chair. The figure approached and sat facing Jack. A pouch of coins was thrown on the table in front of him. Jack picked up the pouch, checking the weight with his hand.

"That's not what ye promised me."

"You did not do the job as *you* promised *me*."

Jack was not happy about this at all.

"Listen ye, I killed the lady at the inn like ye wanted. I waited fer the girl like ye said. I got 'er. I seen 'er go down with me own eyes."

He waited. "Give me the money ye owe me," he

growled, "afore I kill ye with me own two 'ands right 'ere."

"The girl is still alive, as of this morning. Other than a bandage on her shoulder, she is fine and still breathing. You will have the rest when the job is done and not before."

The cloaked figure got up and left the tavern. *Damn!*

****

King Alexander Kazimir Augustine the First of Oldenburg was disturbed. He sat upon his golden throne and contemplated the seriousness of the situation. He was tall and fit with dark silver tipped hair, and startling blue eyes. He rubbed his chin with his long fingers as he thought.

Prince Darius, Crown prince of Oldenburg, as tall and muscular as his father, was dressed in his soldier's uniform, his dark hair neatly combed, his cap at his side. Prince Darius waited for his father to come to some sort of decision.

Prince Percival just returned to the palace and filled the king in on the attempted murder in the woods involving Lord Covington's daughter, Anastasia.

Ever since Lord Covington had been shot, relations between Oldenburg and Lichtenburg were stilted at best. King Alexander wanted to avoid war if it was at all possible. They still did not know who had shot and killed Lord Covington, and now one of his daughters had been shot at, too. If he did nothing, the killer or killers would think they had been undetected and strike again. Maybe next time, they would succeed. Such a thing must not be allowed to happen. If he sent troops to Lichtenburg or searched too deeply for proof that it was them behind it all, he risked war, and the lives of his people.

"Perhaps, Father, I could take a small group of men over the border and investigate a little. Scout around for clues and solve this puzzle without causing a lot of attention to us."

Prince Darius was very good at blending in. He was an excellent soldier and he had his mother's charm. If there was anything to know about Lichtenburg, Darius would sniff it out.

The king nodded his head. "That would help. At the very least give us an idea if they are behind these attacks or not. Be careful. If Lichtenburg is behind this, they would stop at nothing to capture Oldenburg's Crown Prince."

"I will be careful, Father."

The king nodded and Prince Darius left the throne room.

"Percival, we want you to take your men back to the Covington village. Stay in disguise as you have been. Do not reveal your identity or your purpose to anyone. Keep Lord Covington's family under surveillance at all times. We do not want those ladies to be harmed in any way. We owe it to Lord Covington to keep them safe. We do not know how many people know that Lord Covington was a cousin to the crown. We need to know if they are being attacked because of Lord Covington and his diplomatic career, or because they are directly related to us. Do a little looking around while you are there. Find out who is behind this if you can."

Percival bowed to his father and left the room.

That means I am going to be close to her, going to

see her, going to watch her, maybe even talk to her again. He shook his head. *What is the matter with me?* He had not acted like a besotted youth with his first woman since, well, since he had been a besotted youth with his first woman. Anastasia was the same as any other woman, and he had plenty of women to know that the excitement did not last long. Inevitably he got bored and moved on.

Val thought of how she looked that night at the stream. Anastasia had been completely limp, her clothing sticking to her slim body. They thought she might be dead, but then he rolled her toward him and felt the tiny beat of her heart on the side of her long neck. Relief rolled over him, stilling the sudden ache in his chest. They built a roaring fire and after informing his men *he* alone would be the one removing her clothing, he preceded to do so.

She had been so cold, her lips turned blue and her skin felt like ice. He marveled at the fullness of her breasts, as he removed her gown. He measured the smallness of her waist as he undid her skirts. Then he stared at the gentle flare of her hips, as he pulled her sodden gown off, and moved it down over her long shapely legs. Her chemise did nothing to shield his gaze from the beautiful woman he held in his arms. His gaze caught on her pale pink nipples, pressing against the thinness of the fabric. His stomach clenched when his gazed moved over the cloud of dark hair at the juncture of her thighs. Desire slammed into him with an intensity that surprised him. His groin tightened and fire ran though him like a wick of a candle catching flame. God, he was disgusted with himself. She was freezing and nearly dead, and all he could think about was tasting her, touching her, burying himself in her. He inspected the massive scars on her arm too, and rage boiled his blood at the sight. Where had she been and what happened to her? He wrapped her up in his own blanket then to keep his eyes from looking, and his body from wanting. Thank the gods, he had not followed through on his intent to bed her. She was a lady and if he had taken her, the situation would have been a complication he could do without.

He needed to get himself under control. He could not afford to get more involved than he already was. He would go back to the village, but he would simply watch from a distance. He was going to keep her safe, keep her alive and that was all.

Chapter 11

"They have been stolen! My mother's jewels have been stolen!" Rella screamed at the top of her voice.

They all hurried to the library, where Rella was looking in the strong box. She was certain there was some jewelry in there that Lord Covington purchased for Lady Agnes.

"And since every other piece of jewelry in this house is either entailed or mentioned in the will, these jewels belong to me! And only me!" Rella had been on a crusade to find them over the past few days, and she made sure everybody knew it.

Lady Evelyn tried to soothe the girl. "I am sure they are here somewhere, although I have never heard mention of such jewels." she said thoughtfully. "Now, darling, describe them again and we shall all help you look."

"There is a complete set of jewels. They are made of rose-colored stones fashioned like flowers intertwined. There is a necklace, a brooch, earrings, a ring, and a bracelet. They are worth a lot of money. I remember Mama talking about them. Papa bought them for her when I was born."

Lady Evelyn took out the trays of jewels one more time, to look them over. They went through the jewels one piece at a time. After the last tray was lifted out, Rella cried out. "Look!"

There was a rose-colored necklace under the tray, as well as a ring and a bracelet. They were fashioned to look like flowers intertwined exactly like Rella said. There were no earrings or a brooch, though. They checked the strongbox again but could not find them.

"I told you! Someone has stolen them! Someone knew they were there and took them!"

"Who?" Lady Evelyn demanded.

"No one comes into the library at all since Papa died and the key is always with me. Someone would need to be very clever indeed to know that there is a strongbox concealed in your father's desk right there instead of a drawer. I believe only someone in the family would know how to open it. So, you see? No one could have taken them." Lady Evelyn stopped to consider. "Are you sure there are earrings and a brooch as well? Perhaps you were too young to remember."

Rella was furious. "I know there are earrings and a brooch. I remember Mama wearing them. The entire set. And how do you know someone did not take your key? Only the other day I saw it on the same ring as the door to the cellars. It was hanging from the cellar lock. Anyone could have taken it and you would have been none the wiser. I know someone stole those jewels!"

Lady Evelyn was silent. She had left the keys hanging from the cellar lock when she went down there the other day. *If Rella saw them who else had? Surely no one in this household would do such a thing.*

"I am sure we shall find them, dear."

****

It had been several weeks since Anastasia's trip to the distillery. The brandy shipment had been sold and they now shipped regularly again. The next batch of

126

brandy was finally aged, and money was starting to trickle in. Lady Evelyn took the girls to the village to order their gowns and masks for the masquerade ball. Bolt after bolt of fine silk, and satin was brought out while Lady Evelyn and Mrs. Griffin talked about the new styles. At last, Mrs. Griffin sent word that the bodices were ready to be fitted. The girls were excited. They had not had new gowns since Lord Covington died. Lady Evelyn ordered new slippers and stockings for them as well.

Henry brought the coach around. The two young gray geldings were the newest addition to the stables. Lady Evelyn said they must have new horses for the carriage, because she did not think that poor old sway backed Marigold would be able to pull the carriage all the way to Larenia. The geldings had only been with them for a few days, and after a long, heated debate they had been named Hercules and Achilles.

Once they arrived at the dress shop, Mrs. Griffin was busy showing Lady Evelyn what her seamstresses had finished thus far. The bodice must be fitted to each of them to ensure a proper fit. When it was her turn, Anastasia set her reticule on the counter and allowed herself to be led into the back for the fitting. Her dress was of emerald silk, the exact color of her eyes. The bodice had pleats running vertical from the square neck to the tiny waist. There was an inset of exquisite white lace set in the center of the bodice. The gown would have a full skirt of emerald silk with another inset of the white lace in the center of the skirt, matching the one in the bodice. Red rose buds adorned the waist in the front as well as at the wrists of the tight long sleeves that she wore to conceal the hideous scars. It was a simple, yet elegant style, and Anastasia thought she had never seen such a beautiful gown.

Anastasia handed her bodice back to the seamstress and went to the front of the shop. As she picked her reticule up from the counter, something heavy fell to the floor in front of her. Mrs. Griffin bent and picked it up. It was the rose-colored brooch that Rella had been looking for!

Rella let out a shriek. "You stole my mama's brooch! I knew it was you! Give me that brooch!"

Mrs. Griffin looked appalled and her entire face pinched up as she stared at Anastasia. "Well I never! Will you look at that?"

Lady Evelyn took the brooch from Mrs. Griffin and looked at Anastasia in surprise. "What in the world! Anastasia! Where did you get this?" Lady Evelyn asked.

Anastasia had no idea where it had come from. It looked like she dropped it, but she had not. She had never seen that brooch before. "I do not know where it came from. I picked up my reticule and it fell to the floor," Anastasia explained.

"You see how she lies, m'lady!" Mrs. Griffin glared at Anastasia, hard, with her hands fisted on her ample hips.

Lady Evelyn turned the brooch over in her hand, studying it.

"She stole it! I told you she stole it!" Rella shrieked.

Anastasia glanced past Lady Evelyn and saw Lady Darling, a shocked expression on her face. Everyone stared at Anastasia. The shop grew quiet.

"Where did it come from, then? It certainly looked

like it fell from your reticule," Lady Evelyn asked quietly.

"I did not have it. I do not know where it came from," Anastasia answered quietly. "I left my reticule here on the counter and went in the back to try on my bodice. When I picked up my reticule, it fell."

Beatrice turned and walked out of the shop. Lady Darling followed suit, shaking her head and murmuring, "Well, I never would have supposed it of her," as she shooed her maid out with her.

Lady Evelyn studied Anastasia, a sad but thoughtful look on her face.

Mrs. Griffin glared and Rella smiled at her behind Lady Evelyn's back.

"Will you send our things to the house?" Lady Evelyn asked Mrs. Griffin.

"Of course," Mrs. Griffin said. Then as if she could not keep her mouth shut any longer, "I tried to tell you your girl was lying to you, m'lady. I tried to tell you she is mean and cruel and selfish. Why, I have had poor Lady Rella in my shop several times, nearly fainting for food and water she was, because that one," she pointed her long skinny finger at Anastasia, "refused to let her have anything to eat or drink. The poor miss was almost done for. Lady Anastasia didn't care. Oh no! She was flirting and carrying on, as if she had not a care in the world."

Mrs. Griffin jabbed her finger in Anastasia's chest. "She tried to work poor Lady Rella to death. I saw it with my own eyes I did. And that one," she jabbed at Anastasia again. "No, she didn't care one mite. Only concerned for herself she was. Now you understand. She is a wicked, wicked girl and I have no idea what you are going to do with her."

"Thank you, Mrs. Griffin; that will be quite enough. Good day." Lady Evelyn took hold of Anastasia's arm and pulled her out of the shop.

Rella followed along behind. "I told you Anastasia took my jewels," Rella began, but Lady Evelyn stopped her.

"Hold your tongue please. There will be no more talk of this until we are at home. I will get to the bottom of this, but this is a family matter and should not be discussed with the whole village looking on."

Anastasia was thankful for that, at least. Lady Evelyn did not like scenes, and she liked to keep family matters private.

Anastasia stared out the window all the way home, her thoughts as dark as the afternoon sky right before a thunderstorm. She had just lost anybody, and everybody who might have believed her. Lady Darling and Beatrice seemed to be the only friends she had, and now she lost them, too. Anastasia glanced at Rella. The girl was smiling her victory smile. She knew what that meant, of course. Rella planned the whole thing and was enjoying Anastasia's pain. Rella was the only one with any knowledge about the jewelry before today. She also knew that Lady Evelyn left her keys in the cellar door the other day. Even if Anastasia walked past the cellar door, at the time, she would not have noticed the key to the strongbox. She had no idea what it looked like, or what made it different from any of the other keys her mother carried. Rella must have been waiting for her opportunity.

Anastasia left her reticule on the counter while she was fitted for the bodice, making it easy for Rella to hide the brooch. *But how am I going to prove I had nothing to do with it?* Anastasia sighed. She knew Lady Evelyn would not believe her. It looked like she dropped the brooch. She needed to come up with some sort of plan, to protect herself. The earrings to her mother's jewelry set were still missing, according to Rella. Somehow, she had to prevent Rella from using them against her. In the meantime, she would tell the truth and hope that sometime in the future, Mama would forgive her. Anastasia waited patiently in the library for her mother once they got home.

When Lady Evelyn finally entered, she appeared tired and drawn. "Tell me what happened, Anastasia."

"I do not know, Mama. We went to the shop. I left my reticule on the counter. I was fitted for my bodice and when I returned and picked up my reticule, the brooch fell to the floor. That is all I know."

"Yet you do spend a lot of time in the library, as Rella pointed out. You have had access to the strongbox, constantly."

"I do spend a lot of time in the library; that part is true, but I have no idea what key belongs to the strongbox. I do not know where you keep them, and I had no idea those jewels existed before today."

"Perhaps, but somehow they ended up in the bottom of the strongbox. I have been in that box before and I cannot remember ever seeing them. And yet there they were as if somebody was trying to keep their existence a secret."

"If I knew which key went to the strongbox and knew about the jewels, why would I wait for Rella to go looking for them to steal them?" Anastasia shook her head. It did not make sense at all.

Lady Evelyn was quiet. "Rella accuses you of trying to sell them. She says you deliberately hid them in the bottom of the strongbox so you could take them out a piece at a time and nobody would know."

"Where would I sell them? I do not know anyone in the village who would buy them."

"You have been in the village, every day. You have had plenty of opportunity, to ask around as Rella pointed out to me."

"That is true, Mama, but I have been tending the booth. I sold everything and brought you the coins, each day. When would I have had time to sell her jewelry?"

"You also traveled to the distillery, for a day and a night, alone. You have no explanation for your extended absence."

Anastasia stared in disbelief. "I was wounded. You saw the wound the arrow made, Mama. I was gone longer because I was unconscious."

Lady Evelyn nodded. "I dismissed the man who shot at you as insignificant, but perhaps the man saw you with the jewels, or saw you sell the earrings and thought to rob you. I did not at the time consider that the man may have had a reason to shoot at you."

Anastasia studied her mother. She was right. It did all look extremely suspicious, but she was innocent and had no way to prove it.

"Then there is also the matter of the two hundred ducats you gave me. Where did you get the gold, Anastasia?"

Anastasia bowed her head. She was sunk. "I cannot say, Mama."

There was no way she could explain about Val or

tell her mother that she saw him several times after Mama told her not to. She could not tell her what happened in the woods. For Anastasia to have been in the woods all night, alone with a group of men, would be more than her mother could take. Mama would never believe that nothing happened. Anastasia's reputation would be ruined. She would be a disgrace. Mama would never believe that Val simply handed her the gold, either.

"Do you not suppose, Mama, that Rella could have had the jewels all along and just recently took the key and dropped them into the strongbox? She knew more about your key than I did. And there was a perfect opportunity for her to put the brooch into my reticule at the shop."

"Why should she go to so much trouble, Anastasia?"

"She wants to make everyone hate me."

Lady Evelyn looked at Anastasia a long time. "Both of my girls are accusing the other of terrible things. I am having a hard time deciding what is real and what is a lie. There are a lot of things that do not add up, in both of your stories." She paused for a few minutes. "I cannot listen to either sister accuse the other, anymore. You shall both have to work it out between you. I expect more of you, Anastasia; you are the elder by a few months, and I expect you to act like a lady as I have taught you. For now, there will be no more discussion."

As Lady Evelyn was leaving the room she turned back, "You will not be allowed in the library, alone, until this matter is solved." With that she held the door open and motioned for Anastasia to precede her out of the room.

They almost bumped into Rella who hovered right outside the door.

****

This was going much better than Rella planned. Her determination to make Anastasia look guilty, and discredit her was working. No one believed anything Anastasia said. Everyone thought Anastasia was jealous and mean to Rella, stopping at nothing to hurt her and make her miserable. This was exactly what Rella intended, that way if the little green-eyed witch told what she knew; everyone would assume it was merely another lie made to hurt Rella. Rella nearly laughed aloud as she listened to the talk inside the library.

"Did Anastasia tell you what she did with my mother's earrings?" Rella looked from one to the other.

Lady Evelyn paused. "We agreed there would be no more accusations. You two sisters shall act like ladies and shall learn to endure each other for the sake of the rest of the family that must live with you both. There will be no more talk of stolen jewelry. Do you understand?"

Rella's eyes widened at the tone of voice Lady Evelyn was using. She nodded her head and Lady Evelyn walked away toward the kitchens.

What happened? She was sure she overheard most of the conversation. *What did I miss?* This was not part of her plan at all. She needed Lady Evelyn to believe Anastasia to be a liar and a thief.

Rella narrowed her eyes at Anastasia. "What did you say to Lady Evelyn? I know you believe yourself to be clever, but you are not. I am going to take everything you have away from you. I am going to make you suffer more than you have ever suffered. I am going to have my revenge on you, and by the time I am done everyone will hate you, even your mother and your sister. Lady Evelyn will throw you out of the house and tell you to never come back. None of your precious village people will help you either. You will have no one and nowhere to go! You will be too late, as always."

Anastasia did not flinch at the threat; she merely stared at the floor. Then her head came up. "Why do you say such things? What have I ever done to you?"

"You know too much, and I hate you!" Rella spit at her. She would make Anastasia pay if it was the last thing she did!

****

Anastasia turned away and hurried to her room. She shook with shock from the verbal assault and the hate directed at her from Rella. The reference Rella made to the terrible day Anastasia lost Athena and received the bite that scarred her arm had been made purely out of meanness. Anastasia was always too late. She had to come up with a plan. Anastasia sat on her bed and analyzed the situation.

Rella was the only one who knew about the jewels, and she knew Lady Evelyn did not always have the key to the strongbox. Rella also mentioned she saw the key hanging from the lock to the cellar. So, Rella must have taken the key and put the jewels in the bottom of the strongbox. If all the jewels had been accounted for except the brooch and earrings, until today of course, when the brooch made its debut on the dressmaker's shop floor, the earrings must be somewhere close, too. Anastasia rubbed her forehead. *How am I going to find the earrings without Rella knowing? How am I going to prove to Mama that I am innocent?* She decided that she must keep a better eye on Rella and be extra vigilant about her own belongings so that the earrings did not "fall out" of her possessions somewhere too. Having come to that decision, Anastasia got up and carefully went through her room to make sure the earrings were not already planted somewhere.

She went to bed when she finished, pulling the quilt up to her chin. It had been a very long day. She thought about her mother. It hurt her to see the disappointment in Mama's eyes. It hurt that her friends at the village believed Rella's stories about her. She figured they had known her for the last five years, and that they should know she was not the person Rella portrayed her to be.

Then she thought about Val, like she always did when she was upset. He was the only person in her life that she had not disappointed, yet. Where was he anyway? Did he ever think about her and that kiss? Would she ever see him again? Would it matter if she did? She was a lady, and if he was a mere soldier, nothing could ever come of it.

She sighed. Why did everything have to be so mixed up? Her life was so much simpler when Papa was alive. He had been the one she ran to, the one that seemed to understand her. She even disappointed him, and she never told him how sorry she was. Sorry that she disappointed him, and sorry that she had run away. She decided to put forth an extra effort to be the lady her mother wanted her to be.

Chapter 12

Anastasia lasted about a day and a half. They would be leaving for the ball in the next day or two, and everything was in an upheaval. Difficult was a tame word for what Rella had been. She claimed she had a new beau; one who was very much different from the men she had been bringing home. This man was important, and very rich. Rella claimed he was the man she was going to marry, and every day for the last two weeks flowers appeared for Rella. Each one had a little note attached and Rella would grab the note and read it, sighing all the while. Rella appeared to be in love. She claimed she was and that the feeling was mutual. Rella spent most of her time lying on her bed and rereading every single note. It was annoying at best.

Anastasia still waited on Rella in the mornings and still cleaned her chamber for her on top of the other chores her mother lined up for her. Rella was particularly critical and demanding. Anastasia was so tired of Rella threatening to go to Lady Evelyn and tell her about Val, that she was about to go tell her mother herself, almost. Anastasia had not seen or heard from Val since that night in the woods, and she was beginning to despair.

Lady Evelyn was determined to find suitors for all three of them at the ball. Her mother casually mentioned it only three or four hundred times since the invitation arrived. It scared Anastasia to death. She did not want a suitor. She wanted Val. And since that was never going to happen, she decided she would simply remain unmarried for the rest of her life and put the matter out of her mind.

After the last time Rella threatened to go to Lady Evelyn, Anastasia turned, her temper getting the best of her. "What about you? What if I tell her about the men you traipse in and out of your chamber all the time?"

Rella's eyes went wide. "She would not believe you. She would think you made it up again simply to hurt me. Lady Evelyn is convinced I am the sweetest girl in this house. Besides I have a new suitor now, and I am too much in love to take other men to my bed. So, you see? You have no proof and Lady Evelyn will not believe you."

"Really? What about your scheme with the brooch? Mama is not convinced I had anything to do with that whole thing at all. Maybe she will believe me this time, too."

Rella's eyes narrowed.

"What have you done with your mother's jewels anyway, Rella? I have not seen them anywhere since you put the brooch in my reticule at the dress shop. Have you been selling it yourself? Are you hoping to convince everyone I sold the jewelry while you pocket the coins?"

"I would be very, very, careful if I were you," Rella threatened, "you do not want to make me mad. You have no idea what I could do to you."

"Is that so? Is there still something you could do you have not already done. You do not scare me one tiny bit. You have lied about me, hurt me, and got me into trouble for years. I have done absolutely nothing to you but try to be a good sister. I do not know what you hope to gain by all of this, but it seems to me you are not necessarily winning at this point."

*****

Rella stared at Anastasia. She was right. It was time Rella finished the game.

Anastasia left the room to go do her regular chores, completely unaware of the fury she ignited inside of Rella. *How did Anastasia know I sold some of the jewelry? Has she followed me? Has somebody told her something?* Rella thought, hard. She did not see where she slipped, and Anastasia would have found out. She was very careful that no one followed her. She was sure the necklace was far from the village and Covington House, by this time. She needed to do something drastic to get Anastasia out of her life. As much fun as it was to watch Anastasia suffer, she knew too much and if Rella's threats no longer made Anastasia upset, it was time to come up with a new plan.

****

Lady Evelyn believed that physical labor brought health and prosperity to the household. Even though their financial situation improved, she still required the girls to help in the kitchens and with the laundry.

Thank God we will be wearing long gloves for the ball, Anastasia thought as she looked at her hands. They were still calloused. She sighed. Her callouses made her think of Val and the way he had caressed them. Thinking of Val made her oblivious to the present. Her mind focused on him and the kiss and...

She did not see the basket in front of her, and she tripped with the dishes she carried. They landed with a

139

loud crash. Food, Anastasia, and the dishes went in different directions.

"Now what ye gone an' done?" Cook demanded "Ye need to watch where yer goin', girl."

Well, that was true, and she needed to quit thinking about Val. She was going to have to change her clothes now; they had stew dripping from them. Everyone would be waiting, and Anastasia was trying to hurry. Their masks for the ball were finished and they were all anxious to see them.

Anastasia ran into her room and stopped. Someone had been in here. She had taken to arranging her things exactly so, that way she could tell at a glance if anything had been moved or touched in her absence. Her reticule was crooked on top of the wooden chest where it lay.

Cautiously Anastasia picked it up and weighed it in her hand. It was slightly heavier than it had been before. She opened it and two earrings fell into her hand as well as the coins Mama gave her to pay for the masks. She counted the coins. There were two missing. Then she looked at the earrings. They were fashioned like flowers intertwined of rose-colored stones. *Someone put the missing earrings in my reticule!* Of course! Rella had been in the room when Lady Evelyn counted out the coins and handed them to Anastasia to pay for the masks. It looked like Rella had another plan. She removed two of the coins so when Anastasia went to pay, she would be short and would then turn her reticule upside down to find them. Instead of the coins, the missing earrings would fall out.

Anastasia slid the two earrings into the waistband of her gown, making sure they were not visible and could not fall out. Two could play this game, and she was not going to be made a fool of again. She had a plan now, too. She went quietly up to Rella's room. *Perfect, her reticule is still on the bed.* Anastasia slid the earrings into the reticule and pulled the drawstrings closed. Now, she was ready to go to the village. She begged Mama to come with them saying, "Please, Mama, you need a break and the fresh air will do us all some good."

Rella appeared quite happy with the turn of events. Anastasia figured Rella was delighted at the prospect of having Lady Evelyn witness the scene. Another jewel mishap would no doubt convince Mama that Anastasia had stolen her jewels. Neither her mother nor Beatrice knew how cunning Rella was.

Once they arrived at the shop, Mrs. Griffin brought out the masks. They were beautiful. Each one adorned with feathers and precious stones. Beatrice had a white one with pink feathers to match her pink gown. Rella had a pale blue one with rose feathers, to set off her blue gown and the rose-colored jewelry. Anastasia had an emerald green mask with white feathers. Lady Evelyn's gown was purple, so she had a purple mask with black feathers.

After they examined their masks, Anastasia opened her reticule, and took out the coins Lady Evelyn had given her. She counted them out and frowned, then she counted them again. Anastasia took her reticule and turned it upside down, she carefully pulled it inside out.

"I do not know where the other coins have gone," she murmured, "it appears that two of them are missing." She looked up.

Lady Evelyn was frowning, Beatrice was frowning,

and Rella looked confused.

"They must be in there somewhere. Give me that reticule," Rella demanded.

Anastasia held it up for her to examine. "They are not. I even turned it inside out. There is nothing else in there."

Rella grabbed Anastasia's reticule and shook it herself in disbelief.

"See?" Anastasia smiled into Rella's confused stare. "I believe I saw you put some extra coins into your reticule yesterday. You remember? When we came to purchase the hair ribbon for you?"

Beatrice looked at Rella, too. "You do have some coins. I watched you put them in your reticule too. Mama did not bring her money, so we will need to use yours."

Everyone looked at Rella. She took her reticule and dumped it on the counter. Several coins and a handkerchief fell out, as well as two rose-colored earrings in the shape of flowers. Rella tried to cover the earrings as fast as she could with the handkerchief, but Anastasia was faster.

"Mama, look!" Anastasia exclaimed.

"Why Rella, are those the earrings you have been looking for? They look exactly like the other jewels from the set. They must be the missing ones. Oh darling, I am so happy you found them. Why did you not tell me you had found them?"

Beatrice picked one up and studied it. "Where did you find them?"

Anastasia smiled and said, "Please tell us, Rella we are dying to hear where they were."

Rella flushed a bright red color. "Well, um. I…that

is."

"Yes dear?" Lady Evelyn was waiting for an answer. They had been searching and searching for those earrings.

"They were tangled with the other pieces. At first, I did not see them, but then later when I untangled the necklace and such, there they were!"

Lady Evelyn looked squarely at Rella. "You should have told me that you found them. Poor Anastasia has been quite frantic to find them for you. It would have given all of us peace of mind." Then Lady Evelyn smiled. "I do not need to tell you how worried I have been about all of this." She squeezed Rella's shoulders. "And now the mystery has been solved! Thank God, for that. I do not need more to worry about than I already have. Come my darlings, we still have much to do before we leave for Larenia."

She turned to the dressmaker. "Thank you, Mrs. Griffin, for all your help. You have outdone even yourself with the beautiful gowns. I must say these masks are perfect. I am sure no one will be better dressed than we are! Good day."

They left the shop and started toward home.

Anastasia glanced at Rella. Rella was so furious; she looked downright sinister. Her face was turned toward the window, and the anger rolled off her in waves. Anastasia tried not to shiver. Neither Lady Evelyn nor Beatrice seemed to notice Rella at all. Lady Evelyn happily hummed to herself and Beatrice was lost in her own world, as usual. Anastasia thought about the situation. What could Rella do? The only thing Rella could hurt her with would be to tell Mama about the kiss, but as Rella had not been there herself, it would be her word against Rella's. Lady Evelyn had been most adamant the girls work their problems out between them.

Anastasia cheered up at the thought. Maybe everything would be all right after all. Mrs. Griffin had nothing to say today. That was a good start. Mrs. Griffin *always* had something to say, especially lately.

****

A note was delivered during dinner the night before they left for Larenia. Henry appeared beside Anastasia in the pretext of filling her water glass. He slipped the note onto her lap.

Anastasia glanced down. She flipped the note open long enough to see it was sent by "V." Blushing, she tucked the note into her waistband. The note must be from Val. Later that night, when dinner was over, she slipped away to her chamber and shut the door. With trembling fingers, she opened the note.

"My Dearest Lady Anastasia,

First, I must first beg your forgiveness for being away so long. There is much I wish to discuss with you. I yearn to speak with you in person. Will you meet me at the royal ball? I will be in the library at the stroke of midnight. I will be waiting impatiently for you....V."

Anastasia held on to her stomach. It immediately started to quiver. The air became trapped in her lungs. *So, Val will be at the ball, after all. That must mean that he holds some sort of title; the nobility are the only ones invited, other than royalty, of course.* Anastasia felt the unfamiliar sensation of hope fluttering in her chest and in her mind. It sounded as if Val had intentions. God, she really, really hoped he did.

Anastasia laid the note carefully on her pillow. She

still had her nightly chores to do so she left the room and hurried downstairs.

****

Rella had been watching when Henry slipped the note to Anastasia. She watched the blush cover Anastasia's face when she saw who sent the note. *Now, that is interesting.* She kept careful note of Anastasia all through the evening and followed her when Anastasia slipped off to her chamber to read the note. Rella waited in the shadows until Anastasia ran back downstairs, then she slipped into Anastasia's chamber and looked around for the note. She saw it sitting on Anastasia's pillow. She read the note quickly. Obviously, this "V" was somebody Anastasia cared about. Rella's mind raced with possibilities. This could well be her chance. If she was clever enough, Anastasia would finally pay for all she had done. Rella began to plan. She needed to find out who V. really was. She had no doubt this V. was the man who kissed Anastasia. *So, if he is going to be at the ball, he has to be someone important.* She carefully placed the note back on the pillow exactly as she found it and hurried to her own chamber. She would need to make sure Grigori saddled Hercules for her before he retired tonight.

****

The man with the black hair who answered to Blackjack waited in the tavern again. He had given up on his employer ever being on time. His back was against the wall, and he faced the door so he could see who was coming and going. He kept his hat pulled low over his eyes and leaned back into the shadows. About an hour and several pints later, he saw the figure in the dark cloak approach the tavern. *It is about damn time,*

145

he muttered to himself. His employer walked quickly to the back of the tavern and sat down.

"There has been a change of plans. I need two things. First, I must know the real identity of the man who fancies Anastasia. Secondly, I need several uniforms from the army of Lichtenburg...."

"How much are ye payin' for the bloke's name?"

"A hundred ducats."

Blackjack spit and began to get up.

"Two hundred ducats."

"Now tha's more like it." He sat back down. "I want the money in advance this time. Not anymore o' yer promises."

"Do you know who he is?"

"Do ye have the money?"

Two hundred ducats were counted out and passed across the table.

She might need to find a new mercenary; this one was getting too demanding. She had only been able to get four hundred ducats for the brooch and she needed this man to follow through with her plan.

"I kept thinkin' I knew the bloke. Somethin' about 'im get wigglin' in me head. An' then I remembered. 'E is the bloody prince!"

Rella pushed the cloak off her head and leaned closer to the foul-smelling man. "If you are lying to me, so help me God I will kill you myself."

"As if yer could!" The man laughed into her face. The fumes from his breath made her want to gag.

"Which prince? And how do you know it is the prince?"

"'Ow much ye goin' to pay fer me story?"

That settled it. Blackjack was finished as far as she

was concerned. "Another hundred ducats and no more."

He held his hand out. God he was insolent! She slid the coins over to him.

He smiled and waved his cup at the tavern keeper for more ale. "I wer' on me way back from an assignment and I comes upon a group of, oh I would say, maybe thirty soldiers from Lichtenburg. I likes me head fine where 'tis so I lays down in the snow real quiet like and 'opes they don' find me. I 'ears some 'orses comin' up behind me and they run right into the Lichtenburg soldiers. There was four or five maybe, men on them 'orses. Soldiers. Our soldiers. One of 'em the prince 'imself. The younger one. They takes those Lichtenburg soldiers and kilt them all in minutes. The prince, 'e wer a snappin' necks and spines ever which way. They all were. That prince kilt at least five Lichtenburg men without even breakin' a sweat. Seems thes' Lichtenburg soldiers 'ad jus' raided and burned one o' our villages. That prince, 'e was not a 'appy bloke about it, so he kilt 'em all."

Sober, Blackjack Kelly had almost nothing to say, and usually answered in monosyllables. After a few pints of ale, he talked like a washerwoman with a story to tell.

Rella was thinking, hard. *The prince and Anastasia*. Rella's face twisted up. *Well, that sure as hell is not going to happen.* If anybody was going to catch a prince and be a princess, it was going to be her. So, with a few adjustments…it would work.

"How would you like to earn one thousand ducats?" She had no idea where she would get such a sum, but she would think of something. She always did.

Jack was suddenly all ears and she had his focused

attention.

"Here is what we shall need to do...."

Chapter 13

His Royal Highness Prince Percival Mikael Augustine sat on his horse under the shelter of the trees and watched the stone house. He had been watching Covington House for a while now. It had been weeks, but it seemed like years. He kept his distance, as he determined within himself to do. It proved to be one of the hardest things he had ever done. He knew where Anastasia slept, knew exactly where her chamber was, and which window belonged to her. He knew when she blew her candle out at night and knew when she lit it early in the morning. He knew when she went into the village. He knew when she went to church services, knew when she helped in the kitchens, and knew when she went riding.

Lady Evelyn upgraded her stables with two young geldings, Hercules and Achilles. He witnessed the girls arguing over their names, albeit from the shelter of the trees. Hercules was the one Anastasia favored, and she often let him run once she was out of sight of the house. He followed along; of course, it was his duty to keep her safe after all.

He witnessed her laughter as she rode with the wind in her hair; he also witnessed her anger caused by the yellow haired sister. Once he witnessed her tears, and it nearly undid him. He wanted to go to her, take her into his arms, and solve whatever problem it was that had her sobbing so forlornly, but he could not. His father, the king, commanded that he keep out of sight. His resolve to distance himself from her evaporated like dew before the warm rays of the sun.

Percival went looking for the man who dared to shoot an arrow at *his Dorogaya*, but he had disappeared. It surprised him that he thought of Anastasia as his, but he would be damned if he was going to let any other man have her. He realized he would have to reveal his identity to Anastasia, and he was not sure how she would react. She thought of him as a common man, and he was far from that. It would be better if she learned who he was from him, and not anybody else. The masquerade ball would soon be here, and he feared he must make a move quickly. If he did not, Lady Evelyn would almost certainly look for a suitor for her, and her sisters. His chest tightened with anxiety, he must time it exactly right. It was a complicated matter at best.

Until this last year, both he and the Crown Prince Darius had been betrothed. Darius had been betrothed to the Crown Princess of Bulgaria, and he to the Princess Alena of Lichtenburg. Both marriages had been arranged when they were mere babies. The Crown Princess of Bulgaria recently suffered a tragic riding accident and passed away. Darius was, of course, in mourning. The recent hostilities between Lichtenburg and Oldenburg affected the marriage betrothal. King Alexander received notice that Lichtenburg no longer considered Prince Percival as acceptable for the Princess Alena, and so there would be no marriage. Percival was relieved when he received this news. Nothing would make him happier than to have

Anastasia as his princess. But to wed so soon after this news might be considered an insult. Peace with Lichtenburg was tentative at the time. He hoped to God he could convince his father, and Anastasia, that he was the right man for her.

The day before the Covington's were to leave for Larenia, Percival made his decision. He would meet his Anastasia at the ball and declare his love for her. He knew she liked his kisses, and so he decided if she put up much resistance, he would simply kiss her until she agreed. His father was going to be a different matter altogether. Prince Percival wrote a note to have Anastasia meet him at the ball and waited in the shadows to have a private word with Henry. He trusted the man. He witnessed Henry interfere for Anastasia several times in the past few weeks. Anybody that took care of *his Dorogaya* had his favor.

Percival would be leaving for Larenia and the castle as soon as Darok showed up. Darok would follow the carriage and the Covingtons.

When Darok rode up to his side, Prince Percival looked at Covington house and Anastasia's window. "Keep her safe, Darok."

"With my life, sir."

Percival nodded and turned his horse toward Larenia. He had much to prepare before he made Anastasia his.

****

A carriage rolled up the long driveway and Lady Darling stepped out. She had come to see the girls off, and she brought presents with her. She was excited for the young girls and wanted to reminisce about her first ball and the handsome Lord Darling.

Lady Evelyn served tea and they listened to Lady Darling's stories until Henry announced that all was ready for their departure.

There had been a change of plans in their traveling arrangements. Upon hearing that Lady Evelyn would be traveling to Larenia for the Royal Ball, Cousin Heinrich insisted that she and the girls would be much more comfortable riding in his carriage. Accordingly, he sent his nicest traveling carriage to pick them up at Covington House and bring them to Larenia. He also sent six of his outriders to escort them for added safety.

Lady Darling wrapped Beatrice in a hug and handed her an elegant gift box. It contained a beautiful choker. The stones were rose-colored diamonds. Beatrice was overwhelmed by the magnificent gift. Lady Darling merely waved her hand as Beatrice tried to tell her it was too much; she could not accept such a valuable piece of jewelry.

"I am hoping to help you catch a man, my dear, perhaps even a prince. Not that you could not catch one on your own, but a little bit of glitter does not hurt."

Next Lady Darling handed Anastasia a beautiful satin sash and a jeweled comb for her hair. They were rose in color also. Anastasia thought rose must be Lady Darling's favorite color.

"I am hoping to help you catch a man also, dear, but not quite as soon as Beatrice." She hugged Anastasia and then turned to Rella. "And for you." She held out a beautiful rose-colored fan. It had rose-colored stones along each of the spines and rose-colored feathers along the top. It was magnificent. "I hope you find a man too, dear, but you still have a year or two before it becomes serious. So, for now, enjoy being young and beautiful." She hugged Rella and then Lady Evelyn. "Let me know if you need anything, Evelyn. I shall be glad to offer whatever assistance I can." With a wave of her hand, Lady Darling left, her perfume hanging heavily in the air behind her.

"Well, it is time to go girls," Lady Evelyn declared
And so they left.

The journey was long and relatively uneventful. Well, if you do not count the times they stopped so Rella could retch. No one knew she would become sick being jostled in the carriage hour after hour.

At last they arrived in Larenia. Lord Heinrich Dunbar, a cousin of Beatrice and Anastasia's father Edward, inherited the title on Edward's death. He invited Lady Evelyn to stay at the Dunbar Estate whenever she traveled to Larenia, upon her marriage to Lord Covington. She took advantage of the invitation now. They were welcomed into the house with enthusiasm, many of the servants remembered Lady Evelyn and her kindness to them. The girls were shown into the large guest bedroom upstairs and Lady Evelyn was right down the hall from them.

Lord Heinrich was shorter than Lord Edward had been with dark brown wavy hair, brown eyes, and a round stomach. He was a kind man and ensured his guests were comfortable and wanted for nothing while they were in his home.

Rella immediately went to bed saying her stomach was still rolling around and she felt ill. Beatrice and Anastasia however spent the afternoon and evening exploring the estate that had once been their home. They explored the house, found all their secret hiding places, and then went in search of the stables. The horses were all different, but the stable master was the same and they spent a little time asking after his family and reminiscing. From there, the girls walked down to the lake and sat on the bank under the trees, watching the swans swimming so gracefully over the shimmering water.

"Are you nervous about tomorrow night?" Anastasia wanted to know.

"Why would I be nervous?" Beatrice asked.

Beatrice was a shy person under normal conditions, and Anastasia was surprised at her answer.

"Because it is our first ball, because there will be men there, and because we have never really danced before, or attended social events."

"I do not see any reason to be nervous. We shall have our faces covered, until midnight at any rate. No one will even know who it is before then, and as for the men, it is the perfect situation to meet a man."

"Why is it the perfect situation?"

"Because, silly, if they do not know who you are, you can walk away from the ones that are boring and uninteresting without appearing to be rude. No one will know it is you or me. It is perfect!"

"What if I trip? Or spill something on my new gown? What if I step on some poor gentleman's toes while we dance?"

Beatrice thought about this for a minute. "Well, I suppose you can excuse yourself and go clean your gown, and if you step on someone while you dance, simply refuse to dance with that gentleman again!"

It seemed so simple to Beatrice, but she was not the clumsy one.

Beatrice put her arm around Anastasia's shoulder.

"Do not worry so much, sister. We shall be fine. You shall be fine. Tell yourself you are someone else behind the mask. Perhaps a graceful ballet dancer, or a princess, and if you think you are something hard enough, you will be whatever you decide." She squeezed Anastasia's shoulder. "I know you have had a bit of a rough time lately, sister, with the nonsense about the jewels and such, but think dearest, we are off on a wonderful adventure. Our first ball! Did you even think six months ago that we would be in Larenia about to go to a ball at the palace? I did not, far from it. And we are going, Anastasia. Tomorrow night we shall wear those elegant gowns and dance with actual men. And maybe, just maybe, we can find one or two that we like and that like us, too. We could have actual suitors! Why, I am so excited it is doubtful if I shall sleep at all tonight."

"I do not want a suitor," Anastasia whispered, but Beatrice heard her.

"Of course, you do. You do not know what you are saying. Why even Rella has a suitor. You do not want to be the only sister without one. Think how Rella will tease you!" Beatrice sighed. "I used to sit in church and look at the men in the congregation in Covington and despair. The only ones who are unmarried and available are Lord Kanz," here Beatrice shuddered, "Lord Atwold and Lord Reese."

Anastasia looked at Beatrice in mock horror. "Lord Kanz is too old and too arrogant. Lord Atwold is too young, why he still has sores on his face, and Lord Reese," here Anastasia shuddered as well, "he is too fat, has too many children, and is looking for his third wife."

"Exactly." Beatrice nodded, emphasizing her point. "That is why I am not nervous. When I think of the eligible suitors in Covington, my nervousness disappears, and I find I am quite prepared to dance and flirt with any number of men here in the capitol."

Anastasia laughed. "I see the wisdom in your decision."

They both laughed then, enjoying being together, enjoying the peaceful surroundings and enjoying the wonderful opportunity that lie before them.

****

Because she was supposed to be ill in her room, nobody noticed when Rella threw a dark cloak over her head and left the house. The coachman did not think anything was out of the ordinary. Lord Dunbar told them all to care for the guests needs, and so he was delighted to take the young lady into town. He waited outside the bookstore for her as she asked, and he was unaware that she went around the corner instead. Blackjack Kelly was supposed to meet her at the Tinderhorn Tavern in Larenia tonight at seven, and he better not be late. It was not as easy to leave Dunbar Estate without attracting attention, as it was at home. The servants at Covington House were trained to overlook the things she said and did.

Rella entered the tavern, keeping the hood of the cloak well over her face. She did not need any unwanted attention. Blackjack Kelly was at a table in the far corner, his back to the wall, as usual. She hurriedly walked to the same table and sat down.

"Did you find the uniforms?" she asked without preamble.

"Aye"

"Did you hire someone to help you with the, um, goods?"

"Aye."

He obviously had recently gotten here, too and as such had not had much ale, judging from his reluctance to utter more than one syllable at a time.

"And we can count on these men you hired to keep their mouths shut?"

"Aye." Jack took a long swallow of ale. "I wants me gold fer the men. They be askin'."

"No. I said when you have completed the job, then and only then will you get paid."

Blackjack got up.

"Wait." She pulled out the rose bracelet.

"Ye said gold," Blackjack countered.

"I have not had time to sell the bracelet for gold. Take the bracelet or take nothing."

He pocketed the bracelet.

"Now, about the job."

"Ye said one thousand ducats."

"Yes, now to be clear, I want you there at midnight, no later. Once it is done, do not come back to Larenia. I shall meet you in two days' time in Herzig. Is that understood?"

"With me gold?"

"As long as you do your part, yes, I will be there with the gold."

She nodded at the disgusting man once and left the tavern. As soon as this was over, she would find a new man to get rid of this one. She could not afford witnesses.

Chapter 14

The day of the ball arrived, at last. The sun burst over the horizon in glorious shades of yellow, orange, and red as if it too were excited about the festivities that would soon begin. Its light and warmth caused the birds to start singing, the flowers to open their pretty petals and beautiful butterflies to float about. It seemed as if the whole countryside was putting on its finest garments to aid the celebration.

Lady Evelyn let the girls sleep in until twelve o'clock. It was an unheard of, and never experienced before luxury for the girls.

Beatrice wiggled her toes against the soft silk sheets and let out a sigh of pure bliss.

Cousin Heinrich ordered hot cocoa and biscuits brought to the girls' rooms at noontime with their maid who came to awaken them.

The footman followed with a basket of flowers for Rella. Whoever this suitor was, he had followed her to Larenia.

"I am pretty sure this is what heaven feels like." Beatrice giggled.

Anastasia nodded her head; she refused to open her eyes and admit she was awake. She had been having the most wonderful dream about a certain dark haired, blue-eyed man, and she wanted to stay suspended in sleep and let the dream continue. Her emotions were up, then they were down, then up again. Oh, what was the matter with her anyway? She wondered about Val's note for the hundredth time. He said he had much to discuss but did not say what that might be. He also said he was anxious to see her again, and she was as anxious to see him. It had been such a long time since she had seen him, and she was a little uncertain about what he might be feeling toward her. He liked to kiss her that much she knew, and in truth, she liked to kiss him too. She simply did not know what he wanted to discuss, and so she was anxious. *Was he leaving again? Did he want to say good-bye?* She simply did not know. Lady Evelyn wanted her to find a suitor, but she could not, and she would not look either, until she knew what it was Val wanted to discuss. *And if he was leaving? If he did say good-bye?* Well she would never marry, for she did not want anyone but Val. Whatever it was, tonight she would find out, one way or the other.

****

Rella pulled the covers over her head and wished the stupid girls would cease their mindless chatter. She had the worst headache from that God-awful ale in the tavern and she felt like retching. The idiot maid opened the drapes when she came to awaken them, and the light was bothering Rella's eyes. One good thing came of last night; she succeeded in selling the earrings and the brooch in her wanderings. She smiled. Now she had gold in her reticule to pay for any unexpected expenses in accomplishing her heart's desire. She was close to getting everything she wanted, and she was giddy with excitement.

Beatrice threw a pillow at Anastasia's head, and then another one. "Get up, you lazy girl!" she called as

159

she threw a third pillow.

Anastasia sat up and smiled at Beatrice. She started picking up pillows and throwing them back at Beatrice as fast as she could. Soon they were both laughing so hard, they could hardly throw the pillows, and they fell back onto their beds laughing.

"Will you two be quiet?"

Beatrice and Anastasia stilled when Rella yelled. They looked over at each other and then started laughing again. Rella sat up in bed, she was furious. Her hair was sticking out in various directions, and she had a cloth tied over her eyes. "I cannot wait until I have the two of you out of my life for good."

"What is that supposed to mean?" Beatrice inquired.

"What do you mean, out of your life for good?" Anastasia asked at the same time.

"Well," Rella had to think quickly to cover the slip. She had not meant to speak aloud. "I mean when we have suitors and get married of course. You do not think we are going to be living together, surely?"

"Of course not. That is a silly question Rella. Why would we?" Beatrice answered. "The whole purpose of getting married is to go live somewhere else with someone else. To be alone with one's husband and to start a family of one's own and..." here Beatrice blushed deeply, her words fading off with embarrassment.

Rella rolled her eyes at Beatrice's blush and guessed the reason why. Honest to God they were both so stupid and virginal when it came to men, that it irritated her. They were backward country commoners, with backward country ideals and standards. She thanked God she did not have the same problem.

"Yes, yes, I do understand. Don't tax yourself thinking about it overly much? Hmm? Now will you two be quiet?"

And with that Rella lay back and pulled the covers over her head once more.

****

But it was not to be, for Lady Evelyn entered the room right then, followed by an army of servants.

"Did my darlings rest well?" she inquired with a smile as she waved the footmen in. Three separate screens were set up in three different corners of the large room. Twelve footmen carried in three beautiful brass tubs that they placed behind each of the three screens. A steady stream of servants followed carrying pitchers of steaming water. The tubs were soon filled, and the men servants ushered out of the room. Twelve ladies' maids stood in a row in their dark uniforms and crisp white aprons to help the girls with their baths. The maids held scented oils, scented soaps, soft cloths, and towels.

Lady Evelyn smiled at the girls again and clapped her hands. "Come girls, we must start before the water begins to cool. Beatrice, you go to that corner with Adelin, Anastasia, you go to that corner with Hilda, and Rella, you go to that corner with Tamar."

Lady Evelyn took command again. She had everything all planned out and she was determined that this ball would be a success for them. Lady Evelyn had a hard time expressing even to herself, the relief she felt at being merely a guest here. She had so much responsibility on her shoulders, for such a long time, and it was wonderful to leave all the worries behind her. Cousin Heinrich took care of everything, and he was so kind. All she had to do was relax and plan for the ball. It was the perfect opportunity for the girls to meet eligible men, and she intended to make the most of it. She needed to find a suitor for Beatrice, and she hoped the other two as well. Lady Evelyn glanced toward Rella and saw the girl was still under her covers. She walked over and pulled the covers back.

"Come on, dear, wake up. Please tell me you are feeling well today. It will not do to have one of your strange illnesses befall you today. This is the opportunity we have been waiting for, and we must get you ready."

It was the opportunity Rella was waiting for, too. "I do not wish to go!"

Lady Evelyn was surprised. This ball was all anybody had talked about for weeks. "Why ever not, dear?"

"Because someone has stolen my mother's jewelry again and I simply cannot go to the ball without something. I will look too plain. My gown was made to showcase Mama's jewels and now they are gone! Again! No one will notice me, and I will be the laughingstock of the ball. I will not find a suitor. I will be a failure! No! I will not go." She started crying.

Anastasia stopped bathing behind the screen so she could hear what was going on. Rella had a reason for everything she did.

"Now, dear, I do not believe anyone has stolen your jewelry. It must be misplaced. We shall all help you look. But, darling, you must get up and take your bath. Your water will cool, and we shall have to start all over again."

"I looked everywhere! It is not here! I simply cannot go!" Rella wailed and pulled the covers over her head again.

Lady Evelyn lost her patience. They had a lot to do and the girl really must get up. "Then we must think of something else. What might there be, that we could put with your gown, so it does not appear too plain? Surely there must be something." Lady Evelyn was busy thinking about what other jewelry they had brought that might work.

Then Rella said slowly, "Well, I suppose there is the choker Lady Darling gave Beatrice, and Anastasia has a rose-colored sash and hair comb...." her voice trailed off. Rella watched Lady Evelyn under her lashes to judge her reaction.

"That might work," Lady Evelyn began. She walked over to the wardrobe where Rella's dress hung and pulled the paper wrapping away from the beautiful dress. She held Anastasia's new sash up to the dress and nodded her head.

"Yes, that should do nicely."

****

Anastasia leaned back. *Of course. That makes perfect sense. Rella wants the rose choker, the sash, and the hair comb that Lady Darling has barely given us and she has devised a way to get them.* She closed her eyes as the maid poured the scented water over her hair to rinse the soap out. *What does it matter anyway? It is only a sash.*

"I am sure the girls will be happy to share their things with you so that you look nice for the ball." Lady Evelyn was satisfied with the solution and did not even consider that she had just been fooled.

Rella was satisfied too, because not only had she covered up the fact she did not have her mother's jewelry anymore, but she was now in possession of *all* the beautiful gifts Lady Darling gave the girls.

Five hours later, they were ready. Their hair had been washed, dried and beautifully coiffed. Jewels had been strung among the curls and sparkled brilliantly in the candlelight with each turn of their heads. Their silk dresses had been aired out, and the wrinkles removed. They donned their silk chemise, drawers, corsets, and silk stockings. Then, they added layers of silk petticoats and finally the beautiful gowns.

Lady Evelyn had her own bath and was dressed and ready to go. Her purple gown fit perfectly, the color enhancing her dark-haired beauty. She carefully inspected the girls before they went downstairs. Beatrice was like an exotic flower, with her dark hair and coral pink gown. Anastasia like a fairy queen, the emerald silk of her gown perfectly matching the emerald green of her eyes, and Rella as delicate and fair haired as the other two were dark. The pale blue of her gown repeated the color of her eyes, and the rose adornments she wore, echoed the delicate blush of her cheeks. Lady Evelyn was very satisfied with what she saw. They were all striking and would no doubt draw the attention of every man in the palace. She nodded with approval.

"I feel like a wonderful fairy godmother waved her wand and changed our plain work dresses into beautiful princess gowns," Beatrice announced. "I love the way silk feels when I walk, the way it swishes about my legs." She twirled for the sole purpose of watching her silk skirt swirl around her feet.

"Really, Beatrice," Lady Evelyn laughed, "Where do you get such fanciful ideas?"

"From *my* papa!" Rella said furiously. "You have no right to repeat stories my papa told you. They are my stories meant only for me! If anybody is going to marry a prince and be a princess, it is me! I am the one who deserves it!"

"Come dears," Lady Evelyn hurriedly ushered them downstairs before an argument broke out between the girls.

Cousin Heinrich insisted his carriage be brought around. He ordered it late last fall, and it had finally arrived. Cousin Heinrich believed that appearances should be everything, and so he ordered a special carriage for special occasions such as this. It was a gold carriage, with exquisite gold detail, twisting and turning its way over every inch of the carriage body. Red velvet drapes hung from the windows, while golden angels blew their trumpets over the carriage doors. Red velvet lined the entire inside of the carriage, from the roof to the softly padded red velvet seats along both walls. Even the carriage wheels were gold. It was the most magnificent carriage they had ever seen, and Anastasia felt like she must be in a dream. This was so much more, than she ever imagined.

"You see? A fairy godmother." Beatrice breathed.

Anastasia nodded her head. She believed. Anastasia tugged on her long sleeves, fairy godmother or no, she intended her scars to remain hidden.

The footman slid a golden step into place and extended his gloved hand toward Lady Evelyn. One by one, they entered the magnificent carriage, and sank down on the lushly cushioned seats. And then they were off. Anastasia leaned back against the soft seat and closed her eyes as the four prancing white horses pulled the carriage effortlessly through the winding streets toward the palace.

Chapter 15

The palace was breathtaking. It looked like it belonged in one of Lord Covington's princess stories. It was lit with thousands of fairy lights. Its many turrets and spires outlined magically against the dark night sky. Anastasia drew in her breath when she saw it in the distance. It was magnificent. She remembered seeing the palace, once as a child but never lit up so completely and magically, as it was tonight. Brightly lit lanterns sparkled from lampposts on every street that led to the palace. One had only to follow the fairy lights toward the magical palace, and the royal ball that a waited. Carriage after carriage climbed up the narrow cobblestone road. The drawbridge was down, and soon they were rumbling across the wooden structure. The coachman drew up to the stone entrance with a flourish, and then the footman was helping them down.

An elderly man, in a black and red guard's uniform, held out his hand to Lady Evelyn. He bent his powdered head and kissed her gloved hand.

"Lady Evelyn, it is so nice to see you again. His Royal Highness King Alexander welcomes you, and your lovely daughters to the palace. You will find Major Kavandish at the top of the stairs, he will escort you inside."

"Thank you, Lord Everett, it is nice to see you again also."

"Masks must be in place before you will be escorted inside the palace. His Majesty commands the masks be worn until the clock strikes midnight. It is part of the celebration. Have an enjoyable night, my lady."

Lady Evelyn bowed and led the girls up the stairs. Once their masks were all in place, and their full names given to Major Kavendish, he checked his guest list, and they were escorted into the palace. They waited behind several other guests filling the long corridor, until at last they stood at the top of the stairs right inside the ballroom.

Anastasia blinked. Massive gold and crystal chandeliers, with myriads of brilliant lights hung from the golden ceilings. Scores of beautiful women in brilliantly colored gowns circled the floor in the arms of their equally handsome partners. The music from the orchestra floated around and around the massive ballroom. Liveried servants carried trays loaded with champagne offering it to the guests. There were several tables set with delicacies of every kind in the far corner, and chairs set in groups here and there, so the guests might sit and visit with one another.

The king sat upon his golden throne directly across from where they stood. Two very tall, dark men stood on either side of him, both in their red and black dress uniforms, trimmed with gold rope. Medals hung in rows across the front of their uniforms. They would, of course, be Crown Prince Darius, and Prince Percival. It was difficult to tell what they looked like as each wore a mask. She curtsied to the king and his princes with Lady Evelyn and her sisters. Then she stood and gazed out over the ballroom, her right hand clutching the bottom of her sleeve self-consciously. She thought she had never seen so many people in one place at a time. It was all so beautiful, so magical, so wonderful, and every single person wore a mask.

Beatrice squeezed her hand. "Now our lives shall change forever," she whispered into Anastasia's ear.

Beatrice had no idea how true that statement would become.

Rella was done waiting; she pushed Anastasia out of her way and went down the stairs to join the crush. Beatrice nudged Anastasia, and together they went down the stairs.

"Oh, I say, my lady," Someone took Lady Evelyn by the hand, leading her away for a nice long chat. She turned and nodded at the girls to let them know they should go on without her. No sooner had they reached the bottom, than a very tall man bowed low to Beatrice.

The man wore a maroon colored jacket with white braiding about the front and shoulders. With it he wore white breeches, white stockings, and white shoes. Two dark eyes sparkled mysteriously at Beatrice through the slits in his black and white mask. "My lady, may I have the pleasure of this dance?" His voice was very deep.

Anastasia could tell Beatrice was nervous, despite her mask. She nudged her toward the man and smiled when Beatrice looked at her in panic. The gentleman took that opportunity to slide his arm around Beatrice's tiny waist and lead her off in a waltz.

Anastasia headed in the direction of the refreshment table but only made it a few steps before she was asked to dance. She really did not want to feel another man's arm about her, nor did she want to hold another man's hand, but she decided maybe she should for appearance's sake. So, she nodded her head in agreement. That was the last time she had a moment to herself for most of the night. Anastasia no sooner got done with one dance, before she was swept into another. Each time she would covertly study her partner beneath her lashes, to see if she recognized the man. Each time, she drew a negative. It appeared she did not know anybody at all.

Finally, she asked to be escorted to one of the finely cushioned chairs, begging a headache. Once seated, her escort left her to her thoughts with a bow, and she breathed a sigh of relief. She glanced about for Beatrice but could not see her. She noticed Lady Evelyn speaking with a group of ladies across the room. She could not see Rella anywhere, either. Maybe she found her mysterious suitor and was off dancing with him somewhere. Anastasia took a moment to study the men around her, but none of them were as tall as Val. There were many dark-haired men in attendance, but they were either too fat, too thin, too short, too old, or too young. She sighed. *Where is he? What did he want to talk about?* Anastasia glanced at the large clock on the wall and nearly swooned. *It is almost midnight!*

Quickly she got up and made her way to the doorway that led to the long hall. She made inquiries as to the direction of the library and knew it to be five doors down on the left of the hall. Anastasia was asked to dance several times before she reached the door. Each time she shook her head and hurried on. She was so anxious now, she stumbled. She held tightly to the bottom of her right sleeve. *What if I am late? What if he does not come? What does he want to say to me? Does he think of me as much as I think of him?*

Anastasia stopped dead in the middle of the hallway for it suddenly occurred to her, that *she was in love with Val*. That was the reason for her anxiousness about this meeting. She could not bear for this to be good-bye. She realized she would never be able to live without him and it frightened her. *What if he felt differently?* She must not let him see how much she loved him until she discovered the reason he wanted to talk to her. Anastasia took a deep breath and steadied herself. Then, she continued down the corridor. One, two, three, four, five, she stopped. Val would be inside waiting for her, precisely as his note said. Anastasia let go of her sleeve and grasped the brass handle. Slowly she opened the door, as the clock in the tower began to strike the midnight hour. She removed her mask and walked inside.

It took her eyes a minute to take in the scene before her. Anastasia thought at first, she miscounted the doors and walked into the wrong room by mistake. There were two people standing in front of the fire. They shared a passionate embrace, their mouths fused together in a lingering kiss.

The first thing she recognized was Rella's dress. *My God! It was Rella and her new suitor.* Anastasia flushed with embarrassment. She started to turn away, but then focused on the man when he turned toward her. Every bit of the blood drained out of her face. *It was Val!*

Anastasia's knees buckled and her eyes started to swim. Everything was blurry and unreal, suspended in time. She stood frozen to the spot, her heart pounding loudly in her head. She reached blindly for the door handle to steady herself. Then, she noticed Val's

171

uniform. *He is dressed like the prince!* Her eyes widened as she looked from his face to his uniform. Suddenly, it all made sense. The men who followed him everywhere, the amount of gold he had given her. Anastasia shook violently as the realization hit her. *Val is Prince Percival of Oldenburg!* Anastasia gulped in a huge breath. She tried to move her legs, but they refused to work.

Val stood frozen, also. He stared at her, as though he were afraid to move, afraid to breathe.

Rella turned and smiled. Her eyes as evil and satisfied as a cat that just ate a mouse.

"Oh Anastasia, come meet my prince. I wanted to tell you earlier, but as always *you are too late.*" Rella purred with happiness.

The prince un-wrapped her claws from around his neck and started toward Anastasia. Rella put up no resistance. Her smile of satisfaction increased by the second as she witnessed the torment she created.

"No!" Anastasia realized she yelled the word. Her vision became blurred with unshed tears and suddenly she wanted out. Anastasia shook so violently she could hardly think. Images of that other terrible day merged with the scene before her, and suddenly Anastasia was running away, like she had that other time. *Oh God, I am going to be sick*! *I am too late once more, and I have lost everything!* Anastasia quit thinking and ran blindly, her vision a blurry tunnel, her heart pounding furiously in her ears. She needed air, she needed to get away, and she needed to not be here at all! Oh God! Anastasia ran. She tripped on her skirts and almost fell, but she picked them up with both hands, dropping the forgotten mask. She ran like the devil himself was after her to take her soul.

And he was.

She did not care who saw her, or what they thought, she only knew she had to make it out of the palace, and away from Rella's laughter. It followed her out of the library, down the hall and through the massive ballroom. *God, how had the ballroom gotten bigger?* Anastasia ran and ran and ran. She ran from the pain, ran from the laughter, ran from the loss, and ran from the emptiness that followed. She dodged past people, dancers, and servants. Everyone turned to stare at her.

"Anastasia, wait!" She looked behind her. The prince raced through the door from the long hall. She choked on a sob and kept going.

"Anastasia!" This time it was Lady Evelyn plucking wildly at her sleeve, but she did not care, she shrugged her off and continued running. This could not be fixed, not even by Mama. She ran up the stairs and out the entry, dodging soldiers and footmen this time. Then down all the long stairs to the cobblestone road, she ran. At last she reached the bottom and leaned weakly against the stone wall, trying to catch her breath. She had to think. *Which way is it to Cousin Heinrich's? Oh yes! I remember!* She moved away from the palace wall and ran across the cobblestone courtyard. She reached the road leading to the drawbridge when a black carriage pulled right up in front of her! A man in a uniform jumped out and grabbed her around the waist. Anastasia let out a loud scream as the man threw her into the carriage, and the carriage started off!

She fell back with a thud. It was dark inside the

carriage and she could not see a thing. She heard someone move above her head. When she sat up, the smell hit her. Anastasia opened her mouth to scream when she was roughly grabbed by the back of her head, and a rag stuffed into her mouth. She started to gag, and reached for her mouth, but her arms were jerked forward and tied tightly with rope. Next, her feet were tied and a dark hood was thrown over her head. She closed her eyes tight and tried to breath. The stench of unwashed human was foul. If she gagged with this cloth in her mouth, she would choke. Tears streamed down her face and terror set in. She tried to choke back the tears, but this night had been too much. She tried to sit up again, but a blinding pain caught her on the head, and she knew no more.

Chapter 16

Prince Percival was uncharacteristically anxious about this night, and he could not explain why, not even to himself. It settled in his stomach like a stone. He kept checking the perimeter of the ballroom, as if looking for an enemy. Something was off about this ball, and he was not sure what it was. He stood at his father's side as the guests arrived and watched the crowd gather, his senses on high alert. He noted several families as they entered and nodded his greeting. Despite the masks, some people were easy to recognize. He noticed Lady Evelyn enter the ballroom. Her daughters followed right behind her. It could only be her, with her dark hair, followed by two dark haired daughters and one blonde. Even though they wore masks to hide their identities, his whole body reacted the second Anastasia stepped forward.

It was her.

He recognized the tilt of her head and the graceful way she held herself. The breath left his body, as his eyes drank in the sight of her beauty. He would recognize her ebony hair anywhere, the graceful curve of her long white neck, and the swell of her breasts above the square neckline of her gown. Anastasia turned her head and looked straight across the crowded ballroom toward the three of them. His stomach clenched tightly at her glance. She curtsied with her mother and sisters, her movements as graceful as a swan. The king nodded toward them, and she turned away. He drank in the sight of her tiny waist and the gentle flare of her hips, as she turned toward her mother. He was a parched man, hungering for the sweet nectar of her smile, her laughter, her beauty. He stared as the dark-haired sister pulled her toward the dancing. It had been so long, and he was impatient for this night to end. In a few hours, he would be holding his *Dorogaya* in his arms. Time could not pass fast enough to make him happy.

He watched through narrowed eyes, as one young buffoon after another held his Anastasia in their arms and danced with her as he could not. He wanted to grab his sword and run them through for daring to touch her. This watching was an agony he had not anticipated. He did not realize he was getting angry until Darius hit him in the shoulder and said, "Does an enemy approach, Brother?"

"No, why do you ask?" Percival was confused.

"You hand is on your sword, Brother, and you look ready to charge into battle." Darius laughed. He glanced toward the stairs and commented. "Perhaps, it is the lovely Lady Gertrude with her elegant deportment that has you glowering so!" Darius nodded toward the steps leading up to platform where they stood beside their father's throne.

Percival looked in the direction Darius indicated. Sure enough, a very large, very clumsy Lady Gertrude *was* heading their way. There was no denying who the imposing figure was, even with a mask covering her face. The predatory look in her eye was obvious, even from this distance.

"Perhaps she has set her cap for you, Brother." Darius teased.

Percival was not amused. He needed to escape and quickly. He turned to Darius. "As you are the Crown Prince," he pointed out, "the older brother, and I might add, no longer tied to a marriage contract, I think perhaps it is you the lady seeks."

Darius immediately lost his smile. He took several quicks steps backward.

Percival gave his brother a cheeky wink, "And here the lady doth come," he said in a loud whisper and laughed as Darius looked around for a means of escape.

Prince Percival quickly executed a half bow to his father and fled. He was through watching Anastasia being passed from one idiotic oaf to another. He wanted to hold her in his arms; he wanted to kiss her soft lips; he wanted to hear again the little noises she made in the back of her throat when he kissed her. Hell, he wanted a lot of things, and he intended to have them all. He had to make it until midnight somehow, but not in here. He needed some air, so he made his way out to the gardens where he could be alone.

At exactly ten minutes to midnight, Percival came inside the palace and walked down the long hall toward the library. He instructed the servants to see to it the room was emptied of any guests who might be lingering there, by half past eleven. He let himself in and removed his mask. He poured himself a glass of whiskey from the decanter on the table and went to stand in front of the fire. He had a little speech all worked out in his mind, and he wanted time to rehearse it to himself. He needed to get this exactly right. Percival could not say what he felt for Anastasia exactly, he only knew that he could not let another man have her. The thought of anyone else holding her, or kissing her, filled him with rage, and that confused him. He had too much self-control to let a woman under his guard. Yet he could not deny the anger he felt toward the men who held her and danced with her. Percival frowned. The truth was, he needed her like the night needed the sun for it to be day. She chased away the darkness in his life with her innocence and brought light into his world. The thought of her smile and the joy of her laughter made him forget the dark images of battle that often tormented him. He took a long swallow of his whiskey and thought it must be close to midnight. He turned to set his glass down on the mantel, when the library door opened. Percival quickly straightened, a welcoming smile on his face. It was not Anastasia that entered, but Rella. Prince Percival frowned; he gave specific orders that he was not to be disturbed.

"My lady, what are you doing here?" the prince asked.

"I am not well and thought I might come inside and lie down." She staggered a little toward the settees.

Percival frowned but stepped forward to assist her.

Rella put a hand against her forehead and pretended to swoon. Percival caught her in his arms and was in the process of leading her toward the settee when the clock began to strike midnight. The library door opened, again. Rella wrapped her arms around the prince's neck and pulled his mouth toward hers.

Prince Percival was completely taken by surprise. One minute the blonde sister was swooning, the next she kissed him. *What the hell is going on?* Dimly he heard the clock strike midnight, and the library door opened at the same time. He grabbed the claws of the blonde vixen, pushing her away and turned toward the door. His beautiful Anastasia stood there as pale as the sheets that covered his bed.

The yellow haired she devil smiled and called him her prince. She said something about Anastasia being too late. He was astonished at the blonde sister's boldness and thought to correct her error, when it all became clear to him. The she devil was trying to destroy his Anastasia, *and it worked.*

Anastasia went paler still, and he saw her whole body begin to shake. She threw the door wide open and raced away as if all the devils of hell were at her feet. The yellow haired witch started laughing a horrible screeching laugh. He did not have time to deal with her; he must catch his *Dorogaya* before she was lost to him forever.

"Anastasia, wait!" He ran after her, stopping in the long hall. *Which way did she go?*

Percival caught a glimpse of emerald silk disappear through the doorway into the ballroom, and he ran after it. He stopped again at the top of the stairs leading to the ballroom. "Anastasia, wait!" he commanded.

She glanced back but did not stop, in truth it looked as though she ran faster.

"Hell and damnation!" He chased after her, caring neither for the obstacles in his way, nor the scene he must be presenting. Percival caught a glimpse of Darius reaching for his sword as he raced through the ballroom and merely shook his head at him. Down, down the stairs he raced. He toppled Lord Fisk down the stairs with him but stopped to steady the old man. He reached the top of the last flight of stairs and heard Anastasia

scream! He looked cross the courtyard toward the road in time to see a soldier in a Lichtenburg uniform, toss Anastasia into a black carriage and race away down the cobblestone road. Percival ran down the last flight of stairs, his heart thundering in his chest. The members of his guard, after seeing their prince run through the ballroom, raced after him. They all held their drawn swords in their hands.

"What is afoot, Your Highness?" Vroknar demanded, his breathing harsh from the run.

"Quick!" Percival commanded the footmen present. "Fetch our horses!"

He turned to his guard. "A black carriage with Lichtenburg soldiers abducted Lady Anastasia."

Darok and Vroknar exchanged a look. "Lichtenburg soldiers here, Your Highness? At the palace?"

"The men had the uniforms of their soldiers, if not, we shall know soon enough. They cannot hope to beat us to the border. Their carriage will delay them with its weight, allowing us to overtake them."

"And then?"

"We will kill the bastards and bring Lady Anastasia home."

Darius made it to the bottom of the stairs, his sword drawn as well. "Tell me, Brother, what happens here?"

"A plain black carriage with soldiers wearing the Lichtenburg uniform abducted Lady Anastasia."

"And you think to go after her?"

"Yes."

Darius nodded. "I shall relay the tidings to father for you."

Percival nodded but his gaze caught a bit of emerald silk sparkling in the light of the streetlamps. He walked into the drive and picked up a small silk slipper. Rage filled him as he noted how tiny and delicate her slipper was. *Whoever dares to touch Anastasia will die. I will see to it and send them to hell myself.*

"Your horse, Your Highness."

Percival tucked the tiny slipper into his pocket and mounted his great stallion in one fluid motion. He turned to Darius, but Darius already answered before he could ask.

"I shall speak with the king and send soldiers to assist in your search. God speed, Brother."

His words lost in the sound of galloping horses, as Prince Percival and his men raced down the cobblestone drive toward the road that would lead them to the border of Lichtenburg and Oldenburg.

Darius turned and went inside to find his father.

****

The king retired to the throne room after the excitement and, judging from the amount of noise Darius could hear as he approached, was surrounded by hysterical females. Darius winced. The duties of royalty were anything but pleasant on occasion, and this sounded like one of them. It turned out to be one hysterical female, Lady Rella. She screamed like a banshee. The room being very large, was also very empty, and so the sound continued to reverberate.

"Good Lord!" King Alexander said, "Can you not console the lady so I can think?"

Lady Evelyn hurried to Rella; highly embarrassed that Rella made such a scene, and in front of the king, too. Lady Evelyn took hold of Rella and pressed her face into her shoulder. "There, there, child. The king shall know what to do."

It muffled the sound but not much.

"Rella, child, we are all upset but we must get ourselves under control and let the king counsel with his soldiers. He will know what must be done. That is the only way we shall find Anastasia," Lady Evelyn said.

Rella continued to sob against Lady Evelyn's shoulder while Lady Evelyn held her. The noise level had gone down a little.

The king frowned as Darius approached. Darius spoke in hushed tones filling the king in on all that occurred.

"And Percival?" the king inquired.

"Gone after them with his guard."

The king nodded. He expected as much judging from the way his son chased after the girl.

The king considered Lady Evelyn. "We do not mean to be insensitive, Madam, for we are sure that this is a heavy blow to you and your family." He cleared his throat. "We would appreciate knowing your perspective. Do you have any idea who might wish your daughter harm?"

Lady Evelyn's eyes filled with tears and she hastily swallowed. "No, sire," she said slowly, "although, there was an attempt on her life a few months back. An assassin shot an arrow at her in the woods and left her for dead."

King Alexander nodded. "We know of this atrocity."

Lady Evelyn whispered as she said the last part; the terrible realization settled in her mind that someone did, indeed, want her daughter dead.

Darius noted the pallor of Lady Evelyn's face and stepped forward quickly, grasping the poor woman by her elbow. He turned and nodded to several women servants who had been sent for when Rella first started screaming. They took hold of a still sobbing Rella and pulled her from Lady Evelyn. They led her out into the hallway, closing the door behind them.

Darius led the poor mother to a chair, and she sank back gratefully.

****

King Alexander rubbed his chin with his fingers. Would Lichtenburg dare kidnap his little cousin right in front of his palace? Would they be that bold? And why target only the one girl? Was Lichtenburg aware of her relation to himself? Or was the girl out in the public more and an easier target? If Lichtenburg proved innocent in these affairs, who else might want to harm the girl and why? And what about her connection to Lord Covington? That did not make sense because one would suppose that they would have tried to harm the blonde girl who had done all the screaming if it had something to do with Lord Covington. For the loud blonde girl was Lord Covington's blood daughter.

King Alexander turned the thoughts around and around in his mind considering the different answers to each question. At last, he concluded. "Lady Evelyn, you will bring your other two daughters to the palace and stay within our walls until this is all settled. You will be safe here and you will also be close at hand when news comes about your missing daughter. This is a terrible business and we will get to the bottom of this. We shall see the culprits are brought to justice. You may take solace in the knowledge that if anyone can find your daughter, Madam, it will be Prince Percival."

Lady Evelyn stood when the king addressed her and bowed to his command. "Thank you, sire."

The king nodded. "We will see that you are notified of every development."

Lady Evelyn bowed again, and a liveried servant walked with her to the door. Arrangements were being made to bring their belongings to the palace and Lady Evelyn hurried to consult with the soldiers before they left for Dunbar Estate.

Once they were alone, the king addressed Darius. "What do you make of all of this?" He waved his hand about as if to encompass the entire affair.

"I do not know, Father. It seems a far stretch to consider that Lichtenburg would kidnap the girl right outside our palace."

The king nodded. "Exactly."

"Although we must not discount the idea off hand, Percival said the villains were wearing Lichtenburg uniforms." Darius rubbed his chin with his fingers imitating the action of the king only moments before.

"We have to consider that perhaps someone is aware of our difficult peace with Lichtenburg and thinks to deceive us as to whom the real villain might be."

It was Darius' turn to nod.

"Percival will ride toward the border and if he does not find the carriage, he will back track."

The king made his decision. "Darius, you must journey to the Lichtenburg court under the flag of truce and discreetly inquire about the girl. We must ascertain that she is indeed within her borders or that they have knowledge of her and her abductors. We must know of a surety before we act with any force."

"Of course, Father, and if the girl is there?"

"Bring her home." Darius nodded and started toward the door but then stopped. "I must tell you, Father, this mission is personal for Percival."

"How so?"

"I believe my brother has feelings for this girl."

The king nodded again. "It would certainly seem so judging from the way he hastened after her." He was sober.

"Do you believe your brother to be in danger?"

"Only his heart, Father. I believe he is quite smitten with the girl. He could not keep his eyes from her all evening." Darius was silent for a moment.

"I fear if he is too late to save the girl, he will blame himself."

The king nodded his agreement once more, his gaze thoughtful.

Chapter 17

Dear God, her head hurt! What was that foul odor? Anastasia opened her eyes to assess her surroundings. Everything remained dark. Something pressed against her face, and she realized she had something over her head. Her hands and feet were bound tightly. She lay on her side in the bottom of a moving carriage. She bounced as the carriage hit a rut in the road. The bumpy ride must have woken her. She lay still, considering how she came to be here and then in a rush, she remembered the ball, the dancing and the library. Val. *Oh God! Val is the prince! Val was in the library kissing Rella!* She moaned in agony as she remembered the kiss and the look on Rella's face. The pain hit her anew with the force of a blacksmith's blow. She groaned out loud and doubled over. *She had been too late! She lost Val!* A sob broke from her throat. How long had she been unconscious? How long had she been in the bottom of this carriage? Her mind filled with terror. Why was she here? Who abducted her? Where were they taking her? She could not seem to quit shaking. Tremors shook her body violently. Someone kicked her in the ribs, hard. Anastasia curled up in pain.

"'Ere now. Ye don' need to kill 'er afore we gets thar," a deep voice said.

Anastasia froze. She remembered the man that grabbed her. Terror squeezed her chest. *They meant to kill her!* Suddenly, she wanted to retch.

"Tha lady said ta make sure 'er suffers. I wer jus' doin' me job, Jasper," the other man responded in a nasal tone.

The lady? What lady? Who wanted her to suffer? Who wanted her dead?

"'Ere now, keep yer mouth shut, Tom! She can 'ear ye she can. She's awake," the first man's deep voice commanded. "An' don't say our names out loud for Chris' sake!"

"I don' see what difference it makes. She be dead quick enuf. Who she gonna tell?" Tom asked in his nasal tone, chuckling to himself.

Anastasia fought against the horror. If she could tell who they were, or where they were going, maybe she could think of a way to escape. So far, all she had was their names, Tom and Jasper.

"Jus' tha same. Ye shouldn't be yappin' yer beak," Jasper responded.

There was silence for a few minutes.

"Wha' ye gonna do wit' yer share o the gold?" Tom asked curiously.

Now they had her attention. *Gold?* A sudden terrifying thought flitted through her mind. *Val had gold.* Surely it is not he that wanted her dead! She considered the notion for a minute and then tossed it out. The men said the *lady* wanted her to hurt. That meant it was a lady that wanted her dead, too. *But who?* Val may be guilty of hurting her, and deceiving her about Rella, but he would not kill her. She considered the situation. *Who then and why?* A sudden image of Lady Remington went through her mind. Lady Remington tried to blackmail Rella, and she was stabbed in the alley behind the Inn. *Dear Lord! Was it Rella?*

Anastasia considered the possibilities. She was the only one who knew Rella's secret besides Lady Remington and Rella herself. Lady Remington was dead and Rella burned the only proof of her illegitimacy, saying it would be Rella's word against Anastasia's if she ever told. Rella *had* threatened her; she threatened her quite often. Anastasia brushed it aside, figuring it was what Rella did when she wanted something, or wanted Anastasia to keep silent. Now, Anastasia reconsidered. *Was this it? Was this what Rella meant?* If so, where would she get the gold to pay these men? Anastasia thought again about the look on Rella's face when she turned after kissing Val. It was pure evil. The same look Rella wore in her chamber the night her aunt died. Anastasia had to face the question growing in her mind as all the things that happened, suddenly started to make sense. Who disliked her enough to want her dead? It could only be Rella. She must have sold her mother's jewelry to pay the men to kill her. That explained why she "lost" her mother's jewelry again once they reached Cousin Heinrich's. It also explained why Rella tricked Mama into letting her take the gifts Lady Darling gave her and Beatrice. Rella needed to cover up the fact she no longer had her mother's jewels.

But how did Rella know Anastasia would run out of the palace shortly after midnight?

Anastasia puzzled over that for a minute and then realized Rella must have read the note Val sent telling her when and where to meet him. Rella must have known who Val was, and entered the library right before Anastasia. *But how did she get Val to kiss her?* Anastasia frowned and decided she did not want to know. Anastasia must have given away the fact that she had feelings for Val, and Rella used that knowledge to hurt her. So, she made sure Anastasia saw her sharing a passionate kiss with Val. Anastasia thought carefully about what Rella said right after the kiss. Rella told her she was too late, and Anastasia ran away precisely like she did that other time. Rella told her she was too late whenever she wanted to hurt Anastasia. There was so much terror and loss accompanying those words. Rella knew how insecure Anastasia was, and she knew Anastasia blamed herself for what happened.

Anastasia closed her eyes. *God, I am such a fool and Rella played me like a pianoforte.* It must have been so easy for Rella to tell the men when and where to abduct her. The only place Anastasia *could* run to, was Cousin Heinrich's a little after midnight and the scene in the library. Right after Rella said those words. And the men had been waiting for her. It all made perfect sense. Anastasia realized then that Rella did, indeed, hate her enough to want her dead. But how did Prince Percival feel? And what did he ask her to the library to tell her? Anastasia would never know, because she let Rella deceive her with her charade. Anastasia had run away instead of trusting Val. She doubled over in agony at the thought.

"I tol' ye to quit yer yappin. Tha less tha girl 'ears tha better." Jasper's deep voice grew louder.

"O she ain't gonna tell nobody. 'Er will be dead," Tom answered.

"Wha' if somebody rescues 'er eh? Did yer think o that?" Jasper's deep voice sounded irritated.

"Who? Ain't nobody knows where 'er is and we 'ave these fancy uniforms. If'n somebody seen us tha'll be 'eadin' tha wrong way! 'Sides ain't nobody gonna rescue that'n," Tom whined in his nasal tone.

"No more yappin'!" Jasper barked the words out.

The man is right, Anastasia thought miserably. *No one will rescue me! Nobody will care. What was that about uniforms and the wrong way? It looked like Rella thought of everything!* Val had been the only one to notice her or to care, or at least to pretend he cared. She never felt as scared and alone as she did at this moment. The last time she faced death, she had not been alone. Although she lost everything she cared about, in that moment, when death looked her in the face, she had not been afraid, not like she was now. Anastasia started to sob.

"Is yer a cryin'? Good! Ye need to hurt!" Tom said cruelly.

A swift kick was delivered to her middle again.

She bit back the cry that came to her lips. The bastards wanted her to cry and scream and hurt. They also meant to kill her. She held her bound hands together against her stomach to ease the pain. She focused on breathing in and out until the pain subsided. A kind of numbness settled over her then, and she forced her emotions back down, clear back down. Ladies did not cry, nor did they feel sorry for themselves. *If* she was going to live, she would have to be clever and watchful. Grim determination stiffened her spine. If no one was coming to rescue her, and if these two devils were determined to hurt her and kill her, she would have to rescue herself. She needed to tune her senses into her surroundings, so she might be alert to an opportunity.

Anastasia took a deep breath. Last night by the lake, Beatrice said she could be anything she wanted to be, she only had to focus, and it would be. So be it. The first thing she had to do was get her body to quit shaking. Easier thought than done, she decided. She focused on breathing in and then out, breathing in and then out.

The carriage slowed to a stop. The men climbed out of the carriage, kicking Anastasia in the process. They forgot to close the carriage door and Anastasia heard every word they said.

"Why we stoppin'? We ain't to tha cabin yet," Tom's voice said.

"We cain't go that way. Thar be soldiers jus' rode pass 'ere. They be settin' up, checkin' ever' carriage tha' goes that way!" another voice replied gruffly.

"Mmmm. Never figured them soldiers be that fast. Wha' about the well, Jack? Can we make it thar?" Tom asked.

"No, I seen soldiers go that way, too," the man Tom called Jack answered.

"Well, 'ow is we'n supposed ter drown tha girl in tha well if'n we cain't git thar?" Tom whined.

"We'll 'afta think o somethin' else," Jack answered gruffly.

"Wha' about tha cave?" Jasper asked excitedly.

"Wha' cave?" came Jack's gruff response.

"Ye know, tha one 'at fills up with water when tha tide comes in," Jasper explained.

"Widow's cave?" Jack asked sharply.

"Yup, tha's tha one," Jasper's voice answered.

"It could work if'n we 'ad a boat ter row out thar,"

Jack said thoughtfully.

"I 'ave a boat. Thar's one by my cousin's place, right thar on tha beach," Tom's nasal voice sounded excited.

"That'll work. Let's go afore that damn prince comes," Jack's gruff voice answered decisively.

"Or more o' 'is 'ighness' soldiers." Jasper snorted in disgust.

Anastasia's heart fluttered in her throat. Was Val looking for her? Then it sank just as fast. It would not be Val, or rather Prince Percival, but maybe Prince Darius coming to rescue her? Anastasia held the thought for a minute. Either way she had to get out of these ropes and rescue herself. Even if someone *were* looking for her, they had no idea where she was.

She did though. She guessed they were at the turnoff. There was a "y" in the main road. The left road led through the woods to the border of Lichtenburg and Oldenburg. About two miles up the left road one tiny road led off to the right toward a small village. That must be where they were setting up a roadblock. It must also be where this well was. The other road in the "y" veered right. It led to the rocky cliffs and the ocean. She must have been unconscious for some time because it was at least a half-day's ride from Larenia to the "y" in the road. That was by horseback. In a carriage, it would take longer.

The men stepped on her and kicked her again as they clambered back inside the carriage. They started moving along the road to the sea.

She must be quick; she needed to relieve her bladder. Anastasia started kicking her feet and bucking her body while she tried to scream. It was not much of a noise with the gag in her mouth. But it got their attention. Suddenly, she was grabbed by the arm and set with her back against the seat. The hood was ripped from her head, and a large male hand hit her hard across the face. She winced, trying desperately to hold back the tears that formed in her eyes. No such luck. They streamed down her face, partly from the blinding light as the hood was removed from her head, and partly from the sting of the blow. The gag was pulled from her mouth, and the hand raised to strike her again.

"Please, I need a few moments to take care of my personal needs."

The hand struck her, hard. She was knocked backward with the force of the blow.

"Go in yer clothes, we ain't traipsing ye through the woods." Tom said in his nasal tone. He was a thin man with crooked yellow teeth. He stared down at her through black beady eyes.

"Oh let 'er go for a minute. Wher's she gonna run? If'n she goes 'ere we will 'ave to live wit tha smell." An ugly man with a deep voice said in disgust, wrinkling his bulbous nose. He had dark hair, bushy eyebrows, and he smelled horrible. He must be Jasper.

"If'n ye give in ter 'er ladyship she'll 'ave ye be servin' 'er tea next," Tom answered.

"I said let 'er go," Jasper commanded.

"Oh roit, oh roit," Tom whined.

Jasper tapped the roof of the carriage to get Jack to stop. Tom jerked Anastasia from the carriage. She landed on the ground with a thud. He took a knife and cut the rope that bound her feet.

"Ye be quick or I'll be in ter git ye," Tom threatened.

She got to her feet and leaned against the carriage to get the blood to flow down to them. "And my hands?"

The driver jumped to the ground. He was a dark-haired nasty-looking man who smelled like cigars and cheap ale. He stood by the carriage. "Not bloody likely. Ye'll 'ave to 'urry. I ain't waitin'." He was the one they called Jack.

She nodded and hurried to the trees. She walked around behind them until she was out of sight. Her knees knocked violently together. She quickly took care of her needs and turned around.

Jack was right behind her. He grabbed her by the arm. "Ye've 'ad long enuf. We ain't waitin' no more!"

He dragged her around the tree. The bushes in their path caught her skirt and ripped the silk in several spots.

Anastasia cried out with pain. The man had a tight grip on her arm and the jerking made her ribs hurt. The man laughed at her cry of pain, and unceremoniously stuffed her back into the carriage. She landed on the floor again and the hideous man kicked her in the ribs one more time before settling into his seat.

"Thank you." she said quietly and received another kick for her trouble.

They rumbled for another few hours and suddenly, she could smell the sea in the air. Anastasia closed her eyes and prayed that someone would come looking for her, that someone would notice she was missing. The problem with that prayer was that the only person who ever noticed her was Val. Prince Percival, she corrected herself. How had she been such a cabbage head as to consider him nothing but a poor soldier? *Simple,* she told herself, *we have been in the country and have had no social life at* all. Anastasia bit back a groan as the carriage hit a bump in the road. She thought about Mama and Beatrice. Surely, they would notice she was missing, but what could they do? The men who abducted her wore Lichtenburg uniforms, even if Mama noticed she was missing, and somehow convinced the king, or Cousin Heinrich to go look for her, they would look in the wrong place, and she would be dead.

Anastasia thought of Rella and the look of evil satisfaction she witnessed on her face. She shivered. Had Rella known Val was Prince Percival all along? Maybe she had. Rella had gone to Larenia to the formal dinner with Papa and the rest of the family all those years ago. So, she would have recognized the prince. Anastasia choked back a sob. Rella must have sent all those flowers to herself, to get Anastasia to think she had a suitor. The whole purpose was to set Anastasia up for the scene in the library. Anastasia brightened a little. Which would mean Val, rather, Prince Percival was *not* courting Rella.

That explained why he chased after her trying to get her to wait so he could talk to her. She felt her heart breaking. Not wanting the men to hear her, she hid her head in her arm. How many times had Mama told her to not act on impulse? If she had waited, and trusted in Val, she would not be here right now, tied and bruised in the bottom of a carriage. Tears slid down her cheeks, and she stifled the sob that rose in her throat

The carriage came to a stop and the men climbed out, pulling her roughly behind them. Jack jumped to the ground.

"This way," Jasper said and they started off down a

small path that led to the beach. The late afternoon sun warmed her face as they walked. There was a small hut at the bottom and a rowboat tied to a post planted in the sand.

The men cut the rope and grabbing Anastasia by the hands, tried to shove her into the boat. She swung her bound arms wide and knocked Jasper in the head. She kicked sand at Tom's face and started to run. She only made it a few feet before being knocked down and kicked viciously.

"Ye little 'ore! Ye ain't goin' anywhar' but into tha boat. Now git in thar. I don't get me gold unless yer dead so, yer goin' ter die!" Tom yelled.

She thought she might too, with the force of his blows. She went numb. She felt like she was floating when the kicking suddenly stopped.

"Not 'ere ye fool! Get 'er wher' she ain't seen. Tha lady didn' want 'er found! Quick grab 'er feet and get 'er to tha boat," Jack ordered.

She felt herself lifted, and then she was lying in the bottom of the rowboat. She could hardly breathe from the pain in her ribs. She curled up with a small moan and tried not to retch as the boat rocked on the waves. She must have lost consciousness because the next thing she knew, the sun was no longer beating down on her, and the men were no longer rowing. She was being pulled from the boat. She hardly had time to get her bearings, before she was thrown onto a hard, rocky surface. It was cold, wet, and very musty. She shivered violently. She thought she must be in a cave of some sort, judging from the smell, the cold, and the darkness. She could hear the waves slapping against the ledge where she lay, and the roar of the ocean in the background. The men got back into the boat and started paddling away.

"'Ere now put yer back into it! Tha tides a comin' in and we don' want ter be caught in 'ere when it does. The cave fills wit' the sea and thar's nowhar ter go! Ye don' want ter die with tha girl!" Jack's gruff voice rose above the noise of the ocean.

Anastasia lifted her head weakly and looked around. She could see the opening to the cave some distance away. Sunlight barely streamed through the entrance, so it must be evening. The men disappeared and Anastasia pushed herself carefully to a sitting position. She had never been so completely alone in her whole life, and she was terrified! Even the jaws of that horrible beast had not looked as terrifying, as the scene before her now.

Stop it!

She was not going to feel sorry for herself anymore. She was going to live, even if for the sole purpose of thwarting Rella and her clever plan. Rella would not win this time. *I have to get out of here!* She was not going to curl up and die because Rella wanted her to! Besides, there was her mother and Beatrice to think about. Mama would never forgive herself for letting them come to the ball, and Beatrice would be so worried about Anastasia, she would never find herself a suitor. *No, this is not how I am going to die! And Val, Prince Percival?* Anastasia chewed her lip as she considered him. It was too complicated and mixed up. *Prince Percival will have to wait until Mama and Beatrice are taken care of, and then by God, Prince Percival can explain himself.*

Anastasia took careful note of her surroundings.

The cave was rather large and not very tall at all. The only ledge that could be seen was the one she sat upon. She looked at the distance to the mouth of the cave and shivered. It was too far for her to try to swim to it. Especially with her ribs hurting like they did. She knew she would never make it.

The water climbed higher. A wave entered the cave and the water rose to her waist and then receded. Anastasia's teeth chattered with cold. The men were right; the tide was coming in. *I have to get out of here!* She pushed with her legs until she was in a standing position, leaning against the wall of the cave. She fought back the terror gripping her, as she looked for a means of escape. *Dear God, please don't let me die in here! Surely, there is something I can do.* She was so busy looking at her surroundings that she did not notice the next wave come in. It nearly knocked her off her feet. The water was rising fast. She needed to get this rope off her hands! She noted a jagged rock jutting out from the cave wall and worked the rope up and down frantically against it. It worked! The rope gave way and her hands were free!

The next wave came in and surged against the rock she stood on, lifting her completely off her feet. She gasped as the cold ocean water rose to her chest and she lost her footing Anastasia grasped the jagged rock she used to cut her ropes and held on tight. The pull of the wave dragged her sideways. Anastasia tightened her grip on the rock, the sharp edges sliced her fingers, but she did not feel it. She looked frantically for a way to escape. *I am not going to die in here dammit!* When the wave receded, she pulled air into her lungs. *Lord how they ached!* She was standing in ocean to her chest now, barely keeping herself upright with her grip on the rock. She knew she had run out of time. Hopelessness washed over her.

Chapter 18

Prince Percival raced his great stallion toward the border. If the villains in the black carriage came this way, they would overtake them before they reached the border to Lichtenburg. His men rode behind him. They all searched for carriage tracks leaving the main road. Such a thing was not likely with the brush that grew so abundantly along the roads and the hills. The carriage wheels would break off before a vehicle as heavy as a carriage went very far into the brush.

It was a grueling seven-hour ride. The horses were lathered with sweat and breathing heavy when they rode up to the sentries guarding the gates bordering both countries.

The Lichtenburg guards in their blue and red uniforms stood at attention, their muskets by their sides as they warily watched the prince and his guard.

Percival drew up to the gates and dismounted. He approached the Oldenburg guards. "We are looking for a plain black carriage that may have come this way, probably in a hurry. Has a carriage such as this come through this gate in the last couple hours?"

"No, Your Highness. There has been no carriage. We have had no travelers this night."

"If one comes this way, it is not to pass. They are to be arrested and taken to the palace dungeon."

"Yes, Your Highness."

Prince Percival nodded. He saluted the guard and remounted Odin, his great white stallion. "Come, we must backtrack." He nudged Odin and they went back the way they had come.

It was afternoon when they approached the first turn off the main road. It led to a small fishing village. The Oldenburg army had set up a roadblock and was in the process of searching the area.

"Have you searched the village?" Prince Percival asked after he had saluted the men.

"No, Your Highness, we were going there now. We have searched the outer area and found nothing."

Percival nodded. "We shall see to it," he told the officer. Rage and determination pounded within him. *I will not lose Anastasia!* He wheeled his horse toward the village and nudged Odin into a gallop. The longer it took to find her, the better the chance the villains had to get away.

The men spread out once they reached the village. Every house, every barn, every building was checked. There was no sign of her. The prince and his guard rode back to the main road. It was late afternoon and they had not found her! Grimly Percival searched the area around him. *Which way now?* There were still two ways they could have gone. Had they gone down to the village by the sea? Or had they doubled back after the prince and his guard had ridden past? It would be dark by the time they reached the sea if they followed that road, and if the carriage had doubled back, they would have more than a full day's ride on him. The carriage could be headed anywhere. He had to find her and soon. His patience wore thin. He *would* find her, and he would kill the men who had taken her.

Vroknar rode his mount down the road that led to the sea, and then shouted, "Over here Your Highness."

Percival nudged Odin toward Vroknar.

"Look."

Percival turned in the direction Vroknar pointed and spied a small piece of emerald silk clinging to a bush. Suddenly he grinned. "It seems our mercenaries are wanting a little time by the sea. Let's not disappoint them, shall we?"

They rode hard and fast but did not reach the village until well after dark. They rode up to the tavern and stopped.

"Check the stables." Percival dismounted and led his horse to the trough for water. He rubbed the animal's side while he waited for his men.

They returned soon after. Vroknar grinned, his teeth white in the darkness. "There's a plain black carriage in the stables, Your Highness."

Percival nodded. He handed his reins to Darok and the rest followed him inside the tavern.

Blackjack sat at the table in the far corner; his back to the wall. He had a half jug of ale on the table in front of him, his companions on either side. They had been there for a while and Jack was down several pints of ale. The men on either side were well into the pints as well, and none of the men realized the danger they were in. They were happy as pigs in mud, because they completed their mission, and the girl was sure to be dead by now. They were sipping ale and telling each other stories of the things they were going to do with the gold they figured they had coming.

"When's the lady goin' ter bring the gold?" Tom asked.

Blackjack scowled. "She said ter lay low fer a couple o' days. She don' want anyone ter know war we are 'an she will bring the gold ter us."

"I want me gold now! Why do we 'ave ter wait?" Tom asked.

"Because she doesn't wants tha prince ter find us or what 'appened ter tha girl," Blackjack answered, taking a sip of his ale.

"I don't see what diference it makes. Tha girl is dead and nobody will find 'er no how," Jasper observed.

"Tha lady don't want anybody ter see 'er payin' us," Blackjack said.

"Why?" Tom asked.

"Because then they'll be a-knowin' we did a job fer 'er," Blackjack explained. He reached for his ale to take another sip and made the mistake of looking up. His gaze met the ice blue stare of the prince. What he read in the prince's eyes made his hand shake as he set his ale back on the table.

"Good evening, gentlemen." The prince's voice was silky soft.

Terror squeezed Jack's throat shut. "Yer Highness," he managed to get out. Tom and Jasper stared at the table, too afraid to look up.

"Perhaps you can help me with a little problem I am having. It seems I am missing one small lady in a green silk dress. The lady was abducted outside the palace by two gentlemen wearing the blue and red uniforms of the Lichtenburg Guard, precisely like you and your friend are wearing."

Blackjack swallowed. "Is that so?" He pretended to be interested in the story. He was stalling for time, hoping to think of a way to escape the promise he read in the prince's eyes.

The prince nodded, and folded his arms across his chest. "The black carriage out in the stables is the exact one that the bastards used to take the lady. The tavern keeper says that is yours."

Blackjack licked his lips.

Prince Percival's eyes narrowed. "Where is the lady?"

"We 'ad nothin' ter do with it, Yer 'ighness. Twer Jack, 'e made us 'elp 'im take 'er and Jack made us leave 'er ter die. We 'ad no choice! 'E told us 'e would kill us if'n we didn't 'elp," Tom whined.

"Is that a fact?"

Tom and Jasper both nodded in response. They never saw what was coming. One minute they were sitting there, the next they were dead. Percival held the tip of his sword against Blackjack's throat. "Where is she? I will not ask again."

Blackjack shook so hard, he pissed himself. He had never seen anyone so good with a sword. Tom and Jasper were both dead still sitting beside him. He had not even seen the prince move. Now the prince was focused on him. "She be in a cave, Yer 'ighness."

"Is she alive?"

Blackjack swallowed again, "She were when I last seen 'er, Yer 'ighness."

The sword tip pressed a little closer and blood trickled down his neck.

"Please don't kill me." Blackjack whined, he had to think fast, or the prince would slit his throat, too.

"Where is this cave?"

"Right down tha cliffs thar. Ony ye 'ave ter know

where 'tis or ye won't find it. It bein' dark 'n all ye won't see it til tha sun comes up."

Prince Percival was deeply disturbed. They left his Anastasia in a cave, alone, in the dark. She was probably more frightened then she had ever been. Percival's stomach formed a tight knot. *By God! Somebody will pay dearly for this.*

"Is she hurt?"

"I don't rightly know, Yer 'ighness. She were fine when we left 'er." Blackjack lied.

"You better pray that she is alive and unhurt. We will go find this cave at first light, and if I find you have lied, I will cut you into so many pieces the devil himself will not recognize you."

Blackjack could only nod. He would have pissed himself again if he had been able to.

Vroknar jerked him upright and dragged him along to the rooms the tavern keeper had readied for the prince. He spent the night tightly tied to a stiff chair with a sword at his throat.

At first light, Blackjack was jerked to his feet and half dragged down the hill to the sea. The rowboat was still where he and his companions left it. The men climbed onboard and Jack was forced to take an oar and row.

Prince Percival stared at Blackjack. "Who paid you to abduct the lady?"

Percival had done some thinking during the night. Blackjack was a mercenary. He killed for money. He was pretty sure Jack was the man who shot at Anastasia in the woods. His footprints were very familiar. He thought Blackjack was probably the same man who followed Anastasia through town, the night he had kissed her. If these things were true, as he suspected they were, someone was paying him to do these things. Someone wanted Anastasia dead. He thought he knew who paid Blackjack, but he wanted to be sure.

"It wer a lady,Yer 'ighness."

"What lady?"

"I don't know 'er name. I meets 'er at tha tavern."

"The tavern here?"

"No, tha tavern in tha village. She 'ad us follow 'er 'ere. She said t'would be easier ter take the girl."

"Did you follow Anastasia in Covington Village?"

Jack swallowed nervously.

A sword tip pressed against his throat.

"Aye."

"Did you shoot an arrow at Anastasia in the woods east of Covington Village?"

"Aye."

"When were you to be paid for killing the Lady Anastasia?"

"We were ter wait a couple of days and tha lady were comin ter us."

Prince Percival did not like it. He wanted to run the black devil through, but he needed to trap the lady that paid Blackjack to kill for her. He would have to wait.

They reached the mouth of the cave. The tide was going out and they were able to row into the cave. Prince Percival felt his heart drop to his feet when he saw the lone rock ledge.

It was empty!

He whirled toward Blackjack with his sword drawn. "You lie! Where is the girl?"

Jack could hardly talk and for the second time in a matter of hours, he pissed himself. "We left 'er thar! I swear we did! Please don't kill me! She were thar!"

Vroknar jumped out onto the ledge and walked around. "The tide must fill the cave, Your Highness, it is too wide and shallow for it to be otherwise. There is no sign of her here. She must have washed out to sea."

Prince Percival jumped to the ledge also, his heart in his throat. *He could not lose her now!* He needed her! He loved her! God, he loved her. He finally admitted his feelings for her, and he lost her! He inspected the rock closely and found a bit of rope wedged behind a jagged rock. *The bastards had tied her!* Fury such as he had never known ripped through him and he drew his sword once more. *By the gods! The bastards will pay for this!*

"Wait!" Vroknar put his hand on Percival's arm, and pointed up.

Prince Percival looked. The tiniest bit of green silk was visible on the rock overhead. *What the hell is that up there?* It looked like water both from the surface and the sea inside the cave eroded away a vertical cavern about five feet wide and several feet high. The vertical cavern was jagged, and sunlight streamed through the opening at the top. What appeared to be Anastasia, lay on a rock right above his head. *Good God! Is she up there or is it only a bit of her dress? And if it is Anastasia, how the hell did she get up there?*

"Quick, hold me steady!" Percival said.

Vroknar held the prince steady as he braced against the wall of the cave and reached onto the rock ledge above.

"She is here!" Percival could barely reach her arms and he carefully began sliding her toward him. Gently, carefully, he pulled her forward until she was lying on the edge of the rock shelf.

"Darok," Percival called, and the man was instantly by his side. "Catch her and do not let her fall."

Prince Percival gently brought her forward and she rolled right into Darok's arms. Percival climbed down from his perch and gathered Anastasia close to his heart. He was not certain she was alive; she was so cold.

Vroknar stepped into the boat and gently took Anastasia from Percival so he could climb into the boat. Then the prince was holding her close again. He gently turned her head to the side and felt for a pulse. There was the tiniest flicker beneath his fingers. *Thank the gods! She's alive!* At least for now. He noticed the scrapes and the bruising on her face and his frown deepened. He picked up her dainty hands. They were sliced and cut from the rocks inside the cave. He felt along her scalp next and found the bump they gave her when they hit her on the head. His eyes narrowed at Blackjack. "The only reason you are not dead yet is because I want the woman that hired you to kill my lady."

And when Prince Percival had her? Blackjack shivered; he was a dead man. He read it in the prince's eyes.

Chapter 19

They made it back to the tavern in the small village. Percival carried a still unconscious Anastasia into the room he stayed in the night before and laid her gently on the bed. Vroknar and Darok were right behind him.

"Darok, see if there is a physician close by."

Darok bowed and left.

"What about him?" Vroknar indicated Blackjack who was tied to a horse out in the courtyard. The rest of the guard was still mounted and waiting for orders.

"Take him back to the palace and place him in the dungeon. No one is to know he has been arrested or that he is in the dungeon. Tell only the king what you know and tell my father I will explain my reasoning when I return. I must ensure that Anastasia is well enough to travel before I return."

Vroknar looked disappointed. "He must pay for what he did to our Anastasia, Your Highness."

"He will. But first I use him for bait to draw out the woman that hired him. She too must pay."

Vroknar nodded.

"And she is *my* Anastasia."

Vroknar chuckled. "As you wish, Your Highness."

"Vroknar, do not let this man escape or talk to anyone but you."

"I only hope he tries, so I can run him through."

Vroknar bowed. It would be as his prince wished.

The door closed behind Vroknar, and Percival walked to the bed. He looked down at Anastasia and noted the pallor of her skin. He felt the side of her neck once more. The slight flutter was still there. He must get her warm. Percival poked at the fire to rouse the flames and then he set about removing her clothing.

The beautiful ball gown was nearly shredded to pieces. It hung in ribbons from her waist; her long petticoats were not much better off. He unlaced her gown and drew it off her. Then he unbuttoned the long petticoats and removed them as well. She had only one stocking, and her legs had slices, cuts, and bruising, too. Percival examined every inch of her long shapely legs taking careful note of the location of the bruising. He checked the mobility of her knees, as well as her ankles. It appeared nothing was broken there. He unlaced her corset and removed it. It was then he saw the bruising along her ribs.

It was unthinkable that someone could hurt a woman this viciously. Percival drew in a deep breath and fought for the self-control he'd honed through years of training. Carefully, gently, he removed her chemise and what he saw shocked him. She was covered in black-and-blue bruises, from her full pink-tipped breasts to her tiny waist. He gently rolled her over to her stomach and surveyed her back. It was the same. Anger roared through him, and if he had not been alone with Anastasia, he would have ridden after Blackjack and ripped him to shreds. The moment he spotted the bruising around Anastasia's delicate ribs, he turned into a raging beast catching the scent of blood. He wanted to kill someone, very badly.

Anastasia let out a moan. Percival leaned over and very gently, rolled her to her side. It must hurt her to breathe. He picked up one of the blankets left by the tavern keeper's wife and carefully covered Anastasia. A knock sounded at the door and Darok entered with a weathered old man.

"Doctor Horace," Darok said, by way of introduction.

Prince Percival nodded and stepped to the front of the narrow bed.

The old man placed his bag on a chair and turned toward Percival. He adjusted his spectacles. "Nice to make your acquaintance. Now, if you will leave the room, Your Highness, I will see to the young lady."

Percival folded his arms over his chest. "I will stay."

"I must examine the young lady without her gown. It is not proper for you to be in attendance while I examine her." The doctor was looking over the top of his spectacles as he spoke.

Prince Percival did not budge. "I will stay."

"Hmmph," was all the doctor said.

At Percival's nod, Darok left and closed the door behind him. Percival maintained his place at the head of the narrow bed through the whole examination. The doctor looked at Prince Percival for a long minute over the top of his spectacles when he pulled the blanket down and noted Anastasia's state of undress. The prince lifted an eyebrow at the man and the doctor wisely decided to keep his thoughts to himself. The doctor examined his patient thoroughly. He pushed his spectacles up and peered closely at Anastasia's severely scared forearm.

"This girl is no stranger to pain," he commented.

"Do you know what would cause such an injury?" Maybe the doctor could give him a clue.

"A large animal. Wolf, cougar, bear perhaps. Looking at the bite pattern I would say probably wolf. A large one. Although how she lived through such an attack is nothing short of a miracle."

"How so?" Percival frowned.

"Wolves hunt in packs. A wolf would go for the throat. Why did it bite her arm instead of her neck and how did she escape not only this monster but the rest of his pack?"

Percival blanched at the picture the doctor painted. *Where did his sweet Dorogaya meet a wolf and why was she not protected? How did she escape?* He would find out this mystery and kill whoever was involved.

The doctor moved to examine the rest of the patient. He made mumbling noises when he touched the bruised ribs. When Anastasia gave a little whimper, the old doctor felt the tip of Prince Percival's sword against his throat.

Percival was already furious at the image his mind had created of Anastasia being attacked by wolves. His temper was on edge and hearing Anastasia whimper had not helped the good doctor's cause.

"If you hurt her…"

The doctor understood the threat too well. He nervously cleared his throat. "I must bind her ribs, Your Highness, for them to heal. It will hurt her, but it must be done."

He waited. Percival looked hard at him and then nodded his head. "I will help with this task."

The good doctor opened his mouth to protest but at

the look in the prince's eyes he simply nodded his head.

"I will hold her, and you will wrap," the prince commanded.

The doctor did not argue. He got out his jar of salve and liberally applied the smelly ointment to the whole of the poor girl's rib cage. Then he began to wrap her ribs with his rolls of bandages. "I hope you find the person responsible for hurting this girl," he commented.

"I have him, and he will soon be dead." Percival said.

The doctor nodded and continued wrapping. When he was done, the prince laid the girl gently back against the pillows and covered her with the blankets.

Doctor Horace adjusted his spectacles, took out an herbal elixir for pain, and gave the prince instructions for the girl's care. With the statement that he would be by tomorrow to check on the patient and to come get him if anything changed, he left the tavern.

Percival walked to the fire and stoked the flames. He thought about the last twenty-four hours and the cold emptiness that filled his heart and soul when he had not been able to find his Anastasia. The gods were still looking after him, for he shuddered to think of how close he had come to losing her. It was fortunate Vroknar spotted the bit of silk on the road to the sea. It saved hours of empty searching. Percival had no doubt that eventually, he would have searched the village by the sea, and found out where Anastasia had been taken, but he would have been much too late. Vroknar also spotted the edge of Anastasia's gown, barely visible on the rock ledge in the cave where she lay. He must remember to give Vroknar a suitable reward for his diligence. Without Vroknar's sharp gaze, Percival would have left the cave without finding her. Percival thought he would die of emptiness when he lifted her into her arms and felt how still and cold, she was. Percival then faced his greatest fear, when he felt for her pulse. His own heart had stopped beating for a second or two, until he felt the faint flicker of her heart. He could not say when she became so important to him. He would never be the same man he was before he caught Anastasia in his arms, that day in the village.

Anastasia moaned and rolled onto her side. Percival was by her side in an instant, leaning over the bed. Her teeth chattered and she shook violently with the cold her body soaked up in the cave. Percival looked up when Darok knocked and entered with a night rail from the tavern keeper's wife and extra blankets.

"What says the doctor, Your Highness?"

"She has several broken ribs and possibly lung fever from the cold. We will know for sure in a few days."

Darok raised an eyebrow. "Broken ribs, Your Highness?"

"The bastards beat her before they left her in the cave to die. There is not one spot of unbruised skin around her ribs entirely." Percival ground the words out, his hands fisted at his sides.

Darok frowned. "How long does the doctor think she will sleep?"

Percival pointed to the bottles on the table. "He has given her a sleeping draught, and another one for the pain. The doctor believes if she sleeps, she will heal faster."

Darok nodded. "So for now, we wait."

"Aye."

"I will be glad to sit with the girl while you rest, Your Highness."

"Nay. The duty is mine and mine alone. She is mine, Darok, and she must not die."

"I shall be next door if you require my services."

Percival nodded and turned toward the fire.

Once the door closed behind Darok, Percival bolted it and set about getting Anastasia into the clean night rail. He covered her with the extra blankets and settled himself into the chair that stood beside the bed. Her teeth had stopped chattering and she appeared to be in a deep sleep.

He watched the even rise and fall of her chest and thought about all he had seen and heard since he met Anastasia. Percival was certain Rella was responsible. He and his men followed Rella several times as she met the man, they called Blackjack in the tavern, back in Covington Village. Rella was a very clever girl. Percival knew about the rose jewelry. He knew that Rella sold it, and that she had given the coins to Blackjack. Percival heard the stories in the village about Anastasia. Darok had been outside the dressmaker's while Rella told that woman many falsehoods concerning Anastasia. It all made sense. Rella feared Anastasia for some reason, and that is why she told falsehoods, so nobody believed the things that Anastasia said. *But why? What secret did Anastasia have knowledge of that Rella feared?* Percival pondered for a minute or two over the questions. Whatever it was, it scared Rella enough to hire a mercenary to kill Anastasia.

Rella must have found the note he wrote to Anastasia to meet him at the ball. Therefore, she knew where and when to appear and deceive Anastasia with that kiss. Anastasia must care for him a little or she would not have run away the way she had. Rella must know of her feelings for him too, but how? Percival frowned. He scratched his chin with his fingers. *Of course, the man that followed Anastasia in the village the night he had kissed her, Blackjack.* Knowing Anastasia had feelings for him and that she would run from the pain, Rella knew when to tell Blackjack and his two friends to be ready. So, they waited, and snatched her the minute she ran from the palace, shortly after that fateful meeting at midnight.

Percival stood up and began to pace. Now all he had to do was trap Rella and convince the king of the truth of all that happened. *But how?* Rella was an excellent liar and the laws of Oldenburg were precise on how a lady of quality should be treated, even if found guilty of heinous crimes. Rella must be served justice for planning the killing of her sister and for the pain she inflicted. Percival must have hard evidence if Rella were to be condemned.

Percival planned it all out. He needed Blackjack alive, at least for a little while. He meant to kill the bastard once he returned, but he would have to wait. Rella must not be allowed to escape.

Anastasia moaned and thrashed from side to side. Percival reached her side and felt her head. She was still as cold as the cave had been. Anastasia's teeth began to chatter again, and her body trembled. It was a good sign. It meant she was beginning to get warm. He slipped his tunic off over his head and removed his boots and socks. He unlaced his breeches and let them fall to the floor, and then he climbed in the bed and pulled Anastasia into his arms. He pulled the covers over them both and held her close to his heart. Contentment eased the worry from his mind. *God, it felt good to hold her close.* The tension and anxiety from the last few days left his body as he held her. He was never going to let her go again. Percival rubbed the top of Anastasia's head with his chin. She had been through so much; it was a gift of the gods that she was alive and here in his arms. Percival placed a kiss on top of her head and marveled again at the love that filled his heart with her nearness.

Anastasia instantly stopped thrashing the second she felt his touch. It was as if even in her sleep she knew who held her and that she was safe. She rolled into his embrace and snuggled close to his warmth. A smile rested on her soft lips, and she fell into a deep sleep.

Chapter 20

Anastasia decided she was dead, only she could not ascertain whether she had gone to heaven or to hell. First, she was freezing and could not get warm. It was as if Val was there, gathering her into his arms and warming her with his heat. She could feel his arms about her and hear his soothing voice in her ear. Thus, she must be in heaven, she reasoned. Then the pain came, and her lungs burned as if they were on fire. She could not breathe and thought she was suffocating. She wanted to get away from the pain, to run, to get some fresh air! She could not because her feet were tied down with something. Heat and the most terrible pain seared her ribs and lungs. She tried to free her feet so she could run. On one such occasion, her foot made contact with something or someone solid and she thought she heard a man's voice utter a foul word. Maybe there were devils about that she could not see. If that were the case, she must be in hell, for what other explanation could there be?

For several days, Anastasia tossed and turned, crying out with pain and fever. Percival never left her side. He wiped her fevered brow with a cooling cloth as she fevered. He tenderly held her and spooned the clear broth the tavern keeper's wife brought into her mouth, so she could regain her strength. He fed her the elixirs Doctor Horace brought for the pain and the fevering.

He also changed her night rail and held her wrapped in blankets by the fire as her bedding was changed, and her chamber cleaned. He would not let anyone but him, touch her. He often smoothed her hair and whispered words of love into her ear as she tossed fitfully about, and every night, he held her in his arms as he slept. It was on the seventh day, that Anastasia finally awoke.

She felt safe somehow and so warm. A soft blanket was wrapped about her. Her head appeared to be resting on something quite hard. She was held close by someone's rather large arms. She blinked her eyes and tried to remember where she was and how she had gotten here. The last thing she remembered was...Anastasia frowned. She could not remember. Carefully she lifted her head and found herself looking into a pair of sleepy blue eyes. *Good Lord! It is Val.* Reality intruded on her mind. She was in bed with Val and her head appeared to be resting on his naked chest! She sucked in a breath, and then winced in pain. Her ribs were very tender. A sudden coughing spasm racked her body. She tried desperately to sit up but fell weakly back. Her arms flailed about for something to grab. Pain sliced through her as she dragged air into her lungs.

Percival quickly sat up and pulled her to a sitting position against him. He held her as the coughing fit convulsed her body. When it had finally subsided, she sank weakly back against his chest.

"Can you breathe?" his deep voice asked tenderly.

At her nod, he leaned over her to ascertain if her lungs were indeed doing their job. Satisfied with the rise and fall of her chest, he leaned back against the bed and tucked her head beneath his chin.

Virginia Barlow

"Where am I and how did I get here?"

A frown appeared between his brows. "You do not remember?"

"No, I do not think. Wait...I remember the ball, and the dancing."

Percival nodded his encouragement and began to stroke her hair.

Anastasia knew she should move away. This was not proper. She should not be in bed with a man, especially in a state of undress. Anastasia pushed weakly away but it was a puny effort. She simply did not have the strength, and it felt so good to be warm, and to be held. She felt safe. Unable to resist the temptation of his warmth, she gave in and leaned back against him. She allowed him to continue stroking her hair. She would move away later, when she felt better. She closed her eyes and thought about the night of the ball.

"I was to meet you in the library...the library." Her eyes shot open and she went rigid at the memory. Then she shuddered, reliving again the anger, the hurt, the betrayal. "You are the prince and you were kissing Rella...and—"

Prince Percival tilted her head up to his.

"I am the prince," he agreed, "but I was not kissing Rella. She kissed me. I believe she knew that you were coming to meet me in the library. I was waiting for you when she entered. I asked her what she was doing there, and she said she was not well. She went into a swoon. I stepped forward to assist her to the settee, when she wrapped her arms around my neck and kissed me. I believe she heard you opening the door and wanted it to seem as though we were lovers."

He searched her face. Anastasia saw the sincerity in his eyes. "You are the only woman I wish to kiss." His gaze was intense. "Do you believe what I tell you?"

"Aye." Somehow, she did. She knew he was telling her the truth.

He nodded his satisfaction. "Go on, what else do you remember?"

"I remember running, and I remember a black carriage and two soldiers, that were not soldiers." She trembled in his arms. He continued to cradle her against his chest, his hand stroking her hair.

"Go on."

"I remember waking up and I was in the bottom of the carriage. I could not see, there was a hood over my head. I could not move. My hands and feet were both bound with cord. I must have made a noise because the man kicked me hard, right here." She touched the still tender ribs and winced.

****

The prince gritted his teeth, the muscle working in his jaw. It was too bad that two of the men were already dead. He wanted to run them through again.

"I think I lost consciousness, because I remember later listening to the men talk. A lady hired them to kill me and they were talking about how they were going to spend their gold after I was dead. They could not take me where they had originally planned, the army had set up a roadblock, and they decided to take me to the cave."

Fury raced through his blood like quicksilver. *The bastards*. He gripped her waist and pulled her closer to him in a protective gesture. She gave a squeak of pain.

Percival was immediately contrite. "Did I hurt you,

Dorogaya?"

"Only a little. No, do not pull away. I like that you are holding me, it makes remembering not as fearful as it was at the time."

"I would not hurt you in any way. It pains me to see you so. I shall be more careful of the bruises." He kissed the top of her head and then asked. "How did you manage to leave a bit of silk on the bushes so we could find the right path?" *That had been a fortuitous discovery.*

"I remember asking for privacy. It must have been when the man named Jack grabbed my arm and pulled me from behind the tree. I remember hearing my gown tear."

He nodded. *One little mishap and it turned them in the right direction.* He thanked the gods once more for watching over her.

"I remember being in the sand at the beach. I tried to escape. I ran, but Jack caught me, and Tom kicked me so many times I thought for sure he would kill me there." She felt Percival go tense and hurried on.

"They rowed out to the cave. The tide was coming in, and they were afraid they would get caught inside the cave. They left me on the ledge and rowed away. I guessed it was late afternoon."

Prince Percival could only nod. He must not let her see the fury that burned within him at the telling. He knew there was more, and he willed her to go on. He had to hear it all.

"I realized that nobody would know where I had been taken, and that if I were to live, I must rescue myself. I found a jagged rock and worked the cord until my hands were free. The tide was coming in fast, and I knew I would not make the entrance to the cave. My sides were paining me so, and I have never been a very fast swimmer. The water was so high where I stood; I knew I had only minutes before it would be too late for me. A large wave came, and I held fast to the jagged rock, but as it tried to sweep me backward, I looked up and saw the rock shelf above. The next wave swept me up and I rolled onto the shelf. Water was running down from above, so I moved to the back of the shelf where I would be somewhat out of danger. I do not remember anything more."

He sat with his arm about her while he fought to get his anger under control. She must have been so frightened, so cold and so alone, and he had not been able to stop any of it. Percival continued stroking her hair and holding her close. In truth, it calmed him down as well as Anastasia.

"How long have we been here?" she asked.

"Seven days. We found you in the cave and brought you here. We were not certain you would live," Percival said softly. The terror he felt as they waited to see if she would live or die was something he would never forget.

"So, that does not explain why we are in bed together."

He tilted her face up to his once more. "You were cold, *Dorogaya*, I hold you to warm you."

She was feeling the heat. "But why are you...without clothing?"

He shrugged. "It is how I sleep."

A deep blush spread over her face, and she ducked her head. He had been sleeping naked with her for seven days. "But if someone were to come in, or someone to know we have been here like this…"

He leaned down and placed a soft kiss on her lips.

"No one will dare to say a thing."

The man was arrogant.

"I do not believe you could stop them, Your Highness."

He frowned. "You will call me Percival, or Val if you wish, but never again will you call me Your Highness," he commanded.

"I must address you as Your Highness; to call you by your first name is too intimate and not at all proper."

"It is proper because I command it and as for intimate…"

His mouth swooped down on hers. He gently shifted her in his lap taking her mouth in a slow erotic kiss, his tongue mating with hers, stroking, tasting and exploring until they were both out of breath and she pulled back to get some needed air. She felt the hard length of him stirring beneath her, and she blushed vividly against the white of her night rail. She shifted in his lap causing him to grit his teeth. He tilted her face back to his, his eyes warm and gentle as he stroked the side of her cheek with his fingers. Sleeping naked with her was one thing while she was fevering and unconscious. Sleeping naked with her awake would be purgatory. Percival carefully scooted her off his lap and onto the bed by his side, leaning her back against the bed next to him. He picked up one of her hands and held it gently in his larger one. He traced the still visible callouses on the tips of her fingers with the pad of his and watched as she shivered with awareness.

He wanted to pull her into his arms and make sweet love to her, sinking into her softness again and again until she cried out in pleasure. Percival wanted to hear her scream his name as she found her fulfillment, and he, his. The temptation was great, but so was his love for her. He had already hurt her once, albeit unintentionally when Rella surprised him with that kiss, but she *had* been hurt just the same, and he would not hurt her again. This would be done right, so no one could say otherwise. When he finally made Anastasia his, and he *was* going to make her his, it would be with his ring on her finger and his name as her own. Anastasia also needed to heal from her injuries, as well as the terror of all she had been through.

"I had much to discuss with you the night of the ball. Since we were prevented from having that talk as we should have, we shall have it now." He settled her more comfortably against him, gently holding her up.

"I was on my way back from an assignment for the king when I passed through your village. My father often sends me to do certain things for which I must appear as an ordinary soldier. My guards see to my back and protect me from those who would know who I am. I could not reveal my identity to you although I wanted to." He sighed and rubbed his chin against the top of her head.

"I did not at first realize you were a lady or who your family was until the night in the woods after you had been shot with the arrow. It was of import when you revealed you were Lord Covington's daughter, for we are still searching for the men who attacked your father. The king was concerned that the man who shot you might be connected to Lord Covington's death, somehow. My men and I returned and watched from the shadows hoping to catch the assassin or to discover his identity."

She looked disconcerted. "So, all that time, you were there? Close by watching? Watching us? Watching me?"

"Aye. We could not reveal our presence."

****

Anastasia did not know how to answer. She thought of all the times she had gone riding to escape Rella, and the lies. She thought of the time she sat by the stream and cried when Lady Evelyn told her how disappointed she was in her. She thought of how lonely she had been and how she wished he was there. In her mind, she re-played every minute she had with him when she felt like she could not go on, and he had been *right there the whole time!*

He frowned as he noticed her irritation. "What has you frowning, little one?"

"All I could think of was you, and how I missed you, and you were right there the whole time."

"It was hard for me as well, *Dorogaya*. I wanted very much to go to you that day you cried by the stream, but I could not."

She sighed. It did not matter now; he held her close and she was safe.

"We followed the sister, Rella to the tavern in town several times. It is my belief that this sister hired the man they call Blackjack to abduct you and kill you." Percival searched her face intently.

Anastasia simply nodded. She knew it was Rella who hired the men to kill her.

"The one thing I do not understand is why Lady Rella targeted you? What secret do you know that she was willing to have you killed for?"

Anastasia told him about Lady Constance and the letter. She kept that secret for so long, and it was wonderful to have somebody listen to what she had to say.

"Where is the letter now? This letter would be a great help in bringing Lady Rella to justice."

"She burned it, right after Lady Constance was found dead in the alley from a knife wound."

"Have you considered that Rella may have hired Blackjack to kill Lady Constance as well?"

Anastasia nodded. She felt something very sinister when Rella spoke of her aunt's death. "Aye."

"This sister of yours is very clever and we must be more so, and very careful too to catch her in her lies and reveal all the evil she has done."

Anastasia could not agree more.

"But first, I must see to your protection so Rella cannot hurt you." Percival picked up one of her hands and kissed her slim fingers one at a time.

"How will you protect me?" she whispered.

"We will be married, and my guard will see to your protection."

Anastasia was astounded. He wanted to marry her so his guard could protect her? *What about love?* Anastasia searched his face, but all she saw was determination. "You think to command me to marry you so your guard can protect me?" Anastasia asked in surprise.

"Aye. I do."

"Why should I bow to this command?" she wanted to know.

"Because I am your prince and I command it. You are in desperate need of protection, and my guard will keep you safe."

Anastasia dropped her head. She must not be worthy of his affection. She must have disappointed him, too.

Percival frowned at her response

"You do not need to marry me to protect me. I can take care of myself. I thank Your Highness for considering such a sacrifice, but it is unnecessary. As soon as I am well, I will go somewhere safe, and you will never have to worry about rescuing me or protecting me again. I shall be all right."

****

Prince Percival's frown deepened. "The hell you will. We will be married, and I will protect you."

What had he missed? This was not going as he had planned. They should be wrapped around each other sharing sensual kisses by now, not arguing. How could she deny him? How could she deny the feelings he knew she had for him, and he for her?

Anastasia shook her head at him, tears glistening in their emerald depths.

Percival puzzled over her response, the muscle working in his jaw. "You deny me? You would be a princess and you deny me?" he roared. He was not going to accept no for an answer. Anastasia *would* be his.

"Have you no other reason to wish to marry me?" Anastasia asked softly as if she could not help herself.

He was bewildered. He offered to make her his princess, and she would argue with him? "What other reason could there possibly be?"

Tears spilled out of her eyes and she would have turned from him, but he caught her chin and searched her face intently. Her eyes bespoke a yearning, a need she could no longer hide.

At last he understood. Anastasia spent years feeling unworthy, unloved and a disappointment to her mother because of her sister Rella. This was very important to her, that she feel worthy, that she was wanted and loved. Prince Percival immediately picked up her other hand and looked deep into her beautiful green eyes.

"Will you, Lady Anastasia Dunbar Covington, do me the honor of becoming my wife, my princess, my love?"

"Your love?" It was a cry from the heart.

"Aye."

He leaned down and captured her lips in another kiss. His mouth moved over hers; he could not help himself. She wound her arms around his neck and kissed him back with all her love and passion. He growled as she became the aggressor, stroking his tongue with hers, her hands wandering over his back, his chest, his arms, loving and exploring every part of him that she could reach. He shook with need. Perspiration broke out on his forehead.

His hand found her breast through the thin fabric of her night rail and she gasped into his mouth. He weighed her fullness with his hand, and then squeezed gently, rubbing his thumb and forefinger over her nipple until it was hard and aching. He kissed his way down her neck and across her collarbone. Her breath was coming fast, and she trembled in his arms. Then his lips traveled down toward her breast, and he closed his mouth over her taut nipple. She cried out with pleasure. He suckled her, drawing her hardened nipple further into his mouth. She cried out again, and Percival immediately stopped. Had he hurt her? She was not yet well, and he was behaving like a beast in rut.

"I am sorry, *Dorogaya*. I did not mean to cause you pain."

"'Twas not pain," she whispered.

He held her gently against his chest. "If it was not pain, then why did you cry out?"

She blushed and hid her face in his shoulder.

"Then you liked what I was doing?"

"Aye. 'Twas most wondrous."

Percival grinned, satisfied with her answer. 'Twas most wondrous for him too, but he wanted more. He wanted all of her, all her secrets, all her heart, all her soul, and especially all her delightful body.

"Do you answer me, love? I have asked, but you have yet to answer. Will you wed with me? Is it not reason enough when I tell you I love you, Anastasia, and I cannot live without you?"

****

He loves me!

Joy bloomed in her heart and burst into millions of blossoms that raced through her bloodstream causing her entire body to sing with happiness.

"Would you have me on my knees beside the bed instead, when I ask for your hand in marriage? I would willing oblige but I must warn you I am not clothed."

"Yes, I will wed you," Anastasia said quickly, blushing for all she was worth. "I love you too, my prince."

She reached up and kissed him softly, her lips moving over his the way he taught her. He held her gently against him until she licked at his lips and then began to suck on his bottom lip when he did not open his mouth for her.

"Do you think to tempt me?"

"Aye, I do," she answered with a smile.

He looked tenderly into her eyes and stroked her cheek. "I will do this with honor, little one. I want nothing more than to take you into my arms and make love to you, for you tempt me beyond reason. But you have been through so much and you have first to heal, so I do not hurt you. Then, we have a wedding to attend before I can make you my own as I yearn to."

She sighed and leaned back against the bed.

"It is important to me, *Dorogaya*, that you know your worth through my eyes. You are a lady, you are my love, and you are my life. We will be wed according to protocol and tradition; your honor intact, your good name above reproach. I would honor you in this way. Never doubt your worth again, for you are everything to me, and in this way, I show you your value as my wife."

He smoothed her hair back from her face and gently wiped away the tear she felt trickling down her cheek. Then, he kissed her forehead.

She had never felt so loved, so safe or so cherished.

"I must see to our breakfast." He got up and walked toward the chair where his clean clothing lay folded in a pile, completely at ease with his nudity.

Anastasia averted her eyes, but curiosity got the better of her, and she turned her gaze toward him. After all, he was to be her husband, and he had seen all of her, so why shouldn't she see all of him? She gazed upon perfection. Even the statues at the fountain in the center of the village did not compare with this man. Powerful muscles across his shoulders and back gleamed in the morning sun. His waist narrow and lean compared to the broadness of his shoulders. His buttocks were sculpted with muscle and the back of his legs were as sleek and toned as ropes of metal. She openly stared as the blood pounded in her ears, her breathing fast and uneven.

Percival dressed quickly and turned back toward Anastasia. His quick grin told her he caught her staring. She felt the heat rise in her cheeks and looked hastily away, but not before she caught his wink as he closed the door.

Chapter 21

It was another week before the doctor agreed to let Anastasia travel. It was only at the prince's insistence that he reluctantly gave his consent. Anastasia was such a gentle, sweet girl that the doctor found himself looking forward to the next time he must visit her. Often, he dragged the visit out if he could. The girl reminded him of his own sweet Abigail who died in childhood. She had the same gentle spirit and disposition as his Abigail. It was with great reluctance that he agreed to let her go. It would be several weeks still before she was completely healed, the doctor warned them. She must exercise great caution, so the lung fever did not return. He fussed around mixing up extra vials of elixir to take on her journey. Larenia and the palace were only most of a day's ride away, but one could never be too careful.

Messages had been passed often between Percival and the palace by the prince's guard during the two weeks they stayed at the tavern. All was in readiness. Percival wished Anastasia had a little more time to mend before she faced the ordeal ahead, but it was time.

The good doctor tsk, tsked over her as the prince carried her to the royal carriage and lay her gently back against the soft velvet cushions. Doctor Horace saw she was properly covered by a good many blankets before he finally stepped back and allowed the prince to enter the carriage.

Prince Percival pressed a goodly amount of gold ducats into the doctor's hands and thanked him for his service in attending Lady Anastasia. With a promise that he and his good wife would be invited to the royal wedding, the carriage door was closed, and the carriage began the journey to Larenia.

They arrived well after dark, entering the palace grounds through a gate on the east side of the palace. The lamp had been put out, and the carriage entered the grounds in darkness. Percival did not want it known that he returned with Anastasia. Her location was to remain a secret. The prince carried Anastasia up the secret stairway to the chambers that had been readied for her and laid her gently on the massive bed.

Only he, his guard, Prince Darius, and the king knew the truth of what happened, or of Anastasia's whereabouts. They considered telling Lady Evelyn, but in the end rejected the idea. They had no way of knowing what the lady believed, and considering the delicate nature of the situation, because of the involvement of the sister Rella, they decided to leave Lady Evelyn out of the discussions for the time being. The dear lady suffered immensely over the length of time her daughter had been missing, but that could not be helped. Above all, Rella must not be made aware of Anastasia's presence.

Percival settled himself onto the couch that had been brought into the bedchamber and tried to sleep. He awoke each time Anastasia thrashed to a different side of the bed. She seemed to be having a nightmare of some kind. He got up and climbed onto the bed beside her. He gathered Anastasia into his arms and held her close. A blanket of profound contentment settled over him and soon, they both fell into a sound sleep.

****

A conveyance had been sent to Covington House the morning after the ball with a group of soldiers and a letter from Lady Evelyn giving the servants their instructions on what items were needed by the family on their extended stay at the palace in Larenia. Word was also written as to the nature of the extended stay and the reason for it. Henry, the butler, upon hearing that his sweet girl Anastasia had been abducted, packed his own bags. No one was going to stop him from going to her. She would need him, and he would be there when they found her.

Lady Evelyn spent the empty days walking in the gardens, for she found the peace and serenity of the gardens soothed her nerves and helped her to think clearly. She replayed every scene, every talk she had with Anastasia until she felt like she would go mad. The gardens helped to ease the anxiousness that gripped her as nothing and nobody else could. She blamed herself for not listening to the things Anastasia said, and she blamed herself for not taking better care of her daughter. She could not bear to think of what her dear girl may be suffering or that perhaps, she was dead. Her only hope was in the prince. He had gone after Anastasia and not returned. That was a good sign, was it not?

Lady Evelyn strolled toward the palace and caught sight of Henry shuffling toward her. She had to blink back the tears at his welcome familiar face. He would understand the pain she felt.

"Me lady," he greeted her with a partial bow, and

she took both of his worn hands in hers.

"Henry, it is so good to see you."

The butler smiled. "And you as well, my lady."

"How is Covington House?"

"Fair as peaches, my lady. Cook is in charge and having the time of her life."

"I can well imagine." She let go of his hands and led the way to a nearby bench. "Come and sit so we can talk, you and I."

"Have they found my darling?" Henry inquired.

"No." Lady Evelyn blinked back tears. She had a hard time keeping her emotions in control lately. A sad thing, that. A sigh escaped her, and she bit her lip to keep it from quivering.

Henry patted her soft hands with his leathery ones. "None of that, my lady. She is alive. I know it in my bones. She will be back. You mark my words."

Lady Evelyn smiled. Henry was such a dear and exactly the thing she needed.

"Who is looking for her?"

"Prince Percival. He watched Anastasia being abducted from the top of the stairs. He was too far away to catch them, but he and his guard left immediately after. No one has heard a thing since then. King Alexander assures me that if anybody can find my daughter, Prince Percival can."

Henry nodded his silver tipped head and patted Lady Evelyn's hand once more.

****

Rella could not have been happier with the king's decision to move Lady Evelyn and the two girls to the palace for protection. It suited her purposes well, for this is exactly where she intended to be. With the king's guard to protect her, Blackjack would not be able to reach her. Once he realized she had no intention of paying him or his men, he would undoubtedly come looking for her. She had no intention of being found dead in an alley somewhere. With the king's guard about her continually, it suited her purposes. Now, she could hunt for a new mercenary without worrying about Blackjack and his men.

The king commanded the Covington women to stay within the palace walls for protection, but Rella had other plans, besides looking for a new man. She used every excuse she could think of to leave the palace grounds and travel about the beautiful city of Larenia. The royal carriages were the most elegant beautiful conveyances Rella had ever seen, and she delighted in driving about the city waving to the people as the royal guard followed her about. She was sure one of the princes would soon be totally smitten with her. After all, she was born to be a princess and they would soon recognize her superiority to the other women at court. Soon, Rella was making little stops and talking with the curious citizens of the capitol city and although she never *actually* said she was a princess, or soon to be, she hinted at it.

****

Unbeknown to both Rella and the good citizens of Larenia, Crown Prince Darius was suffering from his own fatal case of palpitations of the heart. It had nothing to do with Lady Rella. He had been on his way to his quarters, after the ball to prepare for his journey to Lichtenburg as the king commanded, when he came across the slight figure of a girl, weeping in the garden. The nymph had long dark hair that cascaded down her shoulders, and across her slight form, pooling onto the garden bench on which she lay. She was curled up on her side, her face hidden behind the fall of her silky hair, sobbing as if her heart had been broken into a million jagged pieces. The wretchedness of her sobbing tore at his heart. Unable to resist a maiden in distress, especially a pretty one, Darius stopped, and thought to comfort the girl.

She looked up and brushed her hair aside at the sound of his voice. Flushing deeply, she attempted to rise. "Your...Your Highness," Beatrice stuttered.

Prince Darius waved her back. *The poor girl needs comfort, and rescuing, not protocol, hang it all.* Gallantly he offered to run the cad through, who broke her heart, but at the sight of her tear-stained face and wide-eyed confusion at his suggestion, he apologized instead.

"Tell me what has you weeping so," Darius then inquired. He must know what was wrong before he could fix it.

In broken whispered sentences, interrupted by lots of hiccupping and sobbing, he pieced together that she was Anastasia's older sister Beatrice. Somehow, she felt herself responsible for the abduction. Overcome with sympathy at her forlorn explanation, Darius sat down beside her on the bench, and threw propriety and protocol to the wind. The girl needed kindness and understanding. The Covington family had been through a lot, of late. He pulled her unresisting form onto his lap and tucked her head beneath his chin as if she were a child.

She hiccupped. "I should have stayed close to Anastasia. I should have kept a better eye on her. I never should have left her side. She was nervous about the ball, and once I started to dance, I lost track of her. I was dancing, and flirting, and having a wonderful time and all the while someone was plotting to take my sister. What if they hurt her? What if they kill her?"

Beatrice quivered against him. "It is my fault. I should have been there. I should have stopped them. It is all my fault."

"How can it be your fault? You cannot have known that someone intended to abduct your sister," he reasoned softly, stroking her silky hair.

She ignored his comment. "Anastasia has had such a hard time of late, and I thought the ball would be the very thing to cheer her up, and now she is gone. I cannot do without my sister! It is all my fault! I should have stayed with her. I should have protected her." Then she burst into a fresh fit of weeping.

Darius did his best to convince the sobbing girl that Prince Percival would find her sister, that Anastasia would soon be back, but the lady was convinced that she could have stopped the abduction somehow. So, he simply held her soft body in his arms and let her weep all over his dress uniform. He hated weepy women, yet somehow, he was content to hold this dark-haired beauty against his chest and let her sob and hiccup all over him. His uniform was completely soaked.

When at last her sobbing ceased, and she held still against his shoulder, he thought perhaps, she had cried herself to sleep in his arms. He leaned closer to look into her face, he saw only wide innocent trust in her brown eyes, as she stared back into his. Prince Darius never knew for certain why, but suddenly he found himself kissing her soft sweet lips. Passion quickly ignited between them. She responded shyly at first, and then with a passion that surprised him, mimicking his every move. When he stroked her with his tongue, she stroked back. When he felt along her back, she felt along his, even while she trembled against him. He drank greedily from her mouth, and she drank greedily from his. He growled low in his throat and she whimpered in response. When he found himself losing control, he lifted his head and pressed her face into his shoulder as he fought to control his thoughts and his breathing.

Who would have supposed this dark eyed innocent simmered with the sensuality of a wanton? Darius had to put some distance between them before he did something regrettable. She was a lady, after all, and under the protection of his father. In the end, he did the honorable thing and escorted her to her chamber. He bowed and left the lady standing outside her door, a bemused expression on her face. And then, he rode off to Lichtenburg, hoping to solve the mystery of who abducted Lady Anastasia.

Darius' mission proved to be hopelessly unsuccessful as far as Lady Anastasia's whereabouts were concerned. Darius prayed that his brother was having more success than he was in finding the missing lady. The only good outcome of the mission was a clue found at the sight of the attack on Lord Covington's diplomatic party. The piles of ice and snow finally melted enough to reveal a musket barrel protruding from the mud, a bag of powder and balls nearby. Darius hurried back to Oldenburg with the news. There were only two places possible to obtain a gun like this from, and he was anxious to follow this lead and bring the villains to justice.

Darius had been unable to get Beatrice out of his mind. The entire time he had been away, he kept remembering their kisses, the way she tasted, the softness of her lips. He thought about the way she responded to him, the sexy noises she made at the back of her throat. He thought about her soft lush body pressed against his, the way her breasts felt pressed against his chest. He also thought of the fragrance of lilacs that clung to her skin, and with it came the image of her perfectly shaped form. Darius wondered how such an enchanting lady remained unmarried. Obviously, the eligible lords in Covington were simpletons to let such a treasure remain single for so long. He would need to be more vigilant in checking their skill as knights, if they lacked the intelligence needed to see Lady Beatrice as the beauty she was. He hurried back to Oldenburg.

Lady Beatrice must have been feeling the same way he had been, for when the Crown Prince walked into court after his return, her face lit up as if by a thousand fairy lights, and she blushed hotly when he scanned her body from head to toe. She really was the most delightful lady he had ever met. He found himself making more and more excuses to be in her company.

Word arrived from Prince Percival in the middle of the night the second night after the ball. He found Lady Anastasia! She was alive, but in precarious health. Percival would send word when she was well enough to travel, but the information must be kept secret. No one could know she had been found, not even her mother or her sisters. Darius wanted desperately to tell Lady Beatrice, her sister had been found and that she was alive. He knew she still blamed herself and that she was not sleeping at night, for she still had shadows under her eyes. He also knew she cried when she was alone. Darius understood the reason for keeping the rescue of Lady Anastasia and her whereabouts a secret. They could not risk the evil sister, Rella, learning she was still alive. But damn! He hated keeping the news a secret from his gentle Beatrice.

And then, finally, the message came on the third week. Percival was bringing Anastasia home.

Chapter 22

King Alexander sat on his golden throne and waited. It was time to put an end to this distasteful business. Too much was at stake. Too many lives had been disrupted. War had narrowly been averted. He was going to bring the culprit to justice.

The king had a hard time, at first, comprehending the cleverness and the deviousness of the scheme that led them all on such a risky path. But now he was convinced, and he wanted it to end here, and now, before innocent people lost their lives. He sent soldiers to Lady Evelyn, Lady Beatrice, and Lady Rella, informing them of Lady Anastasia's safe return and requesting their presence in the throne room. His soldiers reported Lady Evelyn's and Lady Beatrice's acquiescence, but Lady Rella was not in the palace walls. *Again!* Soldiers were sent to find Lady Rella, impart the news of her sister's joyful return, and to escort the lady to the throne room without delay. King Alexander then called the whole court into the throne room, so there could be no misunderstanding about the events that were soon to take place.

Major Kavendish arrived with Lady Evelyn on his arm, her face flushed as she anxiously twisted her handkerchief around her fingers. The king watched with interest as his major gallantly escorted the lady to the chair beside the royal platform, and protectively stood by her side.

Crown Prince Darius entered shortly after with a blushing Lady Beatrice clinging to his side. The king nodded his approval to himself. His son had an eye for beauty. *Excellent match. They will make me fine royal grandchildren.* Prince Darius escorted Lady Beatrice to her mother's side and took his place on the platform beside the king.

As soon as Lady Evelyn and Lady Beatrice were seated, the king stood. It was time to get started. He made his announcement. "Lady Anastasia is alive and has been safely returned to the palace!"

The entire court began to clap their approval. Lady Evelyn began to cry silently into her handkerchief. It had been a long, long three weeks.

Major Kavendish offered his arm for support, and awkwardly patted the sobbing lady's shoulder. He ran a finger along the inside of his collar and wiped his brow. Then he began to pat the lady's shoulder, once more.

Lady Beatrice slipped her arms around her mother's shoulder and tried to soothe the poor woman, allowing her mother to lean against her slim body for support.

King Alexander waited for the clapping to die down and then he nodded to the guards. The villain, Blackjack, was escorted into the palace by the royal guard. He was fettered with irons, his hands chained in front of him.

Prince Percival and his guard stood close by, their swords at the ready. Neither the guard nor Prince Percival, for that matter, needed much of an excuse to cut the man into tiny pieces where he stood. Blackjack knew it too for he refused to lift his head or make eye contact with anyone.

King Alexander began the proceedings. "Blackjack Kelly, you are accused of abducting Lady Anastasia Covington and of attempting to murder her in cold blood."

A murmur went through the court. The king held his hand up for silence. "You have also confessed to Prince Percival and his guard, that you are guilty in the killing of Lady Constance Remington, as well as an earlier attempt on Lady Anastasia's life. Both of which took place earlier this year, in and around Covington Village. How do you plead?"

"I be innocent, Yer 'ighness."

Percival had his sword out and the tip pressed against the man's throat before he finished his sentence.

"Hold." King Alexander waved Prince Percival back. The prince reluctantly sheathed his sword but kept his hand on the handle. "We have a witness. Lady Anastasia, herself is here, and condemns you of these crimes."

"Never 'eard of 'er"

The king nodded solemnly at Prince Percival. They hoped to keep Anastasia out of the room if they could, but that was not going to be possible.

Prince Percival withdrew from the throne room and then returned a few minutes later. He carried Lady Anastasia in his arms. The court gasped at the sight of the girl. It was true! She was alive!

Percival gently placed Anastasia in the soft chair beside Lady Evelyn. Once she was settled, he stood protectively beside her. He stared hard at the prisoner; his hand gripped the hilt of his sword.

The king turned toward the girl. "Lady Anastasia,

we feel most sorrowful to have you brought before us in your weakened condition and offer our gratitude for your presence."

"Thank you, sire."

Lady Evelyn gently placed a supportive hand on Anastasia's arm.

The king continued. "Will you tell us, dear lady if the person or persons who abducted you and attempted to murder you is within this court?

"Aye. He is there in chains." Lady Anastasia indicated Blackjack.

"Was there anyone else?"

"There were two other men, sire, but I believe them to be dead."

The king nodded. "You have heard the lady. She gives witness against you. Will the accused answer with a plea?"

Blackjack was about to answer when the door to the throne room was suddenly thrown open, and Lady Rella raced inside, her golden curls bouncing along behind her.

****

Lady Rella had been in Larenia visiting with a crowd of townspeople when the soldiers arrived and delivered the king's message. She had been summarily escorted back to the palace, her mind sorting through a thousand thoughts as she tried to figure out what was taking place. *How can Anastasia be alive? Who could have found her? How can they have found her so quickly? Something must have gone wrong! Or it is a trick! Is somebody lying? Has someone found out and they are trying to trick me? No! It does not make sense!*

She had planned this so carefully, covering her

tracks well. No one could have known about her part in the abduction and the murder. *It must be a trick. It is the only thing that makes sense. Blackjack has never failed me, nor has he ever failed Mama. What if he has failed now?* Lady Rella's eyes narrowed and she felt a moment of fear, but only a moment. No one knew a thing and she had nothing to fear. She was perfectly safe. The king only sent for her because she was Anastasia's sister and it would be expected that she be there, if Anastasia were indeed alive. Realistically, she did need to get back to the palace before people wondered at her absence. She had a part to play, after all, and who would suspect the sister that was so obviously overjoyed at Anastasia's fortuitous return? Besides, she needed to find out for herself if Anastasia had somehow managed to escape, and if she had, she needed to know what had been said about the abduction and attempt on Anastasia's life. So Rella joyfully entered the throne room, her face wreathed in smiles as she approached the court. She even squealed in delight for good measure.

"I barely received the news! Where is she? Where is my dear sister? Oh! I have been simply frantic with fear since she was abducted. Why I have hardly been able to sleep at night, I have been so worried about Anastasia. I simply must see her sweet face so I can be assured of her health."

The whole court turned to watch Rella approach, and she literally glowed with all the attention she received. She caught sight of Anastasia sitting in a chair covered in blankets. Prince Percival stood by her side, his eyes narrow and watchful as she approached.

Good God! It is true! Somehow the bitch lived! But

how? She looked around at the court's watchful eyes. They knew nothing. Several ladies were smiling at her and a couple of the gentlemen nodded. She smiled with relief, and then she caught sight of Blackjack Kelly

"Silence," the king demanded. Everyone went still.

Lady Rella felt a moment of unease. The king never used that tone before. He looked angry. She carefully made her way toward Lady Evelyn and Anastasia. Prince Percival moved to stand directly in front of her. She smiled at him, pretending she had not noticed and tried to skirt around him, but stopped when she noticed two of his guard moving forward to stand next to the prince. *Well, that is not an encouraging sign.* The courtiers noticed the protective action of the prince's guard and stared at her. She decided to pretend she did not notice. Rella smiled sweetly at them all and began to play with her golden curls hanging in front of her shoulder. She swayed side to side as she hummed softly.

King Alexander turned again to Blackjack.

"As I was saying, we have a witness condemning you of the crimes, how do you plead?"

Blackjack turned to Rella. She promised him that he would not be implicated in Lady Anastasia's death or her disappearance, but now pretended she did not know him. She smiled and waved at various members of the court and never even looked in his direction. This was working out better than she planned. The king accused Blackjack, not her. Blackjack would die at the king's command and everything would be fine. There was not one thing in the world that anyone could say or do to prove she was involved in any of this.

"Afore I answer, Yer Grace," Blackjack glanced

nervously at Prince Percival and his sword, "would Yer Grace be willin' ter make a deal fer tha name o tha person what 'ired me ter kill tha girl?"

Rella looked at Blackjack, her eyes narrowed in warning. Then she turned quickly away so the court only saw her innocent smile.

King Alexander fingered his beard with his thumb and forefinger. He glanced at Percival. At Percival's slight nod, the king looked hard at Blackjack. "You are condemned to death for the murder of Lady Constance Remington, for the abduction and attempted murder of Lady Anastasia Covington. Each of these charges carries the sentence of death. I cannot change the law, but I can change the way you die. If you answer truthfully and the answer pleases those who accuse you, your death will be quick. If you seek to deceive and answer with cunning and lies, you will be put on the rack. These are my terms. Do you agree?"

King Alexander looked around the court and nodded, everyone awaited the prisoner's answer. Rella's head swiveled side to side. She looked around for an escape in case the situation got out of control. She forced herself to smile. Even if Jack told the court she was involved, he still had to have proof.

"Aye," Blackjack answered. "It be her."

Blackjack pointed his dirty finger at Lady Rella.

"She be the one what 'ired me ter kill the old lady be'ind tha tavern and ter take tha girl from tha ball and kill 'er whar no one could find 'er. She paid us ter steal Lichtenburg soldier clothes ter make it look like they done it. She be the one what 'ired me ter kill tha girl in the woods when she wer alone."

Everyone looked at Lady Rella and she

immediately started to screech. "Lies, the filthy man tells lies! Why, I have never seen this man before! He is but a common thief and murderer. He thinks to accuse me, a lady of quality to make his death easier. I will not be used! This man is nothing but gutter scum! Surely you all see this man is telling nothing but lies!"

Rella glanced around quickly to see what affect her words were having. "I demand that he be executed at once for making such accusations against me!"

"Silence!" The king roared. He looked hard at Blackjack. "Do you have proof of what you say? The lady professes to not know you. It is a terrible thing to accuse a person of quality, especially a lady."

Blackjack nodded. "'Ere in me pocket is a pretty tha lady gave me ter pay me men wit."

Percival nodded to Darok. Darok cautiously felt the man's filthy pockets and pulled out a bracelet made with rose-colored stones fashioned in the shape of flowers intertwined.

Lady Evelyn gasped and jumped to her feet at the sight of the bracelet. A wave of dizziness washed over her, and she would have fallen but Major Kavendish was quick and caught the dear lady in his arms. He fanned her briskly with his hand, as he had nothing else; Lady Evelyn recovered quickly. Once the major was assured that Lady Evelyn was again in control of her faculties, he helped her sit once more.

"No!" The cry came from Beatrice. She too was on her feet, her face furious, her small hands fisted at her sides.

"He lies! That bracelet is not mine! It was stolen!" screamed Rella

"Silence!" King Alexander yelled.

King Alexander held up the bracelet. "Lady Evelyn, dear lady, tell us, does this look familiar to you?"

Lady Evelyn stood once more; her hands trembled as she clutched her handkerchief to her chest. Realization and understanding dawned on her pale face. "It belonged to Lady Rella's mother and now belongs to her. The last time we saw that bracelet it was in Lady Rella's possession. It could only have been her that gave it to this…this…person. I believe the man tells the truth."

Rella screamed in outrage. "She lies! She lies! Anastasia must have given the man that bracelet. Lady Evelyn lies for Anastasia to protect her. Anastasia has always hated me and always been jealous of me. This is all her fault! You cannot believe these lies!"

"Silence!" the king shouted again. He looked at Prince Percival, "Do you have any further witnesses?"

"Aye." Percival nodded to Darok.

Darok stepped forward and gave his account of following Lady Rella on several occasions to the tavern in Covington village late at night to meet Blackjack Kelly. Coins had been seen changing hands. The court was abuzz with the scene playing out.

King Alexander nodded to the guards standing at attention and they stepped forward, grasping Lady Rella by the arms and bringing her forward until she was directly in front of the king.

Rella tossed her head arrogantly and jerked her arms away from the guards. Then she faced the king, a haughty look on her face.

"Lady Rella Covington, you are hereby accused of hiring mercenaries to kill Lady Constance Remington and hiring mercenaries to impersonate Lichtenburg soldiers implicating Lichtenburg in the abduction and attempted murder of Lady Anastasia Covington. How do you plead?"

"I do not plead."

The court gasped at the audacity of the girl.

King Alexander roared his displeasure. "You have been proven guilty, Lady Rella of these heinous crimes. You have also, almost singlehandedly, destroyed the fragile peace between Lichtenburg and Oldenburg. A peace that your father, Lord Covington, gave his life for, and yet you stand before us and deny it?"

Nothing this good had ever happened in the entire history of their country and every courtier was duly taking note. The events of this day would be repeated throughout all of time. The courtiers all leaned forward to see what would happen next.

"I do. You cannot sentence me." Rella tilted her chin up in defiance.

"What is this? You stand before your king and think to command him? Your insolence greatly displeases us, and we shall pass sentence whether or nay you plead!"

Lady Rella stood and smiled at him, a very smug smile.

"We hereby sentence you Lady Rella Covington to life imprisonment."

"You cannot."

"Do you dare to defy the Crown? God's teeth you shall die for your insolence!" the king bellowed.

Prince Darius and Prince Percival both took a step toward Lady Rella, their swords drawn as they awaited the king's command.

The court drew in a shocked breath! For a lady of quality to be condemned to death was unheard of! The law expressly forbids such a thing. They turned to Lady Rella to see what she would do next.

Rella held up a golden medallion so all could see.

Lady Evelyn drew back in shock.

Rella smiled haughtily at Lady Evelyn, reading the consternation on her face. The medallion belonged to her. Her papa earned it and she intended to use it, now.

"Need I remind Your Highness of the promise you gave when you honored my father Lord Robert Covington with this token and your *word* that whoever held the token would be allowed any favor it was in your power to give?"

Rella stared at the king.

"I demand on your word as king and the honor of my father that I be allowed to remain free. I shall remove myself to Covington Estate, my father's holdings and mine by right of birth." she glanced at Lady Evelyn and Beatrice as she said this, "and I shall live out my days there."

****

The king drew in a long furious breath. Never had he been so disrespected. It was unthinkable, and unforgiveable. And yet, the little chit smiled all the while as if having tea at a garden party. Percival warned him of the deviousness of this devil girl. She thought to defy her way out of the sentence he passed with his token of love and appreciation for Lord Covington. It was an abomination. The token had never been meant to excuse foul and wicked deeds, but to reward good unselfish acts given freely for God and country. Yet here she was, Lord Covington's own daughter, haughty, and full of disdain for everything her father stood for. King Alexander leaned back in his throne, as he thought. He *had* given his word and as king, he must abide by it. But damnation he had never encountered such a wicked scheming evil woman, as this slip of a girl before him. The worst part, to his way of thinking was the girl remained completely unrepentant of her crimes. Not once had she shown the least sign of remorse. How could one so evil be the blood progeny of one so kind and selfless? Reluctantly the king signaled his soldiers to let Rella go. His thunderous expression told them all his thoughts on the subject.

****

Rella smiled at the entire court. The king could not go back on his word, and they all knew it. She escaped by a hair's breadth, but she *had* escaped. She was safe. She smiled widely at Blackjack so he knew how happy she was that he would die for her. She made sure the entire court saw her grand curtsy to the king, and then she turned to go.

A soldier stepped close to the king and whispered in his ear. King Alexander sat up and nodded his head, then he glared at Lady Rella

"Hold the girl, we are not done here," he commanded, and the soldiers instantly took hold of her arms.

"Now what?" Rella was furious. Who dared to challenge the protection the token afforded her?

Prince Percival took a step forward. He stood between her and the king, his hand on his sword. The look in his eye told her he intended to kill her if she so much as twitched. He looked for an excuse to cut her down. Rella swallowed nervously. Surely the king would not allow such a thing. She glanced toward the throne and swallowed again. The king watched Rella with narrowed eyes. Every soldier in the throne room, held the hilt of their swords. It might be best to smile and pretend she was sorry.

Another soldier entered the throne room escorting Henry, their butler, a journal tucked under one arm.

Rella rolled her eyes. *Now what? What can the butler possibly have to say that will be of any import?* He certainly could not affect her! Really, this whole affair was turning out to be vastly trying to her good nature.

"Why Henry! What in the world...?" Lady Evelyn was surprised

"I came to see the king, my lady."

Rella narrowed her eyes at the man. She had never liked him and now she wondered what the old lizard was up to. He walked toward the king quite confidently. He did an awkward sort of bow before the king and took his journal from the soldier.

"My guard tells me you have something of import to add to this occasion."

Henry chuckled. "I do, Your Highness; indeed, I do." He approached the king, or at least started toward him, but was stopped by the soldiers. "I want to hand His Majesty this journal. 'Tis a journal that belonged to His Lordship, Lord Covington."

At the king's nod, the soldier took the journal and handed it to King Alexander.

"I have the place marked where you need to read, Your Highness."

What is this? Her father had a...journal? What nonsense! Rella would have known if he had, for her father always told her everything. Rella was sure he would have mentioned it. *But why is Henry acting like he knows something important? He is up to something and it has to stop!*

"I do not see how this…servant…could possibly have anything to say that will change the fact that you gave your word, *Your Highness*."

Crown Prince Darius had obviously had enough, also. He stepped toward Rella, stopping only when he stood directly in front of her. Fury emanated from every part of his body. "You will show respect for our king when you address him or by the gods, I will throw you in the dungeon myself!"

Rella tossed her head. "You cannot touch me; the king gave his word."

"Yes," Prince Darius agreed, "but I have not!"

Rella swallowed. Prince Darius and Prince Percival were both glaring at her. Their legs braced apart as if preparing for battle, their eyes as glacial as the Alps in winter.

King Alexander took the journal and began to read the part that Henry had marked. A slow smile began to spread across the king's face. He glanced at Henry. Henry was smiling too. The king nodded his approval. He crooked his finger and a guard came forward. The king whispered in his ear and then leaned back, his gaze on Lady Rella once more.

"'Tis a truth, we gave our royal word that who-so-ever had the gold medallion would be granted one favor within our royal power." The king paused. "'Tis also a truth, our law expressly forbids the condemning of a lady of quality, even for the most serious crimes." He looked hard at Lady Rella. "And 'tis also a truth, you have committed crimes that defy the imagination. Hiring mercenaries to commit murder, abduction, attempted murder on several occasions, and treason in that you conspired against the Crown to start a war with Lichtenburg, thus bringing death to hundreds of innocent people."

Lady Rella tossed her head. *So what?*

"Each of these crimes is punishable by death. Were you a man, you would be condemned to death, and executed. As a lady, we can only imprison you for life." The king looked pensive over this statement

"I have here, Lord Covington's journal. I shall read a passage for the court.

August 17,1721

My wife has given birth to a fine baby girl. A daughter. It saddens me to know that she is not my daughter. I know this because it has been years since my wife, Agnes has shared her bed with me. On the discovery of her coming confinement, I have reflected much about the previous winter and who the man was, who fathered this child. My mind has continued to go to a certain party we attended in November of the previous year. One Lord Antone Meyer and his wife Lady Emily hosted a dinner ball and my wife Agnes was quite agitated. At one point I found she was nowhere in sight, but soon saw her appear, coming from the private section of the house. Lord Antone had appeared through the same door only minutes before. He appeared greatly agitated and arrived in different attire than he previously wore earlier in the evening. My wife pleaded a headache and we returned home, but once at home, Agnes appeared much better in health as she spent the evening smiling and humming to herself.

Having known my wife these many years. I knew at once what had occurred. I have looked in the records the clergy keep at christenings and noted that a peculiar birthmark appears on the right inside elbow of those with the Meyer blood. What is interesting to note, is that this daughter has a birthmark on the inside of her right elbow. I shall pretend no knowledge of this and shall love this poor child as my own. It is not the child's fault that she is born a bastard. Her secret is safe with me. For were the world to learn the true circumstances of her birth, they would be most cruel."

King Alexander closed the journal. Everyone in the room was quiet.

Blackjack smirked.

Lady Rella started to screech again, "It is a lie! He is lying! They are all lying! They are jealous of me and they are trying to take everything away from me! It is not true! You have to believe me!"

King Alexander watched the girl and then he held his hand up for quiet. He took the clergy book he sent for from the guard and looked up records on the Meyer family. It was there, precisely as Lord Covington wrote. King Alexander handed the book to Crown Prince Darius and motioned for the guard to bring Rella closer.

"Lord Covington, of whom I had the greatest respect for and counted as a dear friend, condemns you with his own journal. You dishonor his memory with your accusations that he would record falsehoods in his journal. Lord Covington was a man of honor. He held the truth as he held his honor. It was all to him. The record the priests recorded holds this mark on the right elbow as the mark of the Meyer family. Show the court your right elbow and if no mark is there, you shall have your freedom."

"No! I mean...it is not proper. I cannot be forced to show such an intimate area..."

King Alexander leaned back.

"True, but then lady's gowns often have sleeves so short the entire arm is bared, as well as their chest. The gown you have on now is one such as these. Are we to assume you confess to being indecently clothed or rather unclothed?"

Everyone laughed.

"Rella Meyer since you will not consent to revealing so intimate an area as your right elbow..."

The court laughed again.

"We will assume that you bear the birthmark of the Meyer family lineage, thus being born of unwed parents. We name you a bastard and as such have no protection under the law."

Rella paled. This could not be happening. There had to be a way out of this, there always was. She glanced at Lady Evelyn, but the lady turned away after the bracelet had been found, and she had not looked at Rella since. Rella looked at Beatrice, but her gaze was focused on the Crown Prince, and she, too refused to look her direction.

Blackjack was openly chuckling, and both the princes looked like they wanted to run her through. Their hands rested on the hilt of their swords.

Then there was Henry. The traitorous old lizard, she would get him for this. He must have known about the journal for ages, and if she had known about it, that journal would have been burned with her mother's letter.

Rella squared her shoulders and turned to face the

king. He was her only option. Attacking his honor worked once; maybe it would work again.

Chapter 23

"Rella Meyer, you have no claim to Covington Estate or any of its holdings. You cannot claim leniency by right of birth having proven to our satisfaction that you are not born into the privileged class, therefore the sentence we pass upon you for the crimes you have committed is death." At the courts collective indrawn breath, the king continued. "Be it known that although we consider ourselves extremely generous in allowing one such as you to challenge the Crown with a medallion meant to honor, not to forgive, we graciously extend our word that was given as long as it is within reason, for the crimes of which you have been proven guilty. Rella Meyer, what is the nature of the favor you seek?"

"I demand to go free. I shall promise the Crown that I shall stay within Covington lands until the end of my days."

The king coughed. Either the girl was completely daft, or she thought somehow, she could be forgiven for any crime she chose to commit by merely holding the medallion.

The court held their breath. Would she be allowed to go free? Surely not, she was a bastard after all....

"Denied!" The king thundered.

"But you gave your word! You cannot..."

Rella's gaze fell on Prince Percival. He took a

menacing step toward her, his hand held his sword. Prince Darius took a step forward as well, his dark gaze promised retribution.

Rella swallowed and took two steps back.

"We shall grant the favor of your life for the space of a few hours, as keeping our promise. We consider this a most generous favor considering all that has occurred. You have until dawn to leave our kingdom forever. If you remain after the sun rises, you shall immediately be put to death, no quarter given. If any citizen of our realm gives you aid, or quarters you after the sun rises, it shall be considered an act of treason, and they shall be dealt with according to the law. This is the last you shall see of Lady Evelyn, Lady Beatrice, and Lady Anastasia. If you travel across our border at any future time, it shall be on pain of death. You are a traitor and have no claim here."

The court stilled. Not a sound was heard, and every eye looked at Rella.

This is all wrong, Rella thought. *I have every claim here. Why, I am supposed to be queen one day! The prince should be looking at me like some lovesick fool, not Anastasia. Why, I have more royal qualities than most of the people in this room!*

"Your Highness." She made a half curtsy and turned as if to leave. She wanted to get out of the immediate vicinity of both princes before she had her say. Fury burned through her like dry tinder catching fire. *How dare Anastasia take everything from me!* Covington Estate was hers and now it was gone! *This is all Anastasia's fault!* How dare she turn everyone against her, even the king! Rella was the one that deserved to be a princess! She had always been better than Anastasia. It was simply not fair! Anastasia was the one who should be exiled! What had Anastasia ever done to deserve the king's favor? What had Anastasia ever done to deserve Prince Percival? Why, she probably still had calloused hands, and split nails. Rella looked at her own soft white hands and shuddered at the thought. Then there was Anastasia's ghastly arm. Surely the prince was not stupid enough to want a cripple when he could have her. It was laughable that this could happen when Rella was right here! Look at the bitch making doe eyes at Prince Percival while he strutted around acting as her personal avenging angel. She would not stand for it! Rella turned to Anastasia.

"You will not get away with this! I shall make you pay until the day you die! I shall see to it that the whole world knows that I am innocent, and you are nothing but a deformed evil stepsister. No one treats me this way and gets away with it! The whole world shall believe it is entirely your fault. You shall never escape me! I shall make you pay over and over again! Like Athena, you shall try to protect what you love, but you shall always be too late, and shall lose it all! You will see!"

At a motion of the king's hand the guards grabbed Rella's arms and dragged her out of the throne room.

"I want you to think about the fresh meat, Anastasia; I fed the beast to keep him near." Rella wanted to watch the agony Anastasia experienced at her cruel words and she wasn't disappointed. Anastasia drew back as if she had received a deathblow, the color draining from her face. Rella's sinister laughter followed her out into the courtyard.

Percival frowned at Rella's comments and turned

toward Anastasia. One look at her face, and he had her in his arms striding from the court with Anastasia held close against his heart.

Once outside Rella jerked her arms free of the soldier's grasp and headed toward the courtyard. A squadron of soldiers was mounted and waiting in the courtyard. A mare had been readied for Rella. They were to escort her out of the kingdom. Rella had other plans though. She mounted the mare and galloped toward Covington House. She would need money if she were to have the revenge she deserved.

****

After the guards had escorted Rella from the throne room, the king dismissed the court. He was weary of the whole fiasco and had other matters he must attend to.

As Percival carried Anastasia toward her chamber, she insisted she could walk. He insisted that he would carry her.

"How are you feeling?" His breath was warm against her ear.

She shivered in response and wrapped her arms around his neck. "I am all right, only a little tired. It seemed such an emotional scene earlier, in the court that I was not sure for a time how it would turn out."

She started trembling in his arms as she relived all that happened. He looked at her in concern.

Percival wanted to ask about Rella's comments on fresh meat but the look on Anastasia's face stopped him. He saw fear. "Do you doubt that I would keep you safe?"

"Nay. I knew you would. It is simply that years of living with Rella as she twisted her lies around the truth, have made me afraid. I know 'tis not logical, but I have watched many good people fall prey to her lies and stories. And although I know you would keep me safe, 'tis hard to ignore the knot in my stomach as she speaks her lies."

He nodded. In truth, it did not make any sense to him. Either she trusted him to keep her safe, or she did not. He looked at her dark eyes and decided to argue about it another time. For now, she needed rest and he intended to see to it that she got it.

****

Lady Evelyn followed close behind on the arm of Major Kavendish. Shocked and shaken to the depths of her soul, she relived the last few months following Lord Covington's death. There were so many things she wished to talk about with Anastasia. Now that she learned the truth about Rella, she had many questions she wanted to ask. So many things happened over the last few years that did not make sense. She hoped to talk with her daughter, and finally understand what had taken place. Lady Evelyn also had many questions about the night of the ball, and where Anastasia had been taken. She wanted to hear about the rescue and how it was this prince lost his heart so completely, in so short a space of time. For all that Lady Evelyn knew about Prince Percival, was that he rescued her daughter. She had no idea that the man who caught Anastasia when she fell from the roof in Covington Village, was the man standing before her now. Lady Evelyn hurried after Prince Percival's long strides, dragging Major Kavendish with her.

****

Lady Beatrice and the Crown Prince were

following at a much slower pace. Prince Darius needed to assure himself that Beatrice was dealing with the emotional scenes that had taken place in the throne room. It could not have been easy for her, being caught between two sisters and realizing that Rella tried to kill Anastasia. He remembered how Beatrice cried in the garden the night of the ball, and he slipped an arm about her waist and pulled her into an anteroom. He wanted to comfort her in private.

****

Once inside Anastasia's chambers, Prince Percival laid her back against the soft pillows and kissed her lips gently.

"Oh my," Lady Evelyn exclaimed as she suddenly stopped right inside the door.

"I think we have shocked my mother."

Prince Percival turned toward Lady Evelyn with a slight bow. The lady looked from him to Anastasia and back.

"Forgive me, Madam, for I have not had the chance to speak with you about your daughter Anastasia."

"Yes?" Lady Evelyn was still coming to terms with all that had happened in the throne room. She could hardly believe that Rella was responsible for Anastasia's abduction, that Rella plotted to have Anastasia killed. "Was there something more than what was discussed in court?"

Lady Evelyn continued to look from one to the other anxiously. Was something wrong?

"Nay, Madam, 'tis your daughter's future I wish to discuss with you."

"Her future?" Lady Evelyn asked weakly.

"I would like to formally ask your permission to

take your daughter Anastasia's hand in marriage."

So that was it! She breathed a sigh of relief and smiled at the dear prince. "Of course, Your Highness. Forgive me for not understanding. There have been so many surprises and upsets today; I had thought there was something wrong. But of course, you have my permission."

Lady Evelyn walked to the bed and would have hugged her daughter, but Prince Percival stepped between Lady Evelyn and the bed.

"Anastasia is recovering from several broken ribs and lung fever. She cannot be moved about or bumped."

Tears filled Lady Evelyn's eyes. Were it not for this dear prince, her daughter would not be here at this moment. "I would thank you, sir, for rescuing my daughter and for protecting her and bringing her home safely to us."

"It was my pleasure. Madam."

Lady Evelyn dabbed at her eyes. "I cannot bear to think of what would have happened had you not been there, Your Highness, and am most anxious to hear this tale of how Anastasia was abducted and how you found her and rescued her."

"I would be most happy to tell you the tale, although perhaps tomorrow would be a better time, Anastasia tires easily and I fear to push her for I do not want her to suffer a relapse. Anastasia must have rest."

Prince Percival took a step back to allow Lady Evelyn to approach the bed. Anastasia looked so pale against the sheets.

"Of course, Your Highness." Lady Evelyn turned to Anastasia. "My dear girl, can you ever forgive me? I

267

was so frightened that I should never see your sweet face again...and I have been thinking about all the times you tried to tell me...to talk to me...about Rella and I turned you away...."

Anastasia smiled at Lady Evelyn and took her hand. "It is all right, Mama. That was in the past and we should be thanking the gods that we are all together. You are not to blame for what happened. The important thing is Percival found me and I am alive. He has taken great care to see to my health. And I, too was frightened that I should never see you or Beatrice again. But here we are, and you cannot blame yourself. No one could have guessed at the terrible thing Rella was plotting. I have been aware since the day we came to Papa's house that she did not like me, but I never imagined she hated me enough to see me dead."

Lady Evelyn nodded and dabbed at her eyes again with her handkerchief.

****

Beatrice entered the chamber then; her face was flushed, and her lips swollen. Prince Darius was right behind her and could not seem to quit looking at her. Beatrice walked toward Anastasia and picked up her other hand, tears filled her eyes as she, too, thought of all they had been through.

"I am so sorry Anastasia. I should have said something to Mama. I knew Rella lied to her about you, but I did not want to interfere. I thought to not take sides, to let you and Rella work it out between you and you nearly lost your life because of it." Tears streamed down her face.

Anastasia squeezed Beatrice's hand. "It is not any one's fault. We must focus on the fact that we are together and that we are all alive. That is the important part."

"You are right, my darling. We must focus on the good."

"When are you to wed?" Beatrice wondered.

Prince Darius was most insistent in his pursuit of her, even suggesting that they wed at the same time as Percival and Anastasia. Beatrice had yet to answer him on whether she would marry him or not, for she did not want to upset either her mother or Anastasia. So, she wisely kept her secret to herself for the time being.

"Within the month. We have a great many things to prepare and Anastasia has still to heal. She insists that she will walk down the aisle without assistance." It was Prince Percival who answered.

Lady Evelyn leaned down and kissed her daughter on the forehead.

A shadow passed over Anastasia's face. "Do you think we are really free from Rella? What if she has some other plan? Or hires another mercenary? What if she tries to stop the wedding?"

Prince Darius spoke "Do not worry my almost sister. We will continue to have guards following you about during the day and stationed outside your chamber door at night until after the wedding, and then my brother will no doubt follow you around like a pup on its first hunt during the day and personally see you safe and warm in your chambers at night."

Prince Darius winked at Anastasia and bowed to the ladies. He had a personal matter to discuss with the king and hoped to catch his father before he retired.

****

Prince Percival glared at his brother. A pup indeed,

and he had been on more hunts than he could count.

Anastasia cheeks grew rosy at Darius' suggestive remarks. She glanced at Percival. He gave her a heated look; his mind had wandered to how he intended on keeping her safe and warm at night in their chamber.

Anastasia ignored him and turned to her mother. "Are you feeling well, Mama? I am sure all of this has been a dreadful shock."

Lady Evelyn nodded. "It shall take some time to put together all that has happened, but I am doing better now that you are returned to us."

Lady Evelyn leaned over to kiss her daughter's forehead one more time. "Come Beatrice, let us go to our chambers and let Anastasia sleep. She looks so weary and pale. She must rest in order to heal."

Lady Evelyn turned to Prince Percival. "You will let me know if she needs me, or anything?" she ended weakly

"Of course," Prince Percival said.

Lady Evelyn nodded. Beatrice leaned over and whispered "good night" in Anastasia's ear and hurried after her mother, closing the chamber door behind her.

Percival sighed. Anastasia was already asleep, her dark hair spread over her pillow, her face pale as the sheets upon which she lie. He watched her sleep for a few minutes and then quietly left the chamber.

Erik and Darok were stationed right outside her door.

"Let no one in but me," the prince ordered.

"You go to the prison?"

"Aye, it must be done tonight."

Blackjack was given his merciful death. Prince Percival removed his head himself, with one blow of his heavy sword and the body was disposed of properly. It was quick and merciful as the king promised.

Percival went to his chambers afterward to bath and rid himself of the stench of the prison. One he was dressed in clean tunic and breeches, he returned to Anastasia's chamber. His guards watched him walking toward them with a knowing smirk.

"Back so soon, Your Highness?"

"I am come to see that the lady is sleeping well after such a trying day."

"Of course, Your Highness. That's all we were thinking."

The men barely contained their amusement.

"Shut up," Prince Percival commanded with a growl.

He entered the chamber and then bolted the door shut from within. Prince Percival had tried to sleep alone, once, since they had returned to the palace. He had lasted about two hours and then he had given in. He had to have Anastasia close, had to hold her in his arms. It appears she felt the same, for she was restless at night turning from one side to the other, until he pulled her into his embrace, and then they both slept fitfully.

Chapter 24

Rella Meyer arrived at Covington House well after dark. It had taken all her considerable persuasive talents to convince the soldiers that she needed to come to the estate to fetch her personal belongings. Truthfully, she was here for one reason, and that was money. Her money. And her paints. If the idiots believed they could be rid of her so quickly, that was their mistake. A plan had been formulating in her mind as she rode. She was utterly furious and the angrier she was, the better the plan. The problem was she did not have much time, and the palace would be on the lookout.

Rella was sure there would be a royal wedding soon, judging from the way that sappy prince stared at Anastasia. A royal wedding meant many people coming and going. Lots of people coming and going meant there was an excellent opportunity to get to Anastasia. Rella was still working out the details, but she considered it a brilliant plan, nonetheless.

Once she was at the estate she wasted no time. Rella hurried to the library and Lord Covington's desk. She opened the bottom drawer and stepped back in surprise! *Where the hell is the strongbox?* It had completely disappeared. She screamed in fury! She did not have time to search the house. She barely had time to make it outside the border before sunup, as it was. Bellowing with rage, Rella went from room to room throwing everything about as she searched in vain for the strongbox. The vases were gone! The candlesticks were gone! The snuff boxes were gone! *Paintings, I must have the paintings.* They were the only other thing that could be sold for any substantial amount of money. *Damn!* The walls were bare too! *What is going on here? And where the hell are all the servants?* Only Cook and Grigori came to see what the commotion was.

"Grigori!" she screamed. "Harness the gray geldings to the carriage! *Now!*"

"Yes, miss."

Rella ran upstairs to the master suite. Lord Covington kept several of his favorite paintings in his chamber. She threw open the door and looked around. Whoever had taken everything else had forgotten the master's chamber. Quickly Rella took down the three paintings that hung on the wall and wrapped them in the brocade coverlets from the master bed. She ran to the top of the stairs and yelled for the soldiers.

Two soldiers came upstairs, and she commanded them to put the three bundles into her carriage. The men looked at each other awkwardly. "What about yer clothes, miss?"

"Damn my clothes. This is what I am taking! Get them in my carriage. The sooner they are loaded the sooner we can leave. Or do you want to explain to King Alexander why I did not make the border?"

"Nay, miss. We will get them in."

Excellent, now for my paints. She ran to her room and dug the paints from her chest. She glanced about. She could buy more gowns. She had no idea who had taken the strongbox, or what was going on here, but she had no more time to waste. Rella did not intend to find

273

out if the king had soldiers by the border waiting to execute her if she failed to make it across the border in time. She raced down the stairs and out the front door. *Good riddance!* There were other kingdoms in the world and other princes to be had.

The soldiers loaded the paintings as she hurried to the carriage. She dumped her armload of possessions into the carriage and picked up the reins. She clucked to the horses and ran them hard, whipping them if they slowed.

The soldiers took the mare she had been riding and tied her behind the captain's saddle. They raced after her carriage. The king would want a report and they intended to see to it that they watched her cross the border with their own eyes.

Several hours of hard riding later, right as the sun peeked over the horizon, Rella whipped the grays, and the carriage made it across the border into Dusselstein. The king sent soldiers to every border crossing in his kingdom. He was determined that Rella would be outside the border of his kingdom by morning. He gave his soldiers orders to hunt her down if she did not cross before the sun came up.

Rella pulled Hercules and Achilles to a stop. Foam dripped from their mouths and their sides heaved with the exertion of breathing. She tossed her head at the soldiers, and then whipped the geldings into a run once more. Now, all she had to do was find someone to buy her paintings and she could put her plan into motion.

Chapter 25

The wedding took place one month later. King Alexander was extremely pleased with himself. He took credit for the fact that both of his sons, made excellent matches. It had been his idea, after all, to give a ball. It bore no relevance, that Prince Percival met Lady Anastasia before the ball, and had been more than a little in love with the lady at the time, whether he acknowledged it to himself or not. Nor did it bear any relevance to the fact that Crown Prince Darius met Lady Beatrice *after* the ball, while she wept in the garden over the abduction of her sister. The plain fact at hand was, the king had given a ball, and he was solely responsible for his princes' falling in love with two of the most beautiful girls in his kingdom. Therefore, he was the sole orchestrator of the wedded happiness his princes were shortly to enjoy.

The palace grounds were adorned with thousands of blossoms, in every shade of the rainbow, in every shape and size. There were pots, garlands, and vases of flowers. A platform had been erected in the center of the courtyard where the priest, who was responsible for the souls of the royal family, would perform the ceremony. Garlands of red and white roses had been twisted together to form an archway, under which the royal couples would stand as they said their vows. Dignitaries and royalty from the adjoining kingdoms would be in attendance, as well as the local nobility. Separate seating areas had to be arranged to accommodate the status of their royal and exalted guests. King Alexander had a grand time planning and organizing the royal event. By his side was his newly appointed knight, Sir Henry.

King Alexander took Lady Evelyn for a stroll one evening around the castle gardens. He proposed she come and live in the palace, for he noticed the attentions of Major Kavendish toward the good woman. He knew it to be a small amount of time before another wedding was called for. At her gracious, but firm refusal, the king pointed out that her daughters would be in the palace, and Lady Evelyn would be living alone at Covington Estate. Lady Evelyn felt that her duties to her late husband required her to return to Covington land, and see to its holdings. It was a matter of family honor. King Alexander tucked Lady Evelyn's arm in his and explained that Covington Estate and holdings would eventually be dissolved unless there were heirs to carry on the traditions.

"Of course, I understand, Your Highness, but it is my duty as Lord Covington's wife to see to the responsibility that goes with the lands and title."

"We do not like the idea of a gentle lady such as yourself living alone, so far from your daughters and our protection."

"I shall be all right, although it is most gracious of Your Highness to concern yourself with my welfare."

"We would have you here, under our protection, especially until the whereabouts of Rella Meyer are confirmed. Alone you would be a target."

Lady Evelyn sighed. That was a truth she could not

deny.

"We have a solution to this problem that we would like you to consider, Lady Evelyn. We have someone in mind that we would like to vouchsafe the Covington lands and title to."

Lady Evelyn looked up at the king in surprise, "Who did Your Highness have in mind?"

"We have knighted the man Henry, as you know, for his part in bringing Rella Myer to justice. We would like your thoughts on bestowing upon him the lands and title of Covington Estate with all its holdings, thus leaving you free to be by the side of your family."

Lady Evelyn smiled at the king. "What an excellent idea, Your Highness! No one is better qualified and knows more about Covington Estate and all its holding than Henry. I quite like the idea and I commend Your Highness on your cleverness in thinking of him."

King Alexander was pleased. This was an exceptional woman to be sure.

"Then it shall be done. The royal solicitors shall draw up the papers for you to sign. Thank you, dear lady, you are an honor to Lord Covington, and we can see why the fellow was always in a hurry to return home."

Lady Evelyn blushed at the compliment.

And so, it was. Sir Henry the once butler, became the Lord of Covington Estate.

****

Lady Anastasia was better. She could walk about without aid, and she no longer coughed at all. The ache was completely gone from her ribs. The color was returning to her cheeks. It felt so wonderful to walk about the gardens in the evenings and feel the cool breeze on her face. She missed the evening air when she had been confined to her bed, and now she relished it, pulling the air deeply into her lungs.

Prince Percival caught up to her by the fountain and swung her into his arms for a raw open mouth kiss that quickly became carnal. He stroked her tongue with his and she enthusiastically returned his caress.

"I want you Anastasia."

"I want you, too," she whispered shyly.

She was still not used to this handsome man telling her he loved her. It all seemed as if it were one of the stories that Papa told her about princes and princesses, and faraway lands. Only this prince was very real, and he was here with her right now, not in a faraway land Tomorrow she would become a princess. Beatrice would also. Lady Evelyn would be coming to live in the palace with them, and Henry would take the Covington Estate and Title. It was perfect. A shiver suddenly went down her spine.

Percival lifted his head. "What is wrong, *Dorogaya*?"

"I was thinking it was all so perfect. You, me, Darius, Beatrice, Mama, Sir Henry, and then I think about Rella's threats, because it is all perfect, too perfect. It frightens me and I wait for the bad thing to happen because I am so happy."

Prince Percival held her close against him. "It is all right for things to be perfect and for you to be happy."

"I know; it is only that I have never been this happy and it frightens me."

"There is no reason to be frightened. Rella shall never harm you or your family again. I shall protect you and keep you from harm. After tonight you shall be with me always, day and night and you shall see that it can be perfect without the bad things happening."

She wanted to believe him with all her heart.

****

The wedding day dawned without a cloud in sight. A gentle breeze filled the air with the fragrance of the thousands of blossoms that covered every inch of the palace and grounds. Birds sang their happy melodies, as the servants swarmed out of doors to set up the tents, and seating for the hundreds of guests that would soon be arriving. If the palace looked like a fairy land the night of the ball, it now looked like the gods' favorite temple in the heavens.

Anastasia held her arms up as the army of ladies' maids helped her dress for her wedding. Her chemise was made of white silk embroidered with delicate pink flowers around the neck and hem. The corset was made with the finest whalebone available. It, also, had been etched with delicate pink blooms. Next, came the silk stockings, and the silk underskirts. Yard after yard of delicate lace was stitched to the flounces at the bottom of each underskirt. Then came the wedding dress, made entirely of delicate lace etched with roses, it had a low square neck, long tight sleeves and a long full skirt that ended in a graceful ten-foot train. A belt of braided silk was tied about her tiny waist.

The maids did her hair in an intricate weave and added curls that fell gracefully down her back. A diamond tiara was set high upon her head amidst the dark curls.

Anastasia looked at her reflection in the mirror and could hardly believe the beautiful delicate face looking back at her, was her own.

Her chamber door opened, and Lady Evelyn walked in. "Oh my dear, you look so lovely you nearly take my breath away."

That was a good sign. Lady Evelyn never commented on their beauty. She preferred her daughters to keep their minds on more useful things, rather than on the vanities that often beset young girls.

"Thank you, Mama. How is Beatrice?"

"She is dressed and nervous as a cat, pacing back and forth. She looks as lovely as you do."

A knock sounded at the door. "The king is ready, my lady.'

King Alexander would lead Beatrice down the aisle, while Sir Henry escorted her.

It was Sir Henry, who now stood at the door. "Where is your veil, my lady? We must go."

The maids quickly secured the delicate veil over her hair and covered her face. Sir Henry, cut quite a figure in his new red coat with gold braid and cream breeches. *Why have I not noticed what a handsome man he is?* Anastasia wondered. Sir Henry extended his arm and Anastasia rested her arm on his.

"Thank you, Sir Henry for walking me down the aisle. I can think of no one I would rather have other than Papa, of course."

"It is my pleasure, my lady. Your papa would be right proud of you. You are a beautiful bride and the prince is a lucky man."

A shadow passed over Anastasia's face. She sincerely hoped that Papa would be proud. Then Anastasia smiled. "It is I that is lucky. Lucky to have you as my friend. Lucky to have Mama and Beatrice and lucky Prince Percival loves me."

"You deserve it all, my lady."

They reached the courtyard. The king, with Beatrice on his arm, was already leading her to Prince Darius. Anastasia looked toward Prince Percival. His hot gaze traveled slowly over her, lingering on his favorite parts. She left a blush work its way over her cheeks.

****

Prince Percival thought he had never seen a more enticing picture than his lovely bride. She was everything he ever dreamed about and tonight he would finally make her his. He saw the blush on her cheeks and gave her a slow knowing grin in response.

The king reached the platform and relinquished the blushing Beatrice to a smoldering Prince Darius.

He looks like I feel, Percival thought. He recognized the need and the frustration in his brother's eyes. He recognized the love, also.

Percival turned and watched Anastasia as she walked toward him. She was as graceful as a queen, as delicate as a fairy and as beautiful as an angel. By the gods, he loved this gentle lady.

Anastasia looked up and smiled. Percival's heart swelled with love. They were going to live happily together for the rest of their lives.

The ceremony was beautiful and went exactly as planned. Even the king dabbed at his eyes as the love between his sons and their new princesses was witnessed by everyone present that day.

A sumptuous wedding feast was held in the grand hall after the wedding, and the guests gorged themselves on dozens of delicious dishes, before retiring to the grand ballroom. The orchestra began the opening strains of a wedding waltz, and the two happy couples took the floor for their first dance as husbands and wives.

Percival held Anastasia close to him and whispered words of love in her ear. Soon it would be time to retire and he was impatient to have his lovely wife to himself. Tonight, he would finally, make her his.

The dancing and celebration went on for hours. Percival smiled in satisfaction. Everything was going well, and it was nearly time to retire. Prince Percival glanced about for the whereabouts of his wife. *His wife.* Percival shook his head and laughed softly to himself. There was a time when that statement would have sent him running headlong to volunteer for the nearest one-way mission to purgatory. Now, it soothed and warmed his soul with a contentment that he had never known. *The library.* It was the only place he had not thought to check. Lady Evelyn and Anastasia had gone to the library for a quiet moment alone, more than an hour ago. Perhaps his wife was still there.

Darok stopped him. "Not that way, Your Highness, follow me."

"What has happened?" Percival wondered.

Darok led him quietly out into the garden and around to the library terrace as he explained.

"I was having a turn in the garden with a lovely lady when I happened to look through the library doors. The Princess Anastasia was sitting in a chair, facing the other door, Lady Evelyn to the side. My gut told me something was wrong. The princess was sitting so awkwardly and kept leaning to one side looking at me, and then I realized, she was trying to tell me something. There is a man in the library with the two ladies and he has tied Lady Evelyn up and has a knife to Princess Anastasia's throat. He faces the doorway to the hall. We think he is waiting for you to come in search of your wife. Vroknar is outside the door, keeping to the shadows, and I came to fetch you."

Prince Percival simmered with rage. "Then he shall have me. Let's not keep the man waiting."

How did an assassin make it into the palace? Every precaution had been taken. Every invitation had been checked. Every guest had been identified. There were soldiers guarding every door. How had this man gotten in? Percival would find out how this man entered the palace, who helped him, and then he would die for daring to touch his wife. The prince took the steps two at a time and flung open the double doors at the top of the terrace stairs. "Good Evening."

The man whirled toward the sound of Percival's voice, pulling Anastasia with him, the blade of his knife against the side of her throat. The man was dressed as a nobleman in a finely tailored jacket, waistcoat, and breeches. The shine on his boots reflected the light overhead. A man of quality obviously, perhaps even a lord, but with the moral code of a gutter rat. Only a coward hid behind a woman. Only dead ones hid behind his woman.

"So, at last the prince arrives." The sneer was evident on the man's thin pointy face.

Percival leaned against the doorjamb and folded his arms across his broad chest. He glanced at Anastasia's face. She was terrified and he would need her calm for what came next. Percival smiled into her frantic emerald eyes and said, "Who is your friend, darling? I do not believe we have met."

"I…I…do…not…know." She shook so violently it was a wonder she had not cut her own throat against the blade held against her.

Percival relaxed against the door and smiled encouragement at Anastasia. He looked for all the world as if he visited with an old friend. He was furious.

"I am Lord Remington, Your Highness, and I am so glad you decided to finally make your appearance. I had been told that you were quite fond of this piece of fluff, but then I did wonder if it were entirely true, as you did not appear for the longest time. I should think you would be a little more conscientious of your wife's whereabouts. That is, if you truly do care to any degree. It *is* your wedding night is it not?"

"It is."

"It is such a shame you will not be enjoying it. You see, this whore deprived me of what is rightfully mine. The Covington wealth was all but in my grasp, when this creature interfered. My dear wife, Lady Constance, met with an untimely death at her hand, and I simply must have my revenge. A knife through the heart and left to die behind the tavern in Covington village, that is how my Constance died. That is no way for a lady to die. And I thought, what could be more fitting than to kill this bitch in the same manner on the night of her wedding and in front of her prince?"

****

Lord Remington laughed to himself at his own cunning. He was feeling quite invincible. No one had noticed him all night as he stalked the princess and now, she was completely at his mercy. He thought he had the upper hand and he did not see Vroknar and

284

three of the prince's guard quietly enter the library through the doorway that led off the hall.

"So, you are the uncle of my wife's sister, Rella?"

Lord Remington nodded and tightened his hold on Anastasia. He was a little surprised the prince appeared so relaxed, leaning against the doorway as if he had all the time in the world. Rella told him the prince would be furious, so he must act quickly. God's teeth the prince almost looked happy about the whole situation, as if killing his new wife in front of his eyes was what he had wanted all along. Why the bastard was even smiling.

"I am, and I am done talking. My niece Rella wanted me to give you the message that once again you are too late. She swore she would have her revenge and now she has it! Say goodbye to your prince, whore!"

Lord Remington was going to cut the girl's throat, but he was suddenly jerked off his feet and the knife went flying across the room! He had not even seen the prince move.

Anastasia was whisked backward by an unseen arm as Vroknar pulled her to safety. She steadied herself and was now kneeling by the side of her mother. Her head was in her mother's lap and her arms tightly wound around her mother's waist.

Suddenly Lord Remington was on the ground and the prince's boot was across his throat. The prince's sword pierced his chest, right above his heart.

"Did the bastard Rella send you, then?" the prince asked.

Lord Remington was hoping to swoon soon. He did not think he could bear to watch the prince kill him; it was sure to hurt. Rella had not mentioned what a powerful man this prince was, or that there was the possibility that he might die. If she had, he would have reconsidered her offer. One thousand ducats were not worth the pain he was experiencing at the current moment.

"I asked you a question." The prince pressed his sword down a little harder to get the man's attention.

"Yes, she told me what that who—"

"You call my wife that one more time and your death will be extremely painful and prolonged."

Lord Remington swallowed. "She told me what your wife had done to my wife and I came to see that justice was done. No one should die alone in an alley, and certainly not a lady."

"The girl, Rella, tells you falsely. Rella is the one who hired a man, a mercenary to kill your wife. This was made known to many, and the man confessed to the crime. My wife, Princess Anastasia, had nothing to do with it. Rella also hired this mercenary to kill Princess Anastasia because of information Lady Constance and the princess knew about her."

"You lie!" Lord Remington screamed.

Prince Percival leaned toward the thin man. "What reason have I to lie? I am not the one about to die. Perhaps you have not heard that Rella is a named bastard. She does not have the Covington blood in her veins and has no claim on the lands or title. Whatever she has promised you, she has played you for a fool."

"You lie!" Lord Remington screamed again. *It cannot be true! Can it?*

It was the last thing Lord Remington knew. Prince Percival was done talking. Although the man had not known it, he was a dead man the instant he touched

Anastasia.

****

Percival wiped his blade on Lord Remington's coat and sheathed his sword. He turned to Anastasia and saw her weeping in Lady Evelyn's arms.

Major Kavendish burst through the door at that exact moment.

"You are right on time, sir, for Lady Evelyn is in need of your assistance," Percival said.

The prince pulled Anastasia to her feet and held her against his chest. She trembled in his arms.

Major Kavendish hurried to Lady Evelyn, his face red with exertion from the pace with which he had traversed the palace to get here.

"Dear lady, I was recently informed that a person forced his way into the palace and you were in danger. Show me which direction the knave has gone, and I shall end his miserable life so he will trouble you no more."

"I have already taken care of the situation, Kavendish, but I need a proper escort for Lady Evelyn to her rooms. She has suffered through a terrible ordeal and could use a good man to see to her safety."

"It will be my pleasure, Your Highness."

Major Kavendish helped the frightened Lady Evelyn to her feet and tenderly escorted her from the room.

Percival peered down at his bride, a frown upon his face. "I thought Lord Remington was dead. How is it he was not and came to be invited to the wedding?"

"He was not invited. He entered the palace with a delivery of flowers and hid in the stables until the wedding was over. Then he dressed himself in his fine clothes and joined the guests, following me to the library when I went to talk with Mama. He boasted of his cunning and bragged about how he would kill me once you came to find me."

Percival looked down at her beautiful face with the trails the tears made down her cheeks and sighed. This was not what he had planned for his wedding night.

"He will never hurt you again. We must go to the king and tell him of all that happened, and then I shall take you somewhere safe."

"Where is there a place that is safe?"

"You shall see."

Chapter 26

It was well after midnight when they arrived at their destination. Anastasia looked sleepily out the window. The carriage stopped at a lovely little cottage deep in the woods, outside of Larenia.

"Where are we?" she wondered aloud as she accepted the prince's help climbing out of the plain, dark carriage they traveled in.

"This is my hunting cottage. This is not where I wanted to spend my wedding night, but we are safe here. It is where I stay when I am traveling about in secret. There is only one road in, and the entrance is well concealed. My guard will be patrolling the woods while we are here. They know the area well, and will be alerted if anything, or anyone comes near." He smiled at Anastasia and kissed her upturned nose. "Come, little one."

The men unloaded the trunk they carried with them and carried it inside. A fire was started and the trunk hauled upstairs to the bedchamber.

Anastasia looked about her in surprise. It was a charming little cottage. There was a large wooden table in the center of the floor, close to the hearth. Wooden chairs were pushed against the table, and two wooden stools stood on either side of the hearth where a large kettle hung from a metal hook. There was a side table, where a pretty porcelain basin and pitcher sat beneath a carved oval mirror. Wooden shelves held stacks of dishes and eating utensils. The windows were covered with wooden shutters, and the fire cast a golden glow over the entire room. Anastasia was enchanted. The cottage was warm, cozy, and very cheerful.

"Will there be anything else, Your Highness?"

"No, thank you, Vroknar. Let me know immediately if anything appears out of the ordinary."

"Very good, Your Highness. A good night to you both." He winked at Prince Percival and left.

Percival bolted the door behind him and then turned to Anastasia. "Come, love, the bed chamber is up the stairs. You have had a trying day and we must get you into bed."

Anastasia climbed the narrow stairs and found a spacious room at the top of the stairs. A large bed stood in the center of the far wall, covered with a brightly covered quilt. A large stuffed chair stood in the far corner and a fireplace took up the opposite wall. There was a side table with a delicately patterned porcelain pitcher and basin and another oval mirror. The trunk had been set at the foot of the large bed, and a fire had also been lit.

"It is beautiful," she murmured.

Anastasia glanced at Percival. He stood watching her. His hot gaze looked her over from head to foot. She had changed from her wedding gown into a violet traveling dress and the color enhanced her dark hair and brought out the color of her eyes.

Anastasia was suddenly awkward, and unsure. She did not know what she should do. What if she disappointed him? She started to panic. They were alone and this was her wedding night. The prince would surely want to bed her, and she had no idea what was expected of her. Lady Evelyn had not gotten to that part of her talk before they had been interrupted by Lord Remington. She turned her back to the prince and reached for the laces on her gown. Her hand shook and she could not seem to grasp the strings and untie them.

****

Percival saw the panic in her eyes and sighed. It was going to be a long night. He had not taken a virgin to his bed before and he had no idea what kind of patience would be required to woo her sufficiently to bed her. His blood was already heated and pounding in his head. He wanted her like he had never wanted another woman. Thoughts and images of their naked bodies twisted together had been running through his mind for days. Now, they were finally alone, and she was terrified. He walked to her side and reached for the laces at the back of her gown.

"Here, let me. I shall play the lady's maid for you while we are here." He kissed the back of her neck as his fingers deftly untied her laces and he began to ease the dress down over her shoulders.

She shivered at his touch and he pulled her dress down off her shoulders and over her hips. The dress fell in a puddle of silk at her feet. Percival looked at her white shoulders in the fire light and began kissing them one at a time, exploring her with his mouth. She drew in a shaky breath as he reached in front, cupping her breasts with both hands. His thumbs rubbed over her hardened nipples through the silk of her chemise. Her body responded to his touch. Even though she appeared to be uncertain, her woman's body knew what she wanted. Anastasia groaned at his touch and turned in his arms, her mouth finding his, her tongue plunging inside his mouth to mate with his.

Percival groaned at the assault, his hands reaching for the laces that held her corset in place. He wanted to feel her naked against him, all of her, against all of him. Their kisses were hot, wild, and her hands were running over his back and arms, her body trembled with the violence of her emotions.

At last the lace came loose; he ripped the corset from her slight body and dropped it on the floor. He made quick work of her skirts and stockings. He lifted her chemise over her head and pulled her silken drawers from her slight hips. In one quick motion he pulled the covers back and laid her on the smooth sheets. He deftly removed his boots and clothes and slid beneath the sheets to pull Anastasia back into his arms. He was hard, hot, and throbbing. He was not sure how long he had before his control completely snapped. He'd wanted this woman for such a long time, and now he could finally make her his. He knew there would be pain and he wanted to make this as painless as he could for her. So, he had to go slow, and make sure she was ready before he penetrated her. The effort nearly killed him. He covered her with his body and began to kiss her once more.

****

Anastasia drew in a shuddering breath when Percival laid her on the sheets. Her body was on fire and seemed to know exactly what it wanted. Her body wanted Percival, deep inside her. Heat began to gather in her stomach at his kisses, and now liquid fire pooled into the secret place between her legs. Percival slid into bed beside her and moved over her, parting her legs with his knees as he settled himself between her thighs. She squirmed as she felt his arousal pressing against her belly. He was big, hard, and hot. Percival swooped down and settled his mouth on hers, kissing her with hot, wild, carnal kisses until she whimpered in the back of her throat. He kissed his way down her throat and across her breasts. She arched off the bed and grabbed him by the shoulders, her eyes wide with passion.

She sucked in a breath when his mouth settled over her nipple and he drew it into his mouth. White hot heat flooded her entire body when he began to suckle. Percival leaned over and began to suckle her other nipple. She thought she would die from the rapture and more heat pooled into the junction of her legs. She moved her legs restlessly against him, tension building in her stomach.

Percival kissed his way down her stomach and across her hips. She gasped in surprise and then with satisfaction.

Anastasia did not know what was happening to her. She was riding a wave such as she had never known, and it was all centered on Percival and what he was doing to her.

Percival rose to cover her body with his. He gently kissed her mouth as his fingers found her sheath and he slid one finger inside.

Anastasia thought she'd died. She marveled at the pleasure he gave her when Percival slid his finger inside her. Heat pooled around his finger and when he began to move it in and out of her, her body trembled with each movement of his hand. Her breath started coming quicker between her parted lips and she started moving her hips to take his finger deeper inside.

Percival kissed her tenderly and then moved his arousal to the opening of her sheath. He pressed slightly inside and then waited. Anastasia wrapped her arms around his neck and moved her hips to meet his hard length. Perspiration broke out on his forehead; he wanted to take this slow so he did not hurt her, but she would not let him. She lifted her hips against him, and he slid in further. She was so tight, so wet, so hot, he was no longer able to think. He pushed against her and felt the barrier of her virginity. He opened his mouth over hers and plunged forward breaking the thin membrane and seating himself fully inside her. She cried out and he stilled his movement, gently kissing and teasing her lips with his mouth.

"It will feel better in a minute. Do not move, little one." He laid his forehead against hers and willed himself to control the passion that raged within him.

Anastasia had never known anything like the hard full length of him deep inside her. She moved against him curiously and he gripped her hips with his hands.

"Do not move." He ground the words out.

"Why?"

"Because I cannot control myself if you move that way and I want to make this good for you."

"It is already good, my prince."

Anastasia wrapped her legs around his hips and moved against him. Pleasure was beginning to center around his hard arousal, deep inside her, and she wanted more, so much more.

Percival groaned and began to move gently against her. She tightened her legs around his hips and increased the pace, tension beginning to build within her with each movement of his hips. She whimpered with need and pleasure into his ear while she lifted her hips to meet each thrust and take him deeper inside her. He began to move faster, plunging deeper, and moving with a rhythm that she matched, her breath coming fast between her parted lips. Ecstasy streaked through her and she cried out as the waves of gratification crashed over her again and again. Her body shuddered with each wave. Percival thrust harder and harder, his release coming hard and fast, crashing over him with an intensity that had him roaring.

Anastasia closed her eyes. Her body limp with contentment, her mind amazed at the wonder of what she experienced in her husband's arms. They lay wrapped together, marveling at the intensity of their lovemaking.

"Is bedding always like that?"

"Nay." Percival did not want to move, he was spent and wanted to sleep.

"Did I disappoint you?" she whispered the question, but he heard all the same.

"Nay, you could never disappoint me, *Dorogaya*."

Quickly he rolled to his side and took Anastasia with him, cuddling her against him, and wrapping the blankets around them both. He kissed the top of her head and tucked it beneath his chin.

"Go to sleep, little one. I shall keep you safe," Percival said.

Anastasia sighed. She loved being held in Percival's arms. She was warm. She was safe, and most importantly she was loved.

Chapter 27

Anastasia woke to the birds singing outside her window. The bed was empty beside her and Percival was nowhere in sight. She rolled to her side and then gingerly got out of bed. She was a little sore from their lovemaking the night before. She blushed as the images of what occurred came flooding back to her. She heard a sound outside the door and Percival entered fully dressed, carrying a tray with fruit, cheese, and tea.

"Good morning." His gaze took in her rumpled hair, her cheeks still rosy from sleep, and then dropped to the valley between her breasts where she held the sheet against her.

She gripped the sheet tighter and pulled it a little higher against her, as a blush spread over her face. Anastasia dropped her gaze. "Good morning," she said.

Percival set the tray on the side table and walked toward the bed. "Are you still shy, *Dorogaya*, after all we did last eve?"

She could not look at him.

He sat on the bed beside her and tilted her face toward his. He searched her face, and then gently kissed her parted lips.

"You do not need to be shy with me, I have kissed my way across your beautiful body, and you are now mine in every sense of the word."

"I know." She blushed again.

He laughed. "Come and eat your breakfast, Anastasia, the men have found something they want to show you. They are waiting outside, when you have eaten and dressed."

He kissed her again and left.

Anastasia quickly cleaned herself with the water in the basin and dressed in a plain cotton dress of red, the neckline trimmed with a border of little white flowers. She plaited her hair, tied it with a red ribbon, and then picked up the tray and carried it downstairs. She preferred to eat with Percival and set the tray on the table while she went outside in search of him. Anastasia walked toward the group of men and stopped suddenly. They had a small fawn in the grass beneath the trees. It was fitting somehow.

The wounds in her heart and soul were healing under the magic of Percival's love and gentleness. She no longer felt inadequate, or a disappointment. The time had come to let the past go and move forward in her life.

Percival turned at the sound of her footsteps, his hot gaze wandering over her. He smiled and held out his hand. "Come, darling, and see the fawn."

Anastasia approached the fawn slowly; she did not want to frighten her. The fawn was unaware that she should be afraid of them, for she nuzzled their hands and pockets looking for more grass. Anastasia petted the fawn's velvet nose and fed her handfuls of grass. She was such a little thing and Anastasia wondered where her mother was. Anastasia sat on the grass with the fawn in her lap.

"Where did you find her?" Anastasia wondered.

"She was by the river, Your Highness, caught in

the mud. The men and I pulled her out and brought her back. Her mother was nowhere in sight."

It took Anastasia a minute to realize Vroknar was speaking to her. He called her "Your Highness." Anastasia frowned, that would take some getting used to.

"Thank you for bringing her here so I could see her. She is such a little thing." Anastasia hugged the fawn. She was about the age Athena had been when they found her in the woods.

"I had a fawn once. She was younger than this when I found her in the woods behind our house. Her mother had been killed, and she was all alone, like me."

****

Percival glanced at Anastasia. Something had changed. She seemed to want to talk. He lowered himself onto the grass beside her and waited.

"Papa let me keep her in the stables, but only if I took care of her myself. He had the men build a little stall for her with a gate that latched shut. We had been having a problem with a lone wolf near our home, and the men could not seem to kill him. The wolf was too smart. He kept coming closer and closer to the house and stables despite their efforts to trap him or run him off."

"Was he eating your animals, Your Highness?" Vroknar wanted to know.

"No, that was why it was such a puzzle. The wolf had to be eating something, and no one knew what." Anastasia said.

"There was a formal dinner for my father and his family at the palace. Neither I, nor Rella liked to do our stitching, as we were supposed to do." Anastasia wrinkled her nose at the thought.

"I was sixteen summers, and my stitches were that of a small girl. Papa told Rella and I, we had one week to finish our stitching squares, or we would be left home. Mama was done being patient with us. In truth I was a great trial to her because I would rather be outside playing with Athena or riding than learning how to be a lady. I stayed up at night to finish my stitching and played outside with Athena during the day. She followed me everywhere, and she was my only friend, the one I told all my troubles to, and I loved her with all my heart."

Anastasia smiled at the memory.

"The day before we were to leave for Larenia, Mama sent me with a package of fresh meat for the vicar. My stitching was almost done, and I was hurrying to get back so I could finish my square. I stayed up until my stitching square was done and hid it in the corner of my window seat. The next morning when Papa asked for our squares, Rella had hers, but mine was gone. I could not find it anywhere. Rella told Papa I had gone out to play with Athena and had not done my stitching. Papa told me how disappointed he was with me. I told him I had the square, and he allowed me to look for it. I searched the house and could not find it anywhere. No one had seen it. When I returned without my stitching, Papa told me I would stay at home instead of going to Larenia with the family to have dinner with the king, as punishment for my disobedience. I begged and Papa told me he had never been as disappointed in anyone, as he was with me. I ran away into the woods crying and hid by a stream. I decided I would stay in the woods forever, so I did not disappoint anyone again."

Percival nodded. He knew that something important had happened. Anastasia never discussed her past with anyone and here she was, telling his men her story. Suddenly Percival grinned. She trusted them.

Anastasia swallowed. Her hands began to shake so she clasped them in her lap. Percival frowned but he let her talk.

"Papa had been the one person that understood about Rella. It is hard to explain how badly it hurt that I disappointed him. I do not know how long I stayed by the stream, but after a time, I decided to go back home. I remembered there had been a wolf about, and I did not want to meet up with it. When I returned from the woods, I found my stitching square sitting on my window seat in plain sight. Papa and the family had left for Larenia, and I was too late to say goodbye or tell Papa I was sorry."

****

Anastasia choked back a lump in her throat.

"I went out to find Athena, and her corral was empty, the latch was open. I knew I had latched it. I never forgot, especially with the wolf around. Then I heard Athena cry out. I ran as fast as I could. Athena was lying in the grass by a tree. I ran to see what caused her to cry, thinking mayhap she had hurt her legs. When I reached the tree where she lay, I heard the wolf growling. He was only a few feet away, and he was huge."

Anastasia felt her eyes fill with tears as she thought about what had happened next. Percival put his arm around her shoulder and listened.

"I thought I could get to Athena in time. I was

300

wrong. The wolf leaped toward me as I ran toward Athena. I put up my arm in defense. The wolf got my arm and tore it to shreds. The men heard me scream and came running. The wolf heard the men, and he let go of my arm, grabbed Athena, and ran into the woods. He never came back. I was too late to save my Athena. I never saw her again. My arm was torn, bleeding, and I lost the only thing that loved me. The men carried me to the house, and the physician was called. It was a full year before my arm was finally free from infection and pain. With a lot of care and work, I was able to use my arm again. When Papa returned, the men told him that the wolf had come into the yard because fresh meat had been found strewn from the stable to the woods, where the wolf tracks were.”

“Papa was disappointed that I had dropped meat from the parcel I delivered to the vicar. I often asked myself how I managed to drop so much meat without being aware of it. So, because of me, Athena was dead. I was miserable.”

Percival watched Anastasia. “Only it was not you that left the meat.”

“No, it was Rella. I wondered for years where my stitching had been all the time I looked for it. Now I know that Rella hid it, so I would get left behind. Rella told Papa later that I hid it on purpose, so I would not have to finish it. He never knew that it was finished.”

Anastasia stopped; her hands stroked the fawn as she got control of her emotions.

“I disappointed Papa, lost Athena, lost the use of my arm, and nearly lost my life in the same day. I was too late to change any of it. If I had not run away from Papa, Athena would not have gone missing, because I would have been with her. Rella would not have had a chance to let her out. Athena would never have made it to the woods and the wolf. It has taken me years to understand what happened. I never got the chance to tell Papa how sorry I was for disappointing him. When the family returned from Larenia, I was delirious with fever from the infection in the wolf bite. It was months before I was better. Papa was busy then bartering for peace with Lichtenburg until that day they brought him home with a bullet wound in his chest."

Anastasia fell silent. For the first time in a long time, the pain of that day did not hurt.

"Is that why you tug on your sleeve when you are upset, Your Highness, because of the wolf bite?" Darok wondered.

Anastasia smiled. So, they *had* noticed. She took a deep breath as she pulled her right sleeve up and showed the men her arm. Not one of them flinched or turned away. Anastasia let out her breath. It was going to be all right. They accepted her as she was, flaws and all.

"That is not much of a scar," Erik commented. "You should see the one on my back." He reached for the hem of his tunic to show her, but Percival stopped him.

"No, she won't." He growled.

Vroknar chuckled and took the fawn from Anastasia.

"We will look around, Your Highness, and see if we can find the little one's mother."

"Thank you, Vroknar, and thank you for showing her to me. It was a most pleasant surprise."

****

Percival was pleased. His wife was improving in every way possible. She was no longer frightened and there was a glow about her that drew him. He wanted to take her into his arms and show her how pleased he was. He pulled her close and started to nibble on her neck.

"Where did the men sleep last night?" Anastasia asked, gazing at the barn behind the cottage.

"In the barn. There is a room within the stables that was made for the soldiers."

Anastasia blushed.

"What has you blushing now, little one?"

"The men. The barn is very close to the house. Do you think they heard us last night?"

Percival laughed out loud. "If they did it is their own fault for listening."

Anastasia was mortified. "If the men heard, then they no doubt know what we were doing."

"We are married, *Dorogaya*, there is nothing to be embarrassed about. It is expected that we share a bed and make an heir."

****

Later that night in their chamber, she was determined that she would not make a sound. She did not want the men to know what happened between her and the prince once they went to their chamber. She bit her lip to keep her moan inside when Percival suckled at her breasts. She moaned into her elbow, when he kissed his way down her. She totally lost it when the first wave of pleasure washed over her and she found her release, screaming at the pleasure his tongue had given her. She called out his name again when she found her release the second time as he filled her, his hardness pushing her over the edge into a sea of rapture, as he too found his release.

Anastasia had no idea she even made a sound, as they had made love at night. She bragged as much to Percival and he chuckled to himself. He would not tell his little wife that the men heard her and made sure he knew they heard. Anastasia would be extremely embarrassed if she knew, and it was amusing that she thought she had such control. His gentle little wife was a wild cat in bed, and he had the marks on his back to prove it. He never would have guessed that this delicate little woman had such passion, and by the gods, she delighted him.

They stayed at the little cottage for three weeks; they made love every night. At first Percival was worried his little wife would be too sore, but she soon proved she was a fitting match for she reached for him as often as he reached for her.

During the three weeks they were at the little cottage, two of the guards occasionally rode to the palace and back to keep in contact with the king. There was still no sign of Rella, and nothing appeared to be out of the ordinary. Soon, it was time to return to the palace.

Anastasia was sad to leave the little cottage and to return to the palace, she had enjoyed their time alone together. Once they were back at the palace, things would be different. Percival had duties he must attend to, and her mother and sister would be insistent that she join them in whatever activity they were engaged in. They would only have the evenings to be alone together. She sighed as she closed the door to the little cottage and walked toward the waiting carriage. She was more in love with Percival than she had thought possible.

****

Percival watched Anastasia as she closed the door, he could read her emotions as she walked toward him. He wanted to stay, too, but the king had summoned them, and he must attend to his duties. "We shall return, do not be sad, little one."

She looked up at him and smiled. "I have enjoyed this time together Percival, and I am merely sad that it passed so quickly."

"We have a whole lifetime, *Dorogaya,*" he answered

Percival helped her into the carriage, and they sped away toward the palace.

King Alexander was waiting in the throne room when they arrived. His counselors were present also.

"Percival, Anastasia, it is nice to have you back."

"Father, you are looking well. It is nice to be back." Percival stepped forward and bowed to the king.

King Alexander turned to Anastasia and held out his hand. "Daughter."

Anastasia stepped forward and gave her hand to the king with a little curtsy. "Your Highness."

King Alexander waved his hand at her. "Call me father for we are family now," he invited.

"Father," Anastasia said smiling widely.

"That is better. You look to be in excellent health, Daughter. Does my son treat you well?"

"He does." A blush rose on her cheeks as thoughts entered her mind on exactly how well his son treated her.

"Hmmmm." The king watched her blush with

interest. "It does us good to see the glow about you, Daughter, and the color in your cheeks. Perhaps with how well my son is taking care of you, we shall have a royal grandbaby before the year is out, hmmm?"

Anastasia felt her face suffuse with color.

"Father, you embarrass my wife."

The king chuckled. "So, we do, so we do, but we are family now and she will soon be used to our teasing." He winked at Anastasia.

"Your Highness, the envoy from Lichtenburg has arrived." A soldier entered the room with the news.

"Very good, have them wait until Prince Darius arrives, and then show them in," the king said.

"Very Good, Your Highness." The soldier bowed and closed the door.

King Alexander turned to Anastasia. "We have summoned Prince Percival and yourself to the palace because we have received word on the men who attacked Lord Covington. Lichtenburg soldiers have tracked down the men responsible. It appears that there has been a rebel faction living in the mountains. This faction was made up of deserters from both Oldenburg and Lichtenburg armies. They have uniforms from both countries armies and have been trying to start a war. It was they who started the disturbance at the border that threatened peace, causing me to send Lord Covington to Lichtenburg to negotiate a treaty. It was also this rebel faction who attacked Lord Covington on his way home and shot him. Lichtenburg has tracked them down, and now their king sends the guilty men to us as a token of goodwill, and a declaration of peace between us. The envoy is finally here, and we are most pleased that we now have Lord Covington's killer."

Anastasia's eyes filled with tears. *Papa.* That seemed to be another lifetime ago; so much had happened since then.

"Crown Prince Darius, Your Highness," the soldier announced.

The king nodded. "One more thing, Daughter, we have taken extra precautions with delivery men and servants. Anyone entering the palace will need to be approved by myself, Prince Darius, or Prince Percival. You have nothing to fear. That girl Rella shall never harm you again. We shall see to it."

Anastasia nodded and then reached up and placed a quick kiss on the king's cheek. He was such a kind man. She smiled at Percival and with a little curtsy, left the throne room so the king could deal with the envoy from Lichtenburg.

Anastasia went in search of her mother and sister and spent a happy afternoon catching up on the news. Beatrice had a rosy glow about her and a happy smile that spread across her face often as they talked. Anastasia thought she had never seen her sister so happy, and it pleased her greatly. Prince Darius was happy too. The love he had for his new wife was very evident in his eyes as he looked upon her. Major Kavendish was obviously smitten with Lady Evelyn, for the man was in attendance at every opportunity, one could hardly speak with Lady Evelyn without bumping into the man. Lady Evelyn appeared as smitten and blushed like a debutante whenever the major was about. It looked as though another wedding would soon be taking place.

Percival held Anastasia every night and they made love often, their love and devotion apparent to everyone around them.

Two months later, the palace made the announcement that both the royal couples were expecting babies. The king was heard singing in the throne room and waltzing by himself in the hallways. Everyone was overjoyed with the wonderful news. The entire kingdom held a week-long celebration.

****

Henry returned to Covington Estate as Sir Henry Lager, Lord of Covington and knight of the realm.

Cook was most glad to see him and he, her.

Sir Henry thoroughly inspected the large stone house of Covington, for he heard that Rella had come here after her banishment, and he meant to find out if anything was missing. He was disconcerted to find the three paintings missing from the master's chamber. He had, quite frankly, forgotten they were there, or he would have removed them, and hid them with the other paintings in the cellar. He had the strongbox brought out of its hiding place in the attic and returned to the desk drawer. All was returned to its normal place, and Henry set about his wooing of Cook.

It seemed as though they had all found their happy ending, and they would have, if it were not for the small cloud that hung over Anastasia's head, named Rella.

Chapter 28

Rella sat on the bank of the river and watched the boats rowing past. It had been a dismal couple of months, and she was no further in her plan to end Anastasia than she had been before. She really must come up with some sort of plan. What a colossal failure Lord Remington had proved to be. Not only had he *not* taken Anastasia's miserable life as she had intended, but the stupid man had ended up dead himself. One thousand ducats had been paid to the man and all for nothing. She was right back where she started from. She was having a hard time finding anyone willing to sneak into Oldenburg and assassinate the princess. *Princess.* The word stuck in her throat, and she tried not to gag. Rella idly picked up her paints and started to draw a picture of herself on a throne, with a golden crown atop her head. That is how it should have been, what she deserved and what she would get.

Two ladies strolled by deep in conversation and sat upon one of the benches nearby to finish their talk.

"I hear she was absolutely breathtaking, and the prince could not keep his eyes off of her." The lady had dark hair and twirled a purple sunshade idly.

Rella rolled her eyes. She was heartily sick of hearing about the royal wedding and Anastasia.

"I wish my Charles looked at me that way. Why, his eye wanders onto every female healthy enough to walk past him." The second lady took out her fan and began to fan herself. She was heavyset with blonde curls and a tight pink day dress.

"Why, if the bastard girl who tried to kill dear Princess Anastasia strolled by, my Charles would probably look," the blonde woman said.

"He never did have any taste, did he, Doris?"

"Nay, he never did, Enid."

Rella turned her back with a flounce of her shoulders and continued to paint. Her mind seethed at the idle chatter. The people in all the border towns had somehow heard that King Alexander had banished her and named her bastard. It always began something along the lines of: *my cousin told me that her sister said her brother was in the court when it all happened.* It was the talk of the entire countryside. Rella had been unable to find anyone willing to even listen to her plan for Anastasia's assassination. She no sooner brought the subject up when her would-be assassin ran to the nearest constable. Everywhere she turned, the people raved about the grand royal wedding and how beautiful the princesses were. They spoke of how kind and gentle Anastasia was, and how much in love with her Prince Percival seemed to be. Anastasia and her prince were all anybody talked about, and it was enough to make Rella sick. Everyone everywhere seemed to be in love with Anastasia. This was the fourth village she had come to, and she still had not found anybody willing to kill Anastasia. Rella had to rent her room at the tavern under an assumed name to even have a place to stay. It simply was not fair. There had to be a way to make Anastasia pay for what she had done. There must be something she could do.

The ladies continued their talk and Rella listened idly to the conversation.

"I caught my Charles with that tramp Lady Dunhill," Doris said angrily.

"Nooo!" Enid put a hand to her throat in shock.

"I did, and I told Charles I was through, I visited with my solicitors yesterday and had Charles completely removed from my bank and my will," Doris stated.

"You aren't saying that you have cut him off and...are you saying that you are leaving him?" Enid's hand rose to her throat once more.

"I am," Doris confirmed, fanning herself briskly.

"Well, dear, you simply cannot leave him. Think of the scandal. It simply is not done." Enid twirled her sunshade as she considered the notion.

"I do not care. I refuse to be the laughingstock of every party, if there is a scandal, shame on Charles, he brought it upon himself," Doris said. She snapped her fan shut and set it on the bench beside her.

"But what about you, dear?" Enid inquired.

"What about me?"

"Are you not worried that your good name will be bandied about?" Enid was concerned.

"My good name is already bandied about," Doris stated.

"It is too bad you are not a man, so you could challenge him to a duel. It would serve the wretch right to pay with his life for the shame and embarrassment he has brought upon you," Enid said.

Rella perked up. This conversation was getting interesting.

"Oh, I do not want to challenge him to a duel, dear,

or see him dead. Living with the choices he has made will be a far greater punishment than anything I could do to him." Doris reached for her fan and began to fan herself again.

Her companion was astonished. "How could living be a worse punishment than death?"

"Simply because Lady Dunhill is a shrew. She lives for the jewels and trinkets her lovers buy her and without my money, Charles is penniless and will soon rue the day he chose her over me. That harlot will make Charles pay a far greater price then dying ever could."

Rella paused, her brush still in the air where she had begun to reach for more paint. Maybe she was thinking about this all wrong. *What if* instead of killing Anastasia and ending her torment, she made her live with it? Rella looked down at the picture she was painting of herself, with the crown upon her head. *What if* she made everyone that now loved Anastasia hate her as much as she did, and the hate went on and on for Anastasia's entire life and beyond? *What if I could make everybody hate Anastasia forever?* People loved stories. Look how the story of that awful day in court had spread around the whole countryside. *What if I told my story, my way?* The idea had merit. She settled back against the grassy bank in satisfaction and reached for her paints. She started to paint the story of her life, as she wanted it to seem.

****

Rella finally caught up to them in a small village on the outskirts of Dusselstein. She had been looking for them for months, and they were reputed to be inside the tavern enjoying their dinner. Once she was done here, she would go somewhere far away. Romania perhaps, for she had heard a prince lived there with a penchant for blonde hair and blue eyes. First, she had to make Anastasia pay dearly, and she was nearly out of money. So, it was time to move on with a different plan. She glanced at her reflection in the window of the tavern before she entered. She must get this right. Rella pulled a long blonde curl forward across her shoulder and patted the rest of her hair into place. She smoothed her best dress over her hips and with her pages of paintings tucked under her arm, she entered the tavern, a bright smile upon her face.

Two men sat before the fire, eating the thick stew the tavern keeper's wife had placed before them. They spoke quietly together, arguing over a point of view that they both did not share.

"Hello, gentlemen, how nice to meet you both."

The two men looked up from their supper. Who was this beautiful woman who interrupted their dinner, and what did she want?

"Do we know you?" the older of the two asked.

"Nay, but I know you for your reputation has been made known to me. I have searched diligently to find you, and here you are." She made a little giggle and clasped her hands together.

"Why do you search for us?" the older was curious about the woman.

"To bring you the most wondrous story. It is a story of hope, of sacrifice, of endurance and of encouragement, and finally of victory. It is a story that I feel sure every boy and girl in the entire world will revere for years to come."

"Please sit," the older man invited.

"Do tell us this story, for we are most interested in

stories such as this," the younger man said.

With a dazzling smile, Rella set her packet of parchments on the table before the men and began her wondrous story. "Once upon a time there was little girl. She lived alone with her papa in a big house, for the little girl's mother had died when she was young. Her papa loved her very much but was concerned that she had no one to play with and so he married again. This new wife had two little girls of her own close in age to his little girl. Their names were Beatrice and Anastasia...."

The men listened with interest at this amazing story of the little girl, whose father died and of the cruelty of the wicked stepmother. They listened as Rella told them of the little girl being forced to sleep in the cinders of the fire. She told of the girl's sweetness and love for her wicked stepmother and two horrible stepsisters. They listened as she spoke of the handsome prince and the wondrous ball. Rella told of the girl sewing her own dress for the ball and the two stepsisters taking her ribbons and jewels. She told them of her fairy godmother who waved her wand and made the girl a princess. She told them how the prince fell madly in love with the girl, until the clock stuck midnight and the girl ran away. Rella told of the girl losing her slipper on the stairs outside the palace and the prince finding it, and then using it to find the girl he fell in love with. She told them the wicked stepmother tried to keep the two apart, but the prince and the girl found each other.

"So, the handsome prince married the girl and she became his princess and they lived happily ever after." Rella closed her pages with a smile and watched the two brothers.

"How do we know this story is real?"

"We do not even know the name of this girl."

Rella smiled. "Of course, it is true, every bit. The reason I can say that this story is true is the girl is me. It all happened exactly as I have written it here and I yearn with all my heart that you will make this story known far and wide. I truly hope that this story can be a beacon of hope to every girl who is sad, or mistreated, or alone. That every little girl will know that somewhere there is a handsome prince waiting just for her."

"And your name?"

"They call me Cinderella. It is a name they made up because I slept in the cinders." That would teach Anastasia a lesson. Everyone would now believe exactly as she had told Anastasia they would. Rella would be the loved heroine and Anastasia would be hated forever. Satisfied that she had accomplished what she had come for, Rella placed her parchment on the table and left the brothers Grimm to finish their dinner.

Epilogue

Princess Anastasia and her handsome prince lived happily together for the rest of their lives. They had three children a son, and two daughters. Their world was a happy place, filled with love and laughter. When Rella's tale became known, they refused to let it cast a shadow over them or their world.

The tale was published as Rella intended, the story of Cinderella. It was never very famous; however, until well after Prince Percival, Princess Anastasia and all who knew them were dead. For the prince and princess were good, kind, and wise, and all who knew them loved them. They were much beloved of their people. Those who read the story discounted it as a fairy tale, a work of fairies and magic.

Prince Darius and Princess Beatrice lived happily together, as well. Prince Darius took the throne upon his father's death. Together they ruled the kingdom of Oldenburg for many years. The kingdom prospered and grew under King Darius's rule and peace abounded in the land. King Darius and his queen had two children, both sons.

Major Kavendish eventually found the nerve to propose to Lady Evelyn, and the two lived the remainder of their days, happily together, close to the palace and the grandchildren so dear to their hearts.

Sir Henry wooed and married the cook. They were

an honor to the title and lands that King Alexander granted Sir Henry for his service and loyalty to Lord Robert Covington.

Rella went to Romania, but the Crown Prince was much disenchanted with her when she nearly caused a war with Prussia. Eventually she was exiled from most of the European countries and ended up dying alone in a humble little shack from a disease she caught from selling her body for food. For that was the only way she had been able to live, her money gone, her scheming bringing her at odds with the law on many occasions. She never saw her story meet with any success, for it would be years before it became famous. She died penniless, bitter, unloved, and alone, without the happy ever after she had schemed, lied, and plotted to get.

A word from the author...

I have been married to my best friend and partner for thirty-seven years. I am the mother of ten children, six boys and four girls. I have worn many hats over the years including daughter, sister, friend, wife, mother, aunt, grandmother, seamstress, designer, cook, hostess, housekeeper, bookkeeper, teacher, EMT, lieutenant, supervisor, lead, and now I am adding writer!